Readers love MARY CALMES

Change of Heart

"…an incredible story filled with suspense, drama, love and family."

—Fallen Angel Reviews *Recommended Read*

"Mary Calmes has created an intriguing world that I would love to visit again and again."

—Coffee Time Romance and More

"The world built by Mary Calmes in this novel is amazing and refreshing."

—Reviews by Jessewave

Trusted Bond

"Mary Calmes' stories are always wonderfully written and full of drama, excitement, passion and hot steamy sex. And *Trusted Bond* is no exception."

—Night Owl Reviews *Top Pick*

"She throws her readers into a rapture with her engaging narrative and loveable characters. It's hard to take your eyes off the pages."

—Rarely Dusty Books

Honored Vow

"I think you should get this book and lock yourself in a room with a pot of tea and some chocolates and enjoy."

—MM Good Book Reviews

"*Honored Vow* earns 5 Fairies for a captivating book that had me biting my nails and crying tears of joy."

—Amethyst Daydreams

Published by DREAMSPINNER PRESS
http://www.dreamspinnerpress.com

CRUCIBLE OF Fate

Mary Calmes

DREAMSPINNER PRESS

Published by
DREAMSPINNER PRESS

5032 Capital Circle SW, Suite 2, PMB# 279, Tallahassee, FL 32305-7886 USA
http://www.dreamspinnerpress.com/

Crucible of Fate

Cover Art
Cover Design

ISBN: 978-1-62380-181-6
Digital ISBN: 978-1-62380-182-3
First Edition November 2012

Printed in the United States of America
10 9 8 7 6 5 4 3 2
∞
This paper meets the requirements of
ANSI/NISO Z39.48-1992 (Permanence of Paper).

For my wonderful fans
who wanted to know
what was going on with Domin.

Glossary

akhen-aten	King of the semels.
aker	A leadership position in a large tribe that is fought for. The position reports to the maahes. Akers are always appointed in sets of twos, as manu and bakhu.
amenta	A panther who lives in the territory of a tribe not their own without permission.
apophi	A panther who is a disgrace and burden to the tribe.
aset	(Throne) The appointed mate of a semel in the event of the death of their reah. An aset can only be chosen, made, by a reah.
beset	Companion of a reah.
djehu	A leadership position in a tribe that is elected.
duat	A panther who has promised, on pain of death, to live only as human and never shift.
epeboi	An initiate.
hathen	A female servant who oversees the semel-aten's harem.
heru-ur	A bacchanal orgy that takes place during the Feast of the Valley.
khatyu	The soldiers of a semel.
khet	A term literally meaning "separated by fire," each dead to the other.
khonsu	A man standing second.
krates	A person adopted as a brother or sister into a tribe, without having to swear fealty to the semel, a great honor.

maahen/s	Princess/prince of a tribe, the emissary of the semel.
maat	Balance, harmony, correct action.
mastaba	Mistress of a semel's home, normally the widow of the previous semel.
menat	Tribute.
menthu	Guardian of the law.
menthuel	Honor challenge.
phocal	Leader of the Shu cats, an elite group of werepanthers that serve the priest of Chae Rophon.
reah	True-mate of a semel.
sekhem	The chosen mate of the semel-aten who is not a yareah.
semel	Tribe leader.
semel-aten	Tribe leader of the werepanther capital city of Sobek, considered the leading semel of the world who makes werepanther law.
semel-netjer	Tribe leader blessed with a true-mate who is a nekhene cat.
semel-re	Tribe leader blessed with a true-mate, a leader who has found his reah.
sepat	Honor challenge.
sheseran	Mate of a sheseru.
sheseru	(Flail) Enforcer of the tribe, guardian of the mate of the semel.
sylvan	(Crook) Teacher of the tribe, counselor to the semel.
taurth	A yareah who has been cast aside because a semel found his true-mate.
wosret	An unmated reah claimed by the semel-aten as a concubine.
yareah	A mate of a semel who is chosen, not the semel's true-mate.

CRUCIBLE OF *Fate*

First Things First....

WHEN I arrived, before I addressed anyone, before anything, I had to purge my house. I left my new steward, Kabore Nour, to explain it to the two rows of people, the house staff lined up from the steps of the villa into the main hall.

I walked at a brisk clip, flanked by Yuri Kosa on my right and Crane Adams on my left. The guards outside the doors knelt and I told them never again. Just do what I ask, but the bowing and scraping bullshit was over. Taj Chalthoum, my sheseru, was there, having caught up, and fluidly translated my English into Arabic. They seemed surprised but quickly nodded. I understood I was different; it would take time to get used to me.

Mitchell Rayne and Nelson Adams, Jin's and Crane's fathers respectively, had not been placed in a cell per my order, even though their circumstances had, of course, changed. Originally, they had been accepted into the home of the previous semel-aten, so all I had done was place them under house arrest and confine them to a suite in the villa.

Once the doors were open, I strode into the common area between their two rooms. I found the two men there eating, enjoying breakfast, one reading the newspaper, the other finishing up fresh-squeezed orange juice. It would be the last glass he would ever have.

"Who are—"

"Hi there," I said softly as both men gasped.

I didn't make the man who dropped the glass tremble, or cause the hands of the man holding the paper to shake. Crane, my maahes, did that; he was the one. It was his presence there, in the room, that filled both men with dread.

"I used to be the maahes of the tribe of Mafdet," I said slowly, tasting the blood as my fangs, upper and lower, pushed through my gums. The canines were long and wicked sharp, which made the curl of my lip, I was certain, slightly sinister.

"You," the smaller, handsomer man breathed. His face was just similar enough to his son Jin's to remind me of the crime he had committed against his own child.

They fell to their knees, their faces a study in fear, shock, and dawning realization.

"Me," I said and squatted down, cocking my head, studying them. "I won the sepat. I'm the new semel-aten. My name is Domin Thorne, and Crane Adams," I said, pointing to the man on my left, "is the new maahes of the first tribe, the tribe of Rahotep."

Nelson took a shuddering breath.

My eyes went to Mitchell Rayne, Jin Church's father. "And this man," I said, nodding to the second man at my side, "is Yuri Kosa, formally the sheseru of the tribe of Mafdet, guardian of the mate of the semel-netjer, the only male reah in the world."

Mitchell's eyes filled with tears. It surprised me that these men, who for so long had plotted destruction and death, would themselves be so cowardly when faced with their own.

"I'm here," Crane announced, spreading his arms wide. "Still. And Jin is home with his mate, with Logan Church, and they will both soon be fathers. And nothing you did stopped him or me from living our lives."

"At least you will never have children," Nelson spat, speaking of his son's castration as though he was proud to have wielded the scalpel. I was certain he was.

"Yes, I will," Crane corrected. "They might not be mine in blood, but they will be in heart. And I will love them as I was not, as Jin was not, and we'll grow old together, and when I die, they'll miss me and mourn me but remember the love and laughter and what I taught them."

The tears welling up in Crane's eyes were not for the men before him but for the love he would surely have and for that which already was. When he gazed over at me, the smile through his tears made my chest hurt.

"Thank you," Crane said before he spun around and walked out of the room, locking the door behind him.

I refocused my gaze on the men in front of me.

"My son is an abomination," Mitchell spat haltingly. "And Crane Adams is the same for loving him as he does."

I made the *tch* noise in the back of my throat. The man was just so blind.

"You," Yuri said, pointing at Mitchell, "watched your own son nearly beaten to death when he shifted for the first time."

"I—"

"And you," Yuri thundered at Nelson, "castrated your own son. You held the blade."

"I would do it again!" he roared back at my mate. "He's dead to me!"

"As you will be to him shortly," Yuri said, his voice going deathly dark and cold as he began stripping.

Both men rose and stumbled away, Nelson jostling the table and knocking it over, Mitchell walking backward until he hit the far wall.

"You mean to kill us," Mitchell choked out.

"I mean to tear you to pieces and then have you burned with the nightly trash," I stated gamely, smirking at the end.

"You cannot! We need burial rites and to be—"

"I'm the semel-aten." I shrugged as Yuri finished his shift and stood close to me, a massive golden panther bristling with power and fury. "I can do as I please."

"This is inhumane!"

Yuri's roar filled the room before he launched himself at Nelson. Man and panther flipped over the love seat together, hitting the floor hard on the other side. The screams came fast, bloodcurdling and loud.

Mitchell began to shriek as a thick splatter of blood washed the curtains.

"It's sad," I said over Yuri's snarling as Nelson's screaming subsided to wrenching, sobbing whimpering, and I stretched out my hand, the long razor-sharp claws replacing my fingers as I finished the movement. "That only here, now, at the end, will you understand the error of your ways, father of the only nekhene cat in existence."

"I will go to my death believing him to be an abomination."

"That is your right," I said, advancing on him. "But I will no longer have to hear it and neither will he. Let us start with your tongue."

"You're a *monster*!" He screamed his very last word.

But I knew who the real monster was.

Chapter One

IT MADE no sense, and they were all tired of hearing me ask the same questions. But until I had an answer I understood, how was I supposed to simply accept it?

"What did your father tell you when you became a semel?" I inquired of every single tribe leader who visited Sobek.

They all regarded me oddly, the last one being Maroz Amadu of the tribe of Serabit from Giza. He was confused.

Yuri translated. "Specifically, he wants to know what would happen to you if you failed as a semel. Where would the people in your territory go for help, if, let's say, you decided that two panthers of different races couldn't be married in your territory."

"But that's absurd," Maroz said to Yuri. "It doesn't matter who you—"

"The sekhem of the semel-aten is hypothesizing," his yareah, Hesi Amadu, remarked.

Apparently we needed our mates to do the talking for us.

"Oh, I see." He plastered on a smile. "Well, I was told that if I was not a good ruler, that the panthers in my tribe could contact the semel-aten, and he would hear the case against me and pass judgment."

"Exactly." I pointed at him, then whirled around to face Yuri. "You see?"

He crossed his thickly muscled arms across his wide, bulky chest and fixed me with a stare that made me question my sanity. "What do I see?"

"I was a bad semel."

"'Was.' Past tense. What does—"

"So does that mean no one ever reported me to Ammon El Masry when he was semel-aten? That seems odd, doesn't it?"

"I don't know. How would I know?"

"And therein lies my question."

There was a soft clearing of a throat behind me.

Pivoting, I found Maroz and his mate still there. "May we go to the grand salon now, my lord? We're both famished."

"Oh yeah, go ahead," I said, waving them away. "Sorry."

Maroz grabbed his mate by the hand and tugged her away from me quickly. They all ended up doing that, concerned about my state of mind, I was certain.

"Okay, so what now?" Yuri asked, stepping in front of me.

"It's what I was told as a new semel, what Logan was, what we all were."

"That the semel-aten would come get you if you were bad," Yuri paraphrased. "Right? Like the bogeyman?"

"Yeah. And if that's true, if millions of panthers are supposed to be calling me or e-mailing me and complaining—where is it?"

"What? You're asking if there's, like, a command center or something for all this correspondence?"

"That's exactly what I'm asking. I mean, who checks to make sure no panther is ever seen? Who spins an attack? Who basically has kept werepanthers off human radar for centuries?"

His eyes narrowed as he regarded me.

"So maybe whoever it is started small and now covers the entire world."

"You're nuts. You know that, right?"

"Yuri, there has to be a bigger body, a level up from semel-aten, like a werepanther CIA or something. There *has* to be. Someone is handling situations, and we know it's not me. I'm a figurehead with no power."

"You make law for everyone."

I dismissed that with a wave.

"And it just so happens that the tribe of Rahotep is the largest single tribe in the world."

"Yes, but if you put it into perspective and say every panther in the world...." The number was just staggering. "Who does that? Who is responsible for everyone?"

"I think, in all seriousness, everyone is responsible for their own and maybe the tribe closest to them. I mean, it was on Logan to make you stop when you were out of control; maybe that's how it is everywhere."

I shook my head. "That's too simple. Think about it. What if Logan and Christophe were just as fucked up as me? If that was true, then the entire corner of Nevada would have crazed werepanthers running around."

"Yes, but Logan ended your tribe," he reminded me. "He ended your reign as semel. Who's to say that something similar doesn't occur every day?"

"But if single semels are just policing themselves, why doesn't the whole thing just collapse and we're on the six o'clock news everywhere?"

He shook his head. "You're overthinking this."

I wasn't, though; he was just missing it. There had to be a big brother—there simply had to be—but who or what that was, that was the question. I didn't want to be a figurehead. I wanted to make a difference, and on a larger stage than my own tribe. But I had no idea how to do it.

I did have the power to change the law, though, and that was where I was planning to focus all my energy, if I could just figure out what to start with and how. Everything had to be revamped, but I was buried under the weight of what I *should* have been doing versus what I *was* doing. I was on my second rant of the night. If the first was the conspiracy of silence, my next familiar tangent was change.

Yuri said the time for me to simply be had passed. I had to embody the revolution I wanted to see, not simply hope for it. I alone could become a catalyst for action.

"There's no way," I railed, pacing in our room, back and forth at the foot of the bed as he lay stretched out on the mattress watching me. It was how it always went, from firebrand to quitter; I swung back and forth daily. "How do I, the infidel, expect to simply upend thousands of years of *this-is-how-we-do-things*?"

He was waggling his eyebrows.

"What?" I yelled.

"You simply say 'this is the way we're going to do it from now on.' You do what we've discussed—proclaim yourself akhen-aten and begin a new reign with *your* players on the board."

I found myself staring at him. "It's not that easy."

"I think it is."

"That's because you're not the semel-aten!"

"And you're not either." He tipped his head to one side. "Well, at least you don't want to be."

"Yuri—"

"You hate it here," he said, cutting me off. "Not because you're here in Egypt, but because you don't like how the upper class treats the lower, how the priest keeps his temple, or how you are supposed to treat the servants in your own villa. You hate the classes of people instead of one tribe that stands together, and you hate that a hundred semel-atens before you and a hundred priests have kept this city in the Dark Ages instead of letting it join the modern world."

"Yes!"

"Then fucking fix it, my lord," he placated me.

"It's not that easy."

"Change is never easy." He shrugged. "Who lied and said it would be?"

I flopped down on the end of the bed.

After a moment, I felt the mattress lift and dip and realized he was moving behind me. When his strong arms wrapped around my neck, I grunted and leaned back against him.

"You'll do the right thing." He sounded so sure.

"How do you know?"

"Because you always do."

"That's not true." I closed my eyes, savoring the feel of his skin, the heat of his chest against my back, and the stubble-covered jaw grazing mine.

Did he know what a simple comfort his touch was? How did everyone in the world not want a mate? Having someone to listen when you unburden your soul and to sleep wrapped around in the night? How was that not a prerequisite for life?

"You are inherently good," he said, his voice a vibrating purr against the side of my throat. "And once you set your sight on a course of action, you will not be able to push it from your mind."

He was so right.

I was assaulted by everything that needed to be changed on a daily basis and crushed under the weight of the status quo. The landslide of obligations from the vital to the mundane never stopped. There were expectations and demands and endless responsibilities.

I hated it.

SIX MONTHS had come and gone, and still I felt like I was drowning. Every morning when I woke up, I wondered if that day would be the day I finally got my bearings. I was still waiting. I wanted to go back to the night Logan Church had twisted in his seat and stared at me with a glint in his gold eyes, and tell him to go to hell.

"You should be a semel again," he had said with that familiar deep rumble in his voice. He had no idea the effect he had on me, on everyone; it was simply how he was, just Logan. "You're ready, Domin. You need to step out into the light."

Two years before, the man had ended my reign. I had been the semel of a tribe of werepanthers, leader of the tribe of Menhit, and he had fought me in the pit and won. He could have cut out my heart with his claws, but instead... instead he offered the path to redemption. He opened his home, welcomed me into his tribe and into his life. I was trusted, my counsel heeded, my strength relied upon. It was a gift, the second coming of the friendship we had when we were young. I had worried that I would be consumed by bitterness and would turn on him, catch him unawares, betray him, and then kill him. But I had forgotten about my own heart.

I loved Logan. Not like a lover, not with carnal intent, but—and it was so cliché—like the brother I never had. I wanted him back in my life more than I wanted to hurt him.

I had been a shitty leader: the selfish kind, the vindictive kind, the one everyone wished would just die already so they could get someone better, someone who cared at all. So when he beat me in the pit, absorbed my tribe, and took me in, I simply surrendered. Logan was a force of nature, and I had been so tired of fighting him, fighting his nobility and his ethics and his strength, that I let the bitterness go. No good had come from it. Time, instead, to try something new.

Being his maahes, the prince of his tribe, had worked for me. I was easily the second in power. He made the decisions; I carried them out. He navigated; I drove. I was able to be his emissary because I was talking for him, not me. It was so easy.

What came as a surprise was that I changed. I shed my anger, my vanity, and all the pain, and I became everything he'd always seen in me. Logan's faith had made me better, his day-to-day belief invested me in the future of the tribe, in the people, in growth and security and the welfare of all. I was different now, and I owed it all to my old friend, my new semel, Logan Church.

So when he had gazed at me with his honey-colored eyes and told me he wanted me to reclaim my birthright, I couldn't argue, because he believed. I could be, he said, not just a semel, but the semel, the semel-aten, the leader of the entire werepanther world. I would be able to lead those who wanted to follow me because of the changes I had experienced myself. I would be able to get through to those werepanthers who had lost their faith and their way. I would be a catalyst for change and restore prodigals to the fold, Logan was certain of it.

"You're insane," I had replied. "It should be you. You're the strongest."

He shook his head. "You're wrong, it's you."

But no one was stronger than Logan. He was semel-netjer, the only panther in the world whose mate was also a nekhene cat.

Jin Church, his reah, was the most fearsome werepanther I had ever seen, that *anyone* had ever seen, and only Logan had tamed him, could tame him, because only Logan was his true-mate. It was ridiculous for him to even suggest that I could be stronger.

"But you can go anywhere and do anything," he assured me. "I need to stay in the place I was born, rule my tribe, and never leave. All I want to do is go to bed every night with my mate in my arms and wake up every morning to his beautiful gray eyes. Do you understand? You're stronger than me because you can be whatever you want. All I can be is me."

I shook my head. "That doesn't make any sense."

"You're going to be semel-aten."

I was certain I had not heard him correctly. "You have lost your mind."

"No." He lifted one golden eyebrow as he stared into my eyes. "Listen and then tell me what you want to do."

And as he had spoken to me on the long flight to Beijing, I wondered if he even knew what he was talking about.

"What if something goes wrong? What if you and I aren't in the pit at the same time? What if it's just you and Ammon El Masry, the semel-aten, at the end, Logan?"

He shook his head. "It won't be. It can't be. He'll want a guarantee that I'll die. He'll want to make sure. The law says that the semel-aten can challenge me alone or have his maahes with him as well. That's how he'll do it, I have no doubt."

"But he'll find someone else, Logan," I insisted. "If he really wants you dead, he'll find a ringer; he'll get someone from another tribe."

"That won't matter," he guaranteed. "Any cat that's not a semel, I can subdue. You're the one who'll have to kill Ammon. Can you do that?"

Could I?

Had everything led me to a place where leading was again possible? Was I ready to step out of Logan's shadow and take a stand? Did I have the faith in myself that he had in me?

On the high of his praise and faith and love, I gave my answer. "Yes."

Logan smiled, so obviously pleased. "You're going to be amazing."

My prayer had been that he would be right.

It all happened so fast. I became semel-aten and everything fell into place exactly as Logan had said it would. But now I was in Sobek, the ancient werepanther city, semel of the tribe of Rahotep, the tribe of the semel-aten, and everyone was expecting me to lead. They all thought I would just instinctively know what to do and… and instead I was drowning. I was in way over my head and cursing Logan because he was a selfish son of a bitch.

He made me semel-aten because even though he was the best choice for the role, he didn't want to do it. There was no doubt in my mind that Logan would have done a better job than me.

I shared my thoughts with Yuri but no one else. Even as everything threatened to crash down around me, he was the only one I trusted with that secret.

THE PROBLEM was that even though they knew me, with my change of status, the people I brought with me suddenly expected me to simply know what to do. It was, I imagined, what happened when one became a parent. All at once you were expected to know things no one would ever suppose you needed to know otherwise. The weight of their scrutiny made me lash out.

That morning, as I took my usual walk with those closest to me— my maahes, my sylvan, and my sheseru—I was again venting my frustration. There was no way to stop it. I'd tried, but even with all good intentions, the minute they turned to me for guidance, I got pissed and lashed out. I was a horror to be around and I knew it. I was the biggest of ass hats to Crane, my maahes, prince of my tribe. Normally, he gave it back with both barrels. He could speak up for himself. Why he hadn't, why he was just taking whatever I dished out, had been bothering me for the past month. I was ready to have it out with him once and for all.

"So, this Elham," I said softly as I walked the villa with Crane and Taj and Mikhail Gorgerin, my sylvan. "He has a lot to say about me."

"Yes, he does," Crane agreed. "And I'll handle it."

"Which means what?"

"Which means," he said as he sighed, "that I'm talking to him, and it will either escalate and I'll meet him in the pit or it won't and we won't."

Mikhail cleared his throat.

As I glanced at Mikhail over my right shoulder, he gave me a slight shake of his head. But how could I drop it?

"Crane." I took a breath. "You realize that this man, this Elham, is the brother of Ammon El Masry, the last—"

"I know exactly who he is." Crane gave me a slight smirk so unlike him I almost lost my train of thought.

Crane Adams never did anything just *a little*. He laughed big and loud, he had adamant thoughts on subjects that were none of his business, and he poked and prodded until you just confessed your heart to him to get him to shut up. He was strong and kind and fair, and so much more than annoying. But I had never, ever, seen him subdued and quiet. The fact that all his passion and vitality had simply drained out of him was driving me out of my mind. He wasn't himself anymore. He was simply present.

"What the fuck is the matter with you?" I stopped in place.

He kept walking. Everyone else stayed with me, the procession halted.

"Crane!" I barked.

He let out a deep sigh and rounded on me.

I waited expectantly.

He tipped his head sideways because, apparently, he was waiting on me.

"Crane—"

"My semel."

I closed on him fast, pointing at his chest. "Don't fuckin' *my semel* me. What the hell is wrong with you?"

"In what way?"

"In every way!" I snarled.

He crossed his arms. "Am I not the maahes of this tribe?"

"You know goddamn good and well that you're the maahes! What the fuck does that—"

"Then allow me to perform the duties of my station and conduct affairs as I see fit. If I need help, I'll ask for it. If I mess up, you'll definitely hear about it. But until then, don't worry."

"I have to worry! Elham El Masry announced his intention to meet my maahes in the pit!"

"I'm well aware."

"Crane! He was in line to be semel-aten! Since I killed Ammon, he's out, and now he wants to be maahes because he can mess with me and my plans if he's in your spot."

"Again." He sounded annoyed. "I know."

"By law, anyone can challenge your position and—"

"My semel—"

"Crane," I said, my voice rising in anger and frustration. "I don't want Ammon El Masry's little brother in my private circle! As maahes, he would hold considerable power and eventually could sway people to his cause and—"

"Domin—"

"Everyone expected him to be made maahes. Asdiel Kovo, the new priest, never stops asking me when it will happen. He, much like everyone else, never considered that Ammon's brother would not be made maahes. He said that choosing you was—"

"I don't give a shit," Crane cut me off. "The new priest is a dick."

Taj, who'd been listening the whole time, snorted from behind me, and when I looked back at him, he opened his eyes wide and shrugged.

"What? Crane's right, he is a dick."

"He's a man in love with the sound of his own voice," Mikhail chimed in.

"Whatever he believes, or doesn't, is of no interest to us. Crane's right—do not concern yourself with these petty annoyances. Allow your maahes to handle the affairs of his station."

"Thank you," Crane grumbled and stalked away, first down the hall, and then I saw him veer off down the stairs leading to the back entrance and beyond to the gardens.

I faced Mikhail. "Have you lost your mind?"

The expression on his face was pure annoyance. "Here's what's probably going to happen," he said. "Elham will insist on a challenge, and it will be him and one other in the pit with Crane and whoever he chooses."

I figured there was more, and when I realized that was it, I glared. "For fuck's sake, Mikhail, I know that! But it can't be you, and it can't be Taj or any of my khatyu or the Shu, so who the fuck from around here is going into the pit who gives a shit about Crane or me? That's what I'm trying to get him to think about. Whoever he takes in there with him is just gonna fold and let him get beat up, or worse, and if anything happens to Crane on my watch, Jin will—"

"Then you shouldn't have brought him," Mikhail said sharply. "If you'll excuse me, I have a meeting of the sylvans to lead."

He took off before I gave him my permission to go, and Taj gave me a quick nod before he was gone, walking away in the opposite direction.

"Thanks," I yelled. "I really enjoy these morning get-togethers of ours!"

No one was listening to me.

THE VILLA was supposed to be mine. It didn't feel like it. The residence of the semel-aten, while a home, was more like a vast resort and college campus all rolled up together. I had no idea who half the people in the sprawling mansion were at any given time. The place was simply too big, too filled with marble columns and staircases, and statues of gods and goddesses, and balconies and alcoves and just space. So much yawning space. It was supposed to be my haven, but my sanctuary wouldn't be filled with floor mosaics and frescoes that ran through rooms and down halls. Living in the villa of the semel-aten was like living in a museum. The only time I felt any sort of peace at all was when I was in my own quarters.

The area I occupied with Yuri was small—by villa standards—and was located behind the patch of papyrus near the back of the roof gardens. To get to our bedroom, we climbed a winding staircase and there encountered a wrought iron gate that remained locked at all times. Once that was opened, we stepped out onto an enormous stamped concrete terrace that had a view of the main courtyard and, beyond that, miles of desert and hills. Walking the length of the patio brought us to a set of pivoting glass doors, and through them was our area.

Inside the suite, to the left was a wall of floor-to-ceiling pivoting windows that resembled the doors but half the size. When everything was open, a warm breeze blew through the space and it felt open and airy. The room itself was a thousand square feet, with a bathroom and a smaller balcony on the opposite side that ate into the space. On the main terrace section we had to cross to get to our private quarters, one portion of the area was the garden with acacia trees, papyrus, blue lotus that grew near the reflecting pools, and bougainvillea. The other part of the enclosure had a table, chairs, and many lavish chaise lounges. There was also an enormous canopy covering it and drains built in so rainwater couldn't flood the space, though, being Egypt, rain was rarely a problem. It was quiet and serene, and I had moved my bedroom there the second week I was in Sobek. It was supposed to be a place the semel retired to for reflection, but I claimed it for Yuri and me.

The servants had been scandalized by me taking such quaint accommodations, and they were further stunned when I converted the lavish quarters of the former semel-aten into several smaller guest rooms. No one understood why I was so insistent about my privacy. I didn't need people to clean my room or dust it, and I didn't want anyone but Yuri going through my personal things, poking around, or snooping. Laundry could go down the chute, and that was it. No one came in; trays of food were left at the gate and picked up there. I knew it was strange for them—I was strange, and the word kadish was used a lot.

"What is that?" I had asked Taj.

He spoke softly, kindly. "Domin, they say you are kadish, impure, because you do not know the truth of your station. You have to let them serve you."

"I do! All my meals are prepared, the villa is cleaned, and other people who visit are cared for... I don't get it."

"You need to be seen in your home; you can't hide up there in the gardens."

"I don't hide!" I insisted.

The lift of one dark brow said differently.

Alone now, leaning against an enormous stone pillar, I had time to think about the situation I found myself in.

It seemed like an endless problem. The people in my home didn't feel like they belonged to me unless I ordered them around. I wanted to treat them better than that, to ask instead of order and say please and thank you. But apparently, that was very poor manners on my part. It was exhausting. I was supposed to be the kind of semel I could no longer be; going back to being a selfish prick did not seem like a step in the right direction although, after my behavior of the past two weeks, no one would call me anything but a tyrant.

I realized that I would be better—mood, attitude, everything— if my mate was not gone. As it was, the past fourteen days without Yuri were wearing on me. I hadn't even been able to talk to him because he'd taken the wrong phone, and... I missed him and I wanted to see him and touch him. The whole thing was a mess. I shouldn't have let him leave at all. I was an idiot.

"I hate this," I muttered to no one.

"What's wrong with you?"

Turning, I found Mikhail, having reappeared, staring at me like I was stupid.

"I thought you had a meeting," I groused.

"It was moved to four," Mikhail ground out.

"By who?"

"By one of your akers, a manu, Alhaji Yacouba, who was running late getting back from a day trip to Cairo."

"Why do you care?"

"I don't, but apparently Ammon's sylvan, Traore Uago, did and decided to wait for the man."

I studied him, wondering why he let that happen. It wasn't like Mikhail to allow other people to change his schedule. "What are you going to do?"

Mikhail drew in a slow breath. "I'm going to remind Traore that he is no longer the sylvan, that his rank is now shefdew—"

"I think you just called the man a papyrus scroll," I pointed out.

"I did?"

I raised an eyebrow.

"Then how do you say scribe?"

"I'll look it up," I quipped. "Or, more likely, I'll ask someone."

He grunted softly. "Well, anyway, Traore thinks that he still has power. He doesn't and he needs a reminder. Alhaji needs to understand who he should be listening to. He too will be educated."

"How?"

"I'm going to have your sheseru discipline them both."

As if on cue, Taj was there, an enormous bullwhip rolled up in his right hand.

"I'm sorry," Mikhail said quickly. "I know you prefer not to punish, but there is no recourse."

"They're the ones who should be sorry," he replied. "They cannot be allowed to insult you. It's not *maat*."

It was not like Mikhail at all. "You—"

"They continue to test me. I've cited them, I've fined them, and no one responds. I'm done."

I had no idea Mikhail went in for physical punishment. "This doesn't seem like you."

"Respect is earned, and I understand, but barring that, fear will work in the interim. I'm done being talked about behind my back and having them talk about me in Arabic and Egyptian and Farsi. They think I don't know what they're saying, but I do. They think I'm not trained in the law, but I am. I'm the sylvan of my tribe, and anyone who wants to can debate the law with me, but I will win. If they don't like how I conduct the affairs of my station, they're free to challenge me in the pit. But I will no longer stand for insolence."

"I don't remember ever hearing about you having anyone flogged in Logan's tribe."

"Begging your pardon, but until *you* believe that you are semel-aten, the people will not. No one ever questioned that Logan Church was meant to lead and be followed. His respect flowed to me."

"And what, no one respects me?"

His eyes, deep cobalt blue, locked on mine as he waited. He had a good face, chiseled and strong, striking and sharply angled, but he wasn't beautiful, not like Yuri. Normally, Mikhail wasn't the kind of man you noticed, but now, in the middle of a town in Egypt, he stood out. With his fair complexion, his height of six two, and lean muscular build, you noticed him moving through a crowd here. In Nevada, where we had come from, he inspired no second glance, but in our new home, he drew attention.

Sobek lay between Cairo and Giza on land that was almost like another country, with borders patrolled by armed guards and a no-fly zone above it. The land gift dated back to the time of the pharaohs.

"Domin?"

I shook my head. "Just, do you really need to—"

"Yes." Mikhail's voice, normally smooth and silky, was hard and cold. "I do. No one but me changes my schedule. No one."

He left then, Taj walking beside him.

I didn't like the harsh changes I was seeing in any of them, the men who made up my household, who helped me lead my tribe, at all.

After walking down one of the many long staircases, I took a right into the vast library, an endless room filled from floor to vaulted ceiling with shelves of books, ancient texts people from all over the world came to use.

As I crossed the floor, people lifted their heads and greeted me as was custom.

"Sah'eed nahharkoo," they called out.

It meant "good day" in Arabic, and though I was learning the language, the task was daunting. So I waved and walked on. As I passed one of the many small alcoves riddling the library, I saw the place where I had last touched my mate before he left for Ipis two weeks before. I nearly stumbled over my feet getting to the window where he had stood. He had been there, standing still, staring down into the courtyard…

I moved up behind him and put my hands on his hips.

"You know, the semel-aten will have your head if you touch his mate," Yuri vowed.

"Will he?" I whispered, inhaling his musky scent before pressing my face into the side of his neck and kissing him.

"He will," he said, taking one of my hands, easing me closer until my chest rested against his broad, muscular back, and then placing it over his heart. He flattened my palm there, over his hard pectoral, and then slid his fingers between mine. "He's very possessive."

"Why do you put up with that?"

"Because if he stopped it would kill me."

I adjusted my stance so my groin rubbed against his plump, round ass. It was beautiful, solid and soft at the same time, a cushion when I took him from behind, and I could never keep my hands from it. Yuri was heavy with meaty muscle; it was thick over wide shoulders, pecs, arms, and legs. Under his clothes, he was massive and hard, but he could also wrap around me so tight, engulf me in warmth, and….

Yuri.

It was all shit except for him.

Suddenly I wanted him naked in bed with me more than I wanted to breathe. I needed him—his closeness could fix things I never thought possible. Every other lover I'd ever had was treated to me being in charge behind closed doors.

All except him. I could submit to Yuri.

"Come with me to—"

"Are you seeing this?" he asked abruptly, tipping his head, indicating the courtyard below.

I was surprised to see Ebere El Masry, the previous semel-aten's yareah, getting out of a stretch limousine, servants there instantly to welcome her home.

The servants brought a bowl of water for her to wash her hands, a towel, as well, and then lifted an enormous palm-frond shade to keep the sun off her face. It was all still overwhelming for me—the protocol, the training, the standard of service in my home.

"You should go greet your mastaba," Yuri suggested, patting my hand before twisting in place. The warmth in his eyes as he gazed at me... God. I was supposed to walk away from him?

"Domin?"

It had only been six months since I'd claimed him as mine, and I found that every passing day what I felt got stronger, more desperate and clinging. I barely wanted to be parted from him. I would cut out my tongue before I admitted it to him. Confessing my heart was not something I did. I was cool—cold, even—speaking of what lay beneath... no good could come of that.

"My lord!"

"I'm coming," I snarled at the servant who had come to let me know Ebere had arrived.

She recoiled from me. I saw the hurt that I had raised my voice, both in her demeanor and posture, suggesting that I had taken a hand to her, not simply been sharp with my reply.

"Your semel will be right there," Yuri promised her, his tone full of infinite patience and kindness. Funny that he had been a sheseru, as Taj was now, because there was no trace of it left in the man, no enforcer, no punisher. He was simply my rock, and that was all.

"Yes, sekhem," the woman said, bowing and stepping back, her body language conveying that he had smoothed what I had ruffled.

"Why do you take the time to do that?"

"What?" he prodded gently, facing me as I stepped away from him.

It was only then that I noticed what he was wearing. It was like he was dressed to go on a safari; the only thing missing was the big-ass hat. "Soothe their— Where the hell are you going?"

He squinted. "Domin, I'm leaving with Constantine in twenty minutes. I thought you came and found me to say good-bye."

"Shit," I groaned. "That's today?"

"That's *now*," he said, his lip curling up in the corner.

I—*breathe*—how was I supposed to function without my mate? "Why do you need to—"

"The semel of the tribe of Tegeret, Ehivet Milar, says that he is being kept from his son, Garai, who he sent to speak with the semel of Feran, Hakkan Tarek, a month ago. Repeated messengers, even a trip to Ipis, has not yielded any results. The semel refuses to see him and—"

"What? One semel cannot refuse to see another."

"I know, which is why he is asking you to intercede on the point of law."

"How does this—who again?"

"Hakkan Tarek." He supplied the name, his eyes gliding over my face like they always did, with such obvious appreciation. I loved the way he loved me.

I cleared my throat. "How does Hakkan Tarek not let this semel see his own son? That's insane. He can start a tribal war that way."

"Yes, I know," he agreed in his low and gravelly voice. "So before things escalate, Ehivet asked for help. And he's being very gracious. He thinks that because of the ongoing conflict Hakkan Tarek has on his own land that this is the reason for the semel's distraction and inability to answer him."

"What conflict?"

"Apparently in Ipis they have some kind of land dispute that the semel-aten will need to lend a hand resolving."

"I—but why do—"

"The tribe of Feran makes their home close to the catacombs of Abtu, and apparently the catacombs themselves are in dispute. Ehivet says that he's heard of a few fatalities."

"Why would this man send his son to such an unstable tribe?"

"He had to. Years ago, he agreed to a covenant bond with Tarek, that when their children were of age they would be mated. Tarek has a daughter, Masika, who is now sixteen—"

"Sixteen? She should be going to high school."

"Domin," Yuri sighed. "These are not—"

"I'm going to pass a law, Yuri. All children will be educated. All of them. Boys and girls; no one will be exempt."

"It will always be up to the individual semels to do with their children what they will, Domin. You can't change that."

"Watch me."

He smiled warmly. "Your heart is in the right place."

"Just talk to me," I huffed.

"Well, so, anyway, Ehivet says that he simply sent his son to Ipis to let the semel know that they would wait until Masika was eighteen before performing the ritual of handfasting."

"But?"

"But now he has not heard from his son, or the ten men he sent with him, in over a month. All his attempts have fallen on deaf ears, and so now he has reached out to you to come mediate the situation."

"Then I should go with—"

"Domin, you barely have enough time to breathe in a day, so I—"

"No."

"You're being unreasonable."

"No, this Hakkan Tarek is. What exactly is wrong in his tribe?"

Yuri's eyes remained gentle; his tone didn't rise. It was as if being with me, becoming my mate, had changed him, made him the soul of quiet strength and reflection. Not that it had doused his passion for me, but the temper that used to be in him had simply disappeared. He was different, as were the others, but whereas they were all hardening, he had done just the opposite.

"The semel has two factions within his tribe: the peq, made up mostly of farmers and shepherds who live in the hills, and the shen, who are the merchants who live in the city of Ipis. Apparently, the hostility stems from a dispute over the ownership of the catacombs. There has been some kind of discovery there, and so who is heir to the land is in question."

"How do you know all this?"

"The tribal records."

"Oh," I grunted. "Been reading those again, have you?"

He chortled. "Kind of a prerequisite to being the mate of the semel-aten, don't you think? I swear, I have no idea how the tribe of Hatheret has—"

"What?"

"The tribe of Hatheret in Paris. Their semel, Emil Lefevre. His family has compiled and edited the records since the time of the Crusades."

"I know about the tribe of Hatheret!" I barked.

"Then why did you ask me?"

I growled. "So everything you just said, that's all in the tribal record?"

"As you know, it's up to each semel to compose his correspondence weekly and send it to the tribe of Hatheret to be entered into the logs."

"That's not mandatory," I insisted.

"No, but maybe it should be."

"That job has got to be daunting." I sympathized with people I had never seen.

"I'm sure the stipend they receive from each tribe the world over for doing it more than outweighs the annoyance."

"Maybe."

He kissed my forehead, which just reminded me he was leaving and irritated me all over again. "Okay, so if the territory in Ipis itself belongs to the semel, I don't see—"

"But we're not talking about that, we're talking about the land."

"So there is a family that owns the land the catacombs sit on."

"Yes."

"And who is that?"

I got a wicked grin. "I don't know, love. I have to go there to find out."

I grunted.

"But for right now, from what the records say, Hakkan Tarek can see no resolution in sight, but since it affects no one, he has left it in the hands of the two djehus."

"But it is affecting those outside his tribe now."

"This is only a brand-new development, though. Before this, no one knew or cared what was going on in Ipis. Ammon didn't; there's no record that he ever even visited."

"But we care suddenly because of the semel of the tribe of Tegeret."

"Yes."

"If not for him, you would not be making this journey."

"No," he said huskily, gazing into my eyes.

"And what precisely are you going to do?"

"First, I'm going to meet with Hakkan Tarek and insist that he send Garai Milar home to his father immediately. Then I am going to meet with the djehus, the leaders of the two factions in the tribe of Feran, and then report back to you. If it's a question of the law, I might just send for Mikhail. If it's more, then I'll—"

"As soon as you handle the situation with Garai, immediately check in with the two heads of the warring factions and then come back," I instructed. "Don't try and fix anything other than sending the boy back to his tribe. I want you to gather information and that's all."

"I shouldn't stay there and resolve the problem if I can?" Yuri taunted.

I was focused on his words, but it was getting harder. It was difficult not to notice and be mesmerized by the curve of his lip, the dimple in his chin, and his thick expressive eyebrows.

"Domin?"

I cleared my throat. "No. You'll give me a report, and I'll decide what to do at that point."

"Yes, my lord," he said mock seriously, the deference over the top and playfully patronizing.

"That's not what I meant," I growled, not in the mood to banter with him. It was killing me that he was leaving. "You just need to come home!"

"Why?"

"Because it's your duty."

"My duty?" He was still teasing me.

"You're supposed to stand right beside me!" I yelled and saw the surprise register that I was actually upset.

"I will, then," he said quietly. "I'll get home as fast as I can."

I took a breath. "I don't remember you telling me any of this."

"Well, I did. I explained this all to you last night at length, again, as well as several times in the past week."

Had I been listening? Ever?

"Your steward—"

"Kabore, yes," I said sharply. "I've met the man, go on."

Judging from the twinkle in his eyes, I was clearly amusing him. "He suggested that I take this task off your plate by going in your place."

"And what if I don't want you to go?"

His eyes were really the clearest blue I had ever seen in my life, and when they fixed on mine I could feel a comforting weight settle over me, spreading calm. "Is that what you're asking me to do?"

I thought about it for a moment. "Have other mates done these kinds of things?"

"Of course," he said. "Missions of goodwill are what mates of important men do."

"What if it's dangerous?"

"It's not. How could it be? I'll be there to help return a boy that the semel of Feran has probably just not had time to think about. The man basically has a civil war being waged on his land; I'll bet you anything, the boy is an oversight. He'll welcome me with open arms, and when I tell him that I am gathering information for you so that the semel-aten might help him find a resolution, he might even kiss me."

"He better not."

His eyes were warm. "Don't worry about me. Everyone knows that to harm the mate of the semel-aten is a death sentence. No one would risk it."

I was not convinced. "You will take thirty men with you."

"Will I?"

"Stop answering my commands with questions!"

"Am I doing that?" He was so restrained, so calm.

"Yes!" I yelled like a screaming idiot. "And it's very patronizing!"

"Stop ranting," he directed, half grinning, his voice sexy and calming at the same time. "Now, listen. Thirty men on a mission of mediation is overkill."

"I disagree," I said defensively.

"I used to be a sheseru," he reminded me, his tone placating. "I know how many men to take, Domin. Don't fret."

"I don't fret!" I was indignant. "I just want you to be safe and—"

"I will be perfectly fine meeting a semel and the djehus. If I have too many men with me, it will seem like I'm there to impose your will instead of talk. Take my counsel on this."

That was the second time he'd used that word. "What's a djehu? I mean, I get that it's some kind of leader, but the word's new to me."

"A djehu is like an aker, except it's elected. Apparently, this is how the tribe of Feran is. Hakkan Tarek allowed djehus to be picked by the people instead of them just going to the sylvan."

"Why?"

"Because they are two very diverse groups who live apart, don't ever mix, and have basically nothing in common."

"Except that they're all panthers."

"Except that."

"You know you don't have to explain it to me like that. I'm not a child."

"No. You're not," he said, his voice sultry and full of heat.

I swallowed hard.

"So, I'm going to meet with the semel, get Garai home, and then speak to the djehus and bring you back all their concerns, whatever they are."

"Fine," I growled, prickly with frustration.

"Good." His tone soothed me. "Did you want to kiss me or—"

"Just go." I was terse.

Instead of listening, he took my face in his big hands, hauled me close, and kissed me hard and deep and possessive. When he tipped my head back, my mouth opened, and he swept his tongue inside and mated it with mine.

I grabbed hold of the heavy jacket, my hands curling around the lapels as I whimpered in the back of my throat. I needed more, wanted more, and I resented everything, all of it, because being semel-aten meant I could not claim my mate whenever I wanted.

The rules, the protocols, the granted audiences, and the myriad of people I saw in the course of a day kept me continually from his side. And then when I did see him, I often erupted because I was angry and he was the only one I could vent my frustrations to—or on—and it became me attacking him, yelling, picking fights....

I wanted everything to be right between us before he left. I put all of it, everything I was thinking and feeling, into the kiss. He had to know how much I loved him. I needed it ingrained in him, simply recognized and understood.

I sucked his tongue inside my mouth, then slid mine over his, stroking, slipping it back and forth, drawing the kiss out, feeling the shiver run through him. I moaned loudly when his hands gripped my ass tight.

"Domin," he whispered. I kissed him until he had to tear his lips from mine to breathe. "Are you trying to kill me?"

"Just trying to make an impression," I said, lifting my mouth for the next one, tightening my arms around his neck to bring him back down to me.

"I'll never get out of here," he pretended to complain as he fused his lips to mine.

Seconds later when he shoved me away, I was surprised. "What?" I was panting.

"I have to go."

"Yuri—"

"Love." The tone, the lull in it, the adoration, brought me out of my pheromone-fueled haze.

"I have to go," he repeated.

"Take your phone."

"It's in my pocket."

"Okay."

"You're adorable."

Faced with the dancing clear blue eyes of my mate, I couldn't even growl at him. I forced a smile instead, to hide my worry, my fear, my aching heart, and most of all, my devouring need to keep him with me. "How long?" I posed the question as nonchalantly as possible.

"Two weeks, I would think."

"How far away is Ipis?"

"It's a ten-hour drive," he said, taking my chin in his hand to lightly brush his lips over mine. "I'll be home before you know it. I love you."

I dismissed him with a flick of my wrist. The evil glint in his eyes said I wasn't fooling him in the least.

Watching him walk away was almost physically painful. What the hell was I supposed to do without my mate for two weeks?

Chapter Two

YURI HAD called me once from the road and apologized for accidentally taking the wrong phone with him. He'd taken his regular one and not the satellite, so the reception would be spotty at best. I had not been amused.

"You did it on purpose," I groused.

"I really didn't," he said, chuckling. "But please don't worry. I'm under your protection. Who would dare touch me?"

It was not comforting. I had not been able to talk to him since. I wasn't really worried—more annoyed with him for not being more careful—but I didn't even have time to do that properly because of everything swirling around me. I was lucky a new semel-aten wasn't expected to host the Feast of the Valley until the second year of his reign. I would have been royally screwed since it would have been a mere three weeks away. How it was July already, I had no idea.

"Elham," Ebere said, standing when I walked into the room. I still didn't know what she was doing in Sobek. Maybe it was time to pin her down.

"What?" I said curtly, feeling like I had just walked into a conversation already in progress.

"We still haven't talked about him."

"First off, what the hell are you doing in Sobek? Cairo too boring for you all of a sudden?"

"I was getting to that." She was annoyed but trying not to let me hear it in her voice. "And no, I love Cairo. I came to talk to you about Elham. I—"

"What'd you do with your kids? Ditch them somewhere?"

She glared at me. "My children are safe with my mother and their aunt, my lord. Thank you for your concern."

I grunted. "So now you want to talk? You haven't wanted to fill me in about anything since you got here."

"I know, and I'm sorry."

"And now, after days of silence, you want the topic of conversation to be your dead husband's brother?"

"Yes. Please."

"Why would I want to discuss anything about him?"

"Because we must."

I groaned. "Why?"

We were friends after six months, and so, alone, behind closed doors, I could treat her however I liked. She was the mate of the last semel, his yareah, and I had saved her from losing any status at all after I killed him in the pit. Taking her as my mastaba, mistress of my home, put her and her children under my protection. If I never had any offspring of my own, hers would be my heirs. And even though she had two girls and neither of them could ever be semel-aten, whoever was named next would then protect them as my progeny. It was all very tidy, and I liked it. So did she. But now there was a problem, one that she was apparently ready to talk about.

"Because Elham was Ammon's brother," she said. "If he fights Crane in the pit and wins, when he becomes maahes he can ask you for me, and by rights, you cannot refuse him, as his lineage gives him prior claim."

"This is boring old news that I know already," I retorted.

"You're not taking this seriously," she volleyed. "Where is your sylvan? He needs to give you his counsel."

"I don't need my—"

"Elham is going to become your maahes and take me from you if he beats Crane in the pit."

"Crane can beat him." I dismissed her concerns as I walked over to the enormous monstrosity of a desk that came with the whole semel-aten gig. It was all hand-carved out of some extinct wood that surely had been prettier shading a stream somewhere.

"It's not just a simple test of strength in the pit, you know."

My gaze flicked to hers.

"You see," she said as she threw up her hands. "You have no idea what—"

A knock on the door stopped her.

I growled and then yelled for whomever to enter.

The door opened and Kabore Nour, my steward, in charge of the villa and of my private staff, walked into the room. I got the feeling he didn't approve of me, though it definitely had nothing to do with me being gay. He liked Yuri quite a bit, but then, everyone did.

"Yes?" I was irritable.

"You have a visitor, my lord. Korneiley Church from Nevada. He requested an audience at once."

The cherry on the cake of my week. Koren.

"Show him in."

There had been a time when my heart would have flipped over at the news that Koren Church was anywhere near me. I had been wildly, madly, desperately in love with him, and our on-again, off-again relationship had only added fuel to the fire. I had wanted him but couldn't have him, he had wanted me but our timing was bad, and round and round it had gone. We were both stupid, both self-centered, and both of us had wanted the other to cave. The last time he walked away, though, almost killed me. My heart had been too mangled and the jealousy eating away at it just not worth it. You couldn't always wonder if the person you loved, loved you back. There was a time to simply know and be content in that knowledge.

I stood when he walked in.

He stopped by the door. Koren was still very easy on the eyes. The short, thick blond hair, deep olive-green eyes, laugh lines, long and straight Roman nose, full lips, the gold of his skin, the grace of his movements… there was no missing his beauty.

I opened my mouth to greet him as Samani Baro, hathen of my house, slipped past him into the room.

"I must speak to you," she said quickly.

In that instant, I saw his eyes glide over the stunning woman—and he liked what he saw.

Sometimes life gave you reminders without anyone else having to know. Stupidly, for a second, my heart had opened because it was so good to see him. But any words now were empty, as I had seen his interest in another. It was as simple as that. When I was in the room,

Yuri saw no one else. I had gotten used to it, to being the most important thing. I would not give that up for anything.

"I was—" Koren began.

"Wait." I stopped him, rounding on Samani, who had not been distracted at all by the beautiful man in our midst, her focus all on me.

"Yes?"

"The contingent from the tribe of Aswanet has barred me from checking on the concubines in their quarters. Your khatyu must break down the door to gain entrance, and nothing may be destroyed inside your home without your permission."

Why was I being bothered with such mundane crap? Didn't she know I didn't care?

She made a face. "I know you don't like to deal with this kind of thing, but your sekhem, who is normally here to handle these requests, is absent. Because of that, I must come to you."

"What does he usually say?"

"He says to do what I think is best."

"That sounds like good advice. Do that."

"And I have your permission to act in your stead?" She was making sure.

"You do."

She made to leave.

"Wait."

Her eyes came back on me.

"Make sure you let me know if the girls are hurt."

"Of course." She gave me a quick bow, spared a nod to Ebere, and then left.

Koren watched her go.

"I always liked her," Ebere said brightly. "She always handled Ammon so well. He used to come to my chambers fuming because she'd outmaneuvered him again and again."

"Your mate complained that he had missed bedding another?"

She tilted her head, and there was just a hint of a smile.

"It's a wonder you didn't kill him yourself."

Her gaze met mine.

"I'm glad you didn't hate me."

"Nothing to hate." She was adamant.

I cleared my throat. "I enjoy having Samani here."

"You were smart to elevate her to hathen."

"Someone needed to do it, and you certainly wanted nothing to do with the harem."

She scoffed. "No, I didn't."

"I'm sorry." We finally focused on Koren. "You have a harem?"

I waggled my eyebrows.

"All semel-atens have harems," Ebere educated Koren, the censure in her voice evident. "Everyone knows that."

I came clean. "I didn't."

"No?"

My quick laugh made her eyelids flutter before she glanced over at Koren.

"Who are you, may I ask?"

He moved forward, hand extended. "Koren Church."

She took the offered hand. "Oh, yes, I see the resemblance to the semel-netjer now. Pleasure to meet you."

"You know Logan?"

"I've had the pleasure, yes," she sighed, "and of meeting his mate, as well. Your tribe is blessed to have them both."

"We think so."

"When is Yuri due home?" Her focus was back on me.

"In a couple of days."

"Where did he go?"

"Again," I said on a huffed exhale, "he went to speak to a semel for me."

"Yes, but where did he go specifically? I didn't ask and you didn't say."

"You could have questioned Kabore."

"It's unseemly for me to make that inquiry of your steward when I should ask you."

I grunted. "He went to Ipis to meet with the semel and the djehus."

"Whatever for?"

"The semel of the tribe of Tegeret—"

"Ehivet Milar, yes?"

"He's missing his son."

Her eyes narrowed. "If Ehivet is missing his son, why on earth would Yuri be involved? And why would he go to Ipis? He needed to go to Minya, where the—"

"Ehivet sent his son to Ipis."

"I'm missing something."

"He and the semel of the tribe of Feran have a covenant bond for their children."

"*Oh*, I see."

"And he's also speaking to two of Tarek's djehus. There's a land dispute or something. The catacombs figure into it."

Her breath caught excitedly, which surprised me. "And is he going to see the catacombs while he's there?"

"I would think so, yes. Why?"

"Oh, I always wanted to go to see the great cavern, but Ammon would never take me."

"Why?" I was instantly on edge. "Is it dangerous?"

"No, quite the opposite. I understand the catacombs are gorgeous and quite safe."

"So why, then?"

"Ammon said that until the petty feuding was forcibly ended that he would not dignify the semel with his presence or mine. He felt that—oh, and now I can't think of his name—"

"Hakkan Tarek."

"Yes, Tarek." She seemed relieved. "He felt that as a semel he should simply discipline his tribe and take matters into his own hands."

"I hate to agree with a power-mad tyrant, but, yeah. Hakkan Tarek needs to send his sheseru and khatyu to the homes of each djehu, bring them to his house, and everybody stays there until it's fixed or he just executes them and starts over."

"Domin!"

"What? It's true," I insisted.

"You have to understand the problems, not negotiate at knifepoint."

"I think you're missing the point. There would be no negotiating."

"There are two distinct groups," she pointed out. "They have to learn to coexist."

"They're all panthers; they need to get over it."

"You realize that you're not just talking about Ipis, yes? This scenario can be used on the whole world. Why can't people just get along? They're all human."

I shook my head. "It's not the same thing."

"Of course it is."

"Panthers must adhere to the law. We are all bound to our semels and our tribes. The semel made a mistake allowing these two factions to coexist within his tribe. He compounded his error by allowing them to elect their own people to take their complaints to."

"Yes, but now they all have to learn to get along within what they've constructed."

"That's crap. If Yuri comes back and tells me that these two djehus are unreasonable, I will take men back there, sit everyone down, and talk it out. If that doesn't work either—then I will discipline them."

She was glaring at me.

"What?"

"These things are not so simple," she tried to impress upon me.

"Sometimes they are," I said, and then something occurred to me. "So Ammon was aware of these problems as well."

"Yes."

"So it's been going on a long time."

"The struggles with these two groups are ongoing. Everyone knows that the tribe itself has a conflict going on within it, a civil disturbance. But the semel never reached out to Ammon."

"He didn't reach out now; it's Ehivet Milar, who is being kept from his son, who has reached out to me. If Hakkan Tarek didn't want someone in his business, he should have sent the boy back to his father."

"Perhaps there is a reason for his silence."

"Well, Yuri will find out or has already. He'll have a full report for me as soon as he gets home."

She appeared sad.

"Why are you making that face?"

"Oh, nothing, I just—I wish I'd known that Yuri was going out there. I would have loved to tag along and see the catacombs."

"You can go once we know what's going on." I snickered. "I'll send a delegation with you to keep you safe."

"Maybe next time I visit," she said, her eyes warm as she studied me. "So how many men would you send with me? The same as you sent with Yuri?"

She was being funny, but the question made me realize I had no idea how to answer her question.

"Domin?"

Why didn't I know that?

"How many men did you send with Yuri?"

I had no idea. "I'm not sure, besides Constantine. He was the only one Yuri mentioned."

"So it's possible that your mate left simply with one of your khatyu."

"He's the captain of the house guard."

She was studying me. "You really don't know who went with your mate?"

I never did. Yuri took care of himself. He could, of course—he had been a sheseru, he knew what he needed to do to protect himself. Didn't he? "Yuri doesn't need me to coddle him or second-guess him or oversee his preparations."

She furrowed her brow. "You're being very defensive, and I'm not attacking you."

"I—"

"And I beg your pardon, but, yes, he does. The man is your mate, the mate of the semel-aten. He does nothing alone anymore. You are responsible for him, you make the law, and he follows it."

But I had watched Logan tangle with Jin, and Logan never won. "A semel should not rule his mate. He should—"

"A semel should talk to his mate and let them make decisions, yes, but the mate of a semel is a precious thing and should be treated as such."

"I know that."

She didn't seem convinced. "You treat Yuri as I suspect you always have. You put no boundaries on him."

"I want him to know he has his freedom."

"At what cost?"

"At no cost," I snapped. "He's safe, I know he is, and if his damn phone had reception, I'd prove it to you."

"I thought he had a satellite phone?"

"He does."

"Then how is it not working?"

"Just—never mind."

Her eyes widened. "Did he misplace it or—"

"He took the wrong one."

"And you didn't insist that he come back and get the right one?"

"No, of course not."

"Why?"

"Because he was already— Why are you questioning me?" I almost yelled.

"Because even though Ammon was a monster, he was far more possessive of me than you are of Yuri. He never loved me, and yet took far greater care for my safety than you take of Yuri's."

"That's not true."

"It is. You think because Yuri's a man that the same confines are not needed for him, but you're wrong. Your mate is your most precious possession; all care should be taken at all times. He doesn't say, *you* say. You're the semel, he's the mate."

But, again, I had seen Logan and Jin wage the same war over and over: Logan holding tight, Jin pushing the limits. I didn't want to have those same confrontations with Yuri, especially because I wanted the man to be my friend, too, not just my mate.

"Just think about what I said. I would never want you to have regrets."

"I will," I promised.

"Domin," Koren chimed in from where he still stood, close to the door. "You're not actually worried about Yuri, are you? How far away is this Ipis?"

"Ten hours," I said, not taking my eyes off Ebere, repeating what my mate had explained to me.

"You can always have Jamal send members of the Shu after him, now that they are yours to command," she suggested.

"Yes," I agreed.

"You control the Shu?" Koren sounded surprised.

I glanced over at him, interrupting my glaring contest with Ebere. "I do. So I don't ever have to ask the priest to dispatch them, like other semel-atens have had to. I can do it all by myself."

"How?" he queried, closing in on me.

"When Asdiel Kovo disbanded the council of Ennead, the Shu became mine."

"You lost me."

"The phocal announced to all that the Shu would no longer guard the temple of Satis but would instead protect me."

"Why?" Koren wanted to know.

"I just put it to Jamal to decide who he thought more valuable, me or the new priest."

Ebere sighed. "I remember thinking at the time that that was very clever."

"The second in command of the Shu, Shahid Alon, was having none of it."

"Oh yes," she said, nodding. "I remember that too. He said it was wrong for the Shu to abandon their sacred duty to guard the priest and to instead guard you."

"It was quite the speech," I said sarcastically. "Who knew he was so devout?"

"Oh, he was not devout," she said, laughing, the tension from a few moments ago broken. "Or he would have never been in your bed."

"Who was in your bed?" Koren wanted to know.

"That was ages ago," I teased my mastaba.

"And yet he found the priest more deserving than you."

"He thought the priest sacred and me profane."

"Who did you sleep with?" Koren was getting louder.

"Which is funny, considering you became semel-aten in a sepat which was mandated by the old priest," she mused. "And Kovo became the new priest right after he disbanded the council of Ennead, the very council that voted him in."

"I would never have disbanded them."

"But they didn't know that. They thought you were the very devil."

"Even though the old priest, Hamid Shamon, trusted and liked me."

"Which just goes to show you that people really do fear what they don't know. I mean, the council trusted Asdiel instead of you, and he removed them from the temple and left them outside, stripped naked, to rot. He said they were useless old men."

"You don't know what he said," I scoffed.

"I do too. I've talked with each of the nine at length, and they all said the same thing. Asdiel thought they should have been placed in the tomb along with Hamid Shamon when he died. Asdiel decreed that they would never be counsel to another priest."

"And they won't," I agreed. "Now they counsel my sylvan."

"Yes, quite the coup, that."

"Whatever do you mean?"

"When you took the council of Ennead into your home—the very men who had called you a defiler—and gave them shelter, that was when Jamal started to have doubts about guarding the new priest."

"Perhaps."

"No perhaps—that was your plan."

"You give me far too much credit."

"I think not," she whispered. "You are very clever, my lord. I heard that you met with Asdiel Kovo and swore that as long as the council was still with him at Satis, he would never hold true power alone and you would never truly fear him."

"I said that? Me?"

She giggled. "Yes, you, my lord."

"Huh."

"And when Kovo betrayed his own council like the jackal he is, you were there to take those old men in."

"Well, that was kind of me, wasn't it?"

"Yes, it was. And now they teach in the forum, work in the great library, and counsel your sylvan in all matters of the law. He has those men with all those years of knowledge at his disposal and now calls each by their first name, and they address him as master."

"So I've heard."

"You gave them each a home and a new purpose. I have not seen them so happy in years."

I shrugged, because that had been Mikhail's idea, his doing.

"Who are you talking about?" Koren barked. "Who did you sleep with?"

He would keep asking until I answered. I knew he would. I knew him. "Why do you care about something so—"

"Shahid Alon," Ebere said, supplying the name, "one of the many conquests of Domin Thorne."

"Oh, I remember you telling me about... I thought this was a new—" Koren muttered.

"No." Ebere made a face. "Unlike the previous semel-aten, our new lord sleeps only with his mate."

"You make it sound so important."

"It's a greater quality than you think," she said seriously. "Loyalty is never to be undervalued."

"And I need it from everyone now that the priest is gunning for me," I said, chuckling.

"You should take his vendetta more seriously," she cautioned.

I rolled my eyes. "Like it matters what he does. The priest has no say over anything and no resources since he was banned from his old tribe."

"I was surprised when his brother denounced him."

"I wasn't," I quipped. "He declared open war on me. His brother, Selem, semel of the tribe of Dosret—he sent his maahes here to speak to Crane. Selem wanted to be sure that we knew that his brother's sentiment was not his. He didn't want himself, or his tribe, painted with the same brush of treason."

"How sad to be abandoned by your family."

"It's what a real semel does, though, right?"

"I don't know," she said thoughtfully. "Does a true semel put his tribe before anything or anyone?"

"Yes."

"So in your mind, Selem had no choice?"

"No, he didn't."

Koren broke into our conversation. "I wonder about the role of a semel sometimes."

"What do you mean?" My tone had an edge it didn't have when I was speaking only to Ebere.

"I mean, would a semel who loved his mate still put the tribe first?"

"I think so," I said. "A good one, anyway."

He smirked. "In that case, the tribe of Rahotep trumps Yuri."

But even the sound of the words seemed wrong.

"Well?" he posed.

"Do you think I would?"

"Yes," he replied. "I do."

Ebere spoke up. "I don't. I think it's Yuri first and then the tribe."

"That's not the way of a true semel." Koren was adamant. "A true leader always puts the needs of the whole before the needs of the few or the one."

I was quiet and his eyes met mine.

"I think you'd do what was best for the tribe, Domin."

"Why doesn't that feel like a compliment?"

"I think every true semel would. Even Logan."

"You think Logan, if it came down to a choice between his reah or his tribe, would pick the tribe?"

"Yes," he said, sounding very certain.

"Why?"

"Because if he chose Jin, he would have to see the disappointment on Jin's face for the rest of his life and know that he failed his reah. I think if push came to shove that Logan would choose the tribe."

"I think you're wrong."

"Well, God willing, we will never have to find out," Ebere offered, before her eyes glowed softly. "So, will you have dinner with me later?" she added.

"Of course."

"Good." She smiled as she moved forward into my open arms, coming to give me a kiss before she took her leave, giving Koren a little wave as she did so. The first time the servants had seen her do it, they had been stunned. Apparently she showed me greater affection than she had ever given her mate, the former semel-aten.

As she was going out, Samani was on her way back in, and the women clasped hands quickly as they passed each other.

"What?" I grumbled at my hathen, sitting on the edge of my desk as she moved to step in front of me.

"I just wanted to tell you that everyone's fine—the semel's son just thinks he's in love and was trying to sneak Salome out of the villa."

"Which one is Salome?"

"The one with the dark black curls and green eyes," she jogged my memory.

I couldn't recall her, but that wasn't surprising. I had met the harem once, and that was it. "Does she want to go?"

"Who?"

"The girl, the"—I snapped my fingers—"Salome. Does she want to go?"

"Well, yes, but—"

"Then let her go," I said quickly. "If the semel's son wants her, and if she wants to go, and if it's okay with the semel—let her go. I'm trying to decrease the number, remember?"

"Of course I remember, but—"

"If there's no harem, then you don't have to be here and you can actually go and live your life out of this hellhole. Don't you want that?"

"I—"

"Don't you?" I pushed.

"I… you…," she began. "It's not a hellhole. We live in luxury, and I—"

"Domin," Mikhail clipped my name as he walked in. "I need you in the courtyard immediately."

"I am speaking to him," Samani said indignantly, her voice rising as she glared at Mikhail.

"Am I invisible?" Koren yelled, throwing up his arms.

"Is your concern a matter of life and death?" Mikhail rasped.

"I—"

"A simple yes or no will suffice."

"No, but—"

"All right, then." His eyes flicked to me. "I need you in the main courtyard *now*."

"Why?"

"I was disciplining those that opposed me, and several have challenged me. You need to come be a witness."

My stomach clenched. "Mikhail."

"Just do it," he said, heading toward the door and catching sight of Koren. "What are you doing here?"

"That's my greeting?" Koren scowled at my sylvan. "You're not happy to see me?"

"Why on earth would I be happy to see you?" Mikhail growled, charging toward the door.

"Since when does he hate me?" Koren was at a loss.

I snickered. "He's always hated you."

"He has?"

I gave him a patronizing nod.

Samani ran after Mikhail and caught his arm before he could get out the door. He stopped and their gazes locked.

"A sylvan does not fight in the pit. You have those to champion you," she insisted.

"I do my own fighting," he said through clenched teeth.

The animosity between them from the very first day had been palpable. They were like oil and water—there was no mixing. The hatred amused me, but Yuri said I was wrong, that what I saw as cold and frosty was everything but.

"You shouldn't fight. What if—"

"I'll be fine," he muttered, easing his arm loose as he continued toward the door.

She slipped around in front of him, bringing him up short. "You cannot."

"I need to," he said firmly but gently.

Her hand lifted toward his face but stopped, froze and then lowered. "I could not bear it."

"Don't watch," he ground out, stepping around her.

"You should be careful!" She was almost shrieking.

He stopped again and leaned his head back like she was simply exhausting to deal with. "You should mind your station."

She was still fuming as he left the room.

"Samani?"

"That man!"

Her anger startled me as she charged toward the door, picking up speed like she was going after him. "Why does he always have to prove something?"

Normally, she was unflappable. I didn't even know she *could* get mad. The open hostility was really only ever directed at Mikhail.

"Samani?" I repeated.

When she was facing me, I saw that her lips were pressed tightly together, that her beautiful teak-colored eyes were red-rimmed, welling with tears, and that her hands had balled into fists.

"Why can't he just give in? Why can't he just… rest?"

Dear God, I was so blind. "You want him," I whispered, thoroughly stunned.

She caught her breath. "More than anything."

You could have knocked me over with a feather. I had completely missed it.

"Does he want you?"

"Yes!" She started crying.

I really needed Yuri there to deal with—

"But he wants me to see the world and complete my education that I started but was not allowed to finish because of my father's debt. He hates me being here as your hathen. He wants me but he won't allow me to settle."

I gestured at the open door. "How is being with him settling?"

"Tell him, not me!" she complained bitterly.

"That's why you won't let all those girls—"

"I have to go see what he's doing," she rasped, rushing from the room without my permission.

I hurried after her and saw her bolting down the hall. Following fast, it took me a moment to realize Koren was running beside me.

"Your home is kind of exciting," he teased.

"You don't know the half of it," I muttered.

Because I was moving, suddenly everyone else was too. There were guards clearing the hall for me, and Kabore was sprinting at my side as well.

"Where are we going, my lord?" he asked pleasantly even while jogging.

"After Samani and Mikhail."

"Excellent," he said, like it was all perfectly normal.

Lush papyrus and shower trees trimmed both sides of the main courtyard, shading it in the afternoon. When I got there, I saw Mikhail on one end and another man maybe fifty feet away. Taj was behind my sylvan, who was stripping off his clothes.

"Wait!" I yelled from the top step that led down to the cobblestone quad.

Samani was on the first landing, bent over the railing, crying. "Please!"

"I said no!" Mikhail barked.

I stopped beside her and put a hand on her back. "What?"

She was trembling. "I'm forbidden from going down there, and he can order me to stay here because a hathen is below a sylvan and so he—"

"I give you permission."

She moved fast, wheeling around and then flying down the steps. I leaned over the side to watch her descend.

"Do you love him?" I called after her.

"Oh, you have no idea," she shouted back as she reached the bottom and then ran over to him.

My sylvan pivoted around, and Samani froze, shivering, every part of her, I could tell, screaming for her to move, to go to his side.

"Mikhail, you dick!" I yelled. "Why didn't you fucking tell me?"

All eyes on me, every single one.

"It was not my semel's affair, and is still not," he assured me as he yanked off his shirt, flung it at Taj, and then started on his belt.

"Who is the challenger?" I inquired as I came down the stairs, followed closely by Kabore. My guards kept Koren from trailing along.

"Traore Uago, Ammon's old sylvan."

I couldn't see Mikhail for a few seconds while I descended the winding stairs before arriving on the sandy ground, but I heard him and started toward where he and my sheseru stood.

"Taj."

He gave me his attention.

"Bring the old sylvan and his second down here."

As he left, I saw Mikhail's eyes flick to Samani.

She lifted her chin even as it quivered.

"Claim her now and I will strip her of her station as hathen and she will be only your intended mate, with no other duty. I will perform the ritual of handfasting when Yuri gets home, as the ritual, performed by a semel, must be witnessed by his mate. So says the law."

"No," Samani rasped, her wet eyes beseeching. "I have a say too."

"Done," Mikhail said, reaching out a hand to her. "Come and be mine."

She was torn. If she accepted her demotion, she would be Mikhail's intended mate, and no one but he would have dominion over her. But... she would have to do whatever he told her, follow whatever course he laid out. Most women did not accept the role of betrothed anymore, as it gave their intended the right to do with them as they pleased. Normally only those marrying semels accepted the ritual of handfasting—they already were bound to the semel whether by being a member of his tribe or by being his intended.

"Samani," Mikhail said, and I saw his eyes soften in a way I didn't think they could. I had no idea his gaze could ever melt at the sight of another.

She flung herself into his arms, and he clutched her tight to his heart. They were beautiful together: her dark skin compared to his fair coloring created a gorgeous contrast. The way he held her, as though she were a precious, fragile thing, pleased me. I loved seeing Mikhail's heart beating out there in the open, enjoyed his vulnerability as he buried his face in the hair of the woman he loved. I wished Yuri were here to see it.

"You belong to me now," Mikhail assured her. "And you'll have the life back that Ammon El Masry took from you when your father sold you to him."

I knew that part of the story because she had shared it with me. Her father had covered his gambling debts with the semel-aten by selling his daughter. She had been studying abroad when suddenly her werepanther life intruded on her human one, and she went to live in the home of the semel-aten, expected to be a harem girl and service not only Ammon El Masry but any of his guests as well.

"You don't understand," she wept. "I just want you, you ignorant man."

He laughed softly as she coiled her arms around his neck and hung on for dear life.

I threw up my hands. "I miss everything."

I noticed Koren chuckling as Taj brought Traore and his second to me. Each seemed ready for his challenge.

"My sylvan isn't going to fight today," I announced. "I am."

Several in attendance gasped, Mikhail's head jerked up, and everyone started yelling at once.

"Silence!" Taj roared, and the courtyard, now filled with easily a hundred people, went quiet and still. "My semel jests. *I* will fight today."

Even though I would have really loved taking Ammon El Masry's former sylvan apart, it was not my place. I bowed to Taj, who came forward and started undressing.

Traore scuttled toward me. "My lord," the demoted sylvan began, hand over his heart. "I would have to be a fool to accept such a challenge as—"

"Yes." I fixed him in place with my stare. "So, really, Traore Uago, do you wish to press this rebellion of yours, or will you swear allegiance to my sylvan and we'll hear no more of disrespect masquerading as tardiness?"

He stared, and I held his gaze until it moved from my eyes to the ground at his feet.

"Forgive me, my semel."

"My lord," I corrected.

"My lord. Please forgive me."

"Granted," I said, bored, tipping my head at my sylvan. "Now ask for his."

Mikhail pivoted to face the man, but I noticed he did not release Samani's hand.

"Since when does Mikhail have a girlfriend?" Koren was dumbfounded, and when I glanced over my shoulder at him, I saw that Jamal was there as well. The phocal knew who Logan was and had probably made certain my men knew that the brother of the semel-netjer was no threat, thus allowing him down into the courtyard.

"What if he were trying to kill me?" I asked Jamal, indicating Koren.

"He would have been dead before he reached for a weapon, my lord."

"So you say," I muttered.

Jamal's sigh came fast because he understood I was messing with him. It had taken a while for him to understand the teasing and sarcasm, but he did now.

"Domin—"

"No." I faced Koren. "Don't presume to speak to me as though we are friends."

"Domin, I—"

"No," I cut him off again and turned to Kabore. "See to Mr. Church's comfort, have him quartered in the guest wing. I'm having dinner with my mastaba alone."

"Yes, my lord."

"Domin—"

"The semel-aten is addressed as 'my lord,'" Kabore educated my former lover.

I didn't wait to hear what Koren said.

Chapter Three

EBERE WAS watching me pace.

"And my own mate kept from me that my sylvan and my hathen were in love!"

When I realized she wasn't saying anything, I whirled around to face her.

She was knitting.

"What are you doing?"

"Oh, are you speaking to me?" She feigned surprise.

"Do you see anybody else here?"

Her grunt conveyed how annoying I was.

"Well, it's no wonder your former mate preferred the company of other women if you were this interesting when you were married."

She would not be baited; she only yawned. "Perhaps your mate travels because he needs a break from your company."

I narrowed my eyes.

She arched an eyebrow before giving her attention once more to whatever it was she was making.

"What is that?"

"A hat for the semel-netjer's son, Ilia."

I crossed my arms as I gazed down at her. "That's nice of you. I still need to send a gift. Yuri wanted to go, but I made him wait until we could make the trip together in the fall."

"Why?"

"What if he didn't come back?"

She scoffed. "That man would never willingly leave your side."

"He just did!" I barked. "He went off to Ipis!"

"Oh my, I had no idea you missed him so desperately."

"He left me," I said again, as petulantly as the first time.

"On a mission of diplomacy that only he could undertake," she said in an attempt to mollify me. "But he plans to return as soon as possible. I've seen the way he stares at you; he will always fly home as fast as he can."

My grunt was loud as I flopped down onto the chaise across from her.

"Was your mate upset when you had him wait to see Jin and Logan's new son?"

Maybe he was; I wasn't sure. Lately, when Yuri talked to me, I sort of tuned out and instead focused on a patch of his freckled skin, the play of muscles in his back, or the plump bottom lip he would bite sometimes when I sucked on one of his nipples or when I stroked—

"That sound was absolutely decadent."

I was startled. "What?"

"You moaned and it sounded like sex to me."

I scowled.

She tittered. "Since you know, please tell me how Jin and Logan have a son already?"

I was lost. "What?"

"I must have missed something about the child."

"About the—"

"How do they have a child already? Explain it to me."

"What do you mean *how*?"

"The child was born four months after they got home from Mongolia. How?"

"Oh, well, that's simple. Jin's child is the son of a nekhene cat," I said matter-of-factly. "As it was explained to me, the werepanther in his blood overrode everything else so the gestation was not human, but cat."

"Meaning?"

"Meaning, as you know, the average gestation for a big cat is ninety to ninety-six days. For a leopard, I think its 101 days. Jin's child was born three months after the surrogate was inseminated."

"That's amazing, right?"

"It would be for anyone but Jin Church."

"His DNA must be something. I'm sure any scientist in the world would love to get their hands on him."

I snorted. "As if Logan would allow Jin or his child or the surrogate who bore his child anywhere near a human hospital."

"I'm not arguing. It's just an observation."

"I know."

"Is it true about the baby?"

"What?"

"Was he really born in his werepanther form?"

"Yes."

"So there's no doubt that he's a semel, then."

"No, everyone there said they'd never seen anything like it. I mean, none of us ever shift before adolescence, but Jin and Logan's kid comes out shifted."

"Well, Jin and Delphine's kid," she corrected.

"Make no mistake," I cautioned her. "Logan's bloodline mixing with Jin's—that is only their child."

"No, I know, I just… it's… I can't imagine."

"I know," I agreed. "Apparently it took Logan holding his son for him to shift to human."

"Not Jin?"

"No, I guess Jin's pheromones just made his son want to shift to full panther."

"So, wait," she said, making sure she'd heard me right. "The only cat Jin the reah can't soothe is his own son?"

"Yeah, and apparently he's all in a twist about it. I know you don't know Jin that well, but I will tell you there's no way he's taking something like that in stride. I'm sure he's feeling very hurt and useless right about now."

"But he's still his son's father."

"But you know as well as I do that semels bond with their fathers and not—"

"Jin is his father."

"I mean, semels bond with their fathers who are *semels*. So Ilia will naturally relax around Logan, will want Logan. It's just how it is."

"But that's not to say that Jin isn't necessary."

"No, but if Jin were a woman, he would be giving his son nourishment, but as he's not…."

"Oh, I see: what precisely is he doing, then."

"Exactly. Nothing. I'm sure he feels utterly worthless."

"Poor Jin."

"I should probably let Yuri go to him."

"Maybe another, instead."

Only she and Yuri gave me any counsel—ever. "Crane?"

"Yes. Just think how the reah must be missing his beset, especially now."

"I could never do that to Crane."

"Do what?" She eyeballed me. "Take his maahes status from him?"

"Yes."

"But perhaps it will be taken from him if he loses in the pit to Elham."

"You just don't want to have to be Elham's mate."

"No, I don't. And I also don't want to watch him flay Crane's skin from his body."

"If they're in the pit together—"

"It's not that kind of challenge. He gets to have one of his men fight one of Crane's. A fight for the position of prince is not done by the maahes and the challenger, but by men that they both pick."

"So Crane won't be in the pit to fight for his position?"

"Of course not." She was scowling now. "Have you talked to your sylvan about this?"

"No, my sylvan's been too busy disciplining his people and having sex with my hathen!"

"Your house is in disarray, my lord."

"You think?"

She tipped her head sideways as she regarded me. "May I ask a question?"

I gestured for her to go ahead.

"Why do you stay? Why do you remain semel-aten?"

I didn't answer because I wasn't sure what she meant.

"Domin?"

"Fate."

"I'm sorry?"

How to explain…. "So I was a semel, and then that was taken from me, but now I am a semel again."

From the expression on her face, I could tell she had never considered that before. "But you could step down, release the seat to

Elham, and then he wouldn't go after Crane, he wouldn't even begin this campaign to usurp you."

"Is this your advice?"

"No, I simply wonder at you. Are you trying to hold on to something that should not be held?"

It was a very good question.

AFTER DINNER, I walked through the lower gardens with Mikhail, around the pools, watching the koi swim from one pond to another, and realized how pissed I was at Yuri. How could he keep secrets from me?

Maybe he didn't know, Ebere had said earlier.

Mikhail set me straight, inhaling the night air and all the scents swirling through it. "He knew. I confessed, but I also made him swear to tell no one, especially you."

It was a betrayal... and yet I understood. Friends had to be counted on to keep secrets.

"If you knew, it would have weakened you and the choices you made for her and me," Mikhail mused.

"And now what will you do?"

"I'll send her back to Boston to finish her master's degree so she can have the life she wanted."

"And never marry her."

He shook his head. "This is not where she belongs."

"Maybe not three years ago, when her father had her brought here, but people change, and maybe she wants to be by your side. Did you think of that?"

"She's young. She doesn't know what she wants."

"She's twenty-six, Mikhail. My guess is she knows herself all too well."

He didn't want to hear it. I didn't want to yell, so I let him go to his quarters so he and Samani could talk.

Later, as I sat on the thick stone edge on the balcony of one the sitting rooms on the second floor, I heard movement behind me.

"May I come out there with you?"

"Sure," I mumbled. With my head resting against the wall and my ankles crossed, I was sort of precariously balanced. It was funny; Yuri never allowed me to sit like that, too afraid of me falling. Heights made him nervous.

Koren moved quietly near me but stopped far enough away that he couldn't touch me.

"How can I just walk up on the semel-aten?"

"The guards are on the first floor," I answered. "Only trusted people are allowed on the second, and only Yuri and I are allowed on the roof."

"I see," he said, and I saw his green eyes glint in the lantern light.

"Why are you here?" I was annoyed as I studied him.

"Because, of course, I figured out who I really wanted the second I was informed that you weren't coming back."

"Of course."

He moved closer. "What are you playing at?"

"Meaning?"

He was staring at me, missing nothing. "Yuri?"

"What about him?"

"Since when, Domin? Since when do you even *see* Yuri?"

The dark blue summer sky was slowly succumbing to dusk. It was beautiful. "I saw you stare at Samani Baro, the former hathen of my house, today. She is lovely, isn't she?"

"She belongs to Mikhail."

"Not what I asked. I asked if you thought she was lovely."

"Well, yes, very."

"When I got here, I found out that my predecessor had a harem. In fact, every semel-aten has one. Did you know that?"

"No, like I said earlier, I had no clue."

"And why would you? But for me, without her, I would have been lost. I mean, what in the world was I going to do with a female harem? I've been gay all my life."

"I don't get what—"

"But had you become semel-aten and found yourself with a harem, you would have had no problem with that."

"Domin—"

"I have no issue with you loving women," I said, pinning him with my eyes. "What I do have a problem with is you confessing to one thing while your gaze betrays you."

"You're serious?" he scoffed. "I'm in trouble because I checked out Samani earlier? You notice a beautiful woman when—"

"Yuri doesn't see anyone but me."

It took him a second. "It's new, Domin! It's brand new! Of course he doesn't! If I had been carrying a torch for you since I was sixteen years old, I—"

"Precisely," I interrupted. "If."

The silence was brutal, awkward and drowning.

"You're being ridiculous," he finally said. "You can't compare years of us to months of Yuri. I know you. He has no idea."

"Whatever he doesn't know, he can learn," I said, getting down off the railing, ready to slip by him.

He grabbed my bicep tight. "You can't love him just because you think you should—because you'll be safe."

My eyes met his.

"You have to let your heart get hurt. You know Yuri would never hurt you, and because I did it so many times, too many times, you picked him when he offered himself up on a silver platter."

I eased my arm from his grip. "You don't know anything about Yuri."

"But I know you."

"No, you don't, not really, and that was the problem."

"Domin—"

"Tell me," I said as I faced him, "have you ever really been in love?"

"That's the most—"

"No." I put my hand up to stop him. "Really, Koren, think about it."

"Yes." He studied my face before his dark olive gaze finally settled on my mouth. "With you."

"Koren."

"I missed you."

But when I read the intent in him to kiss me, I took a quick step back.

"I—"

"You live with Jin and Logan."

He narrowed his eyes. "Yeah? And?"

"Don't you want someone to look at you the way Jin looks at Logan and vice versa?"

"Jin is Logan's true-mate. You don't just go out and—"

"Please. All that is, is love."

"It's not. They have a perfect bonding. No one gets that unless they are a semel and a reah."

"That's crap. The chemical, biological pull on your body does not create love. It makes need, but that's not what Jin and Logan have. They *love* each other."

"They love each other *because* of the bond. If Jin was not Logan's reah, Logan would be mated to Simone right now, plain and simple."

"You're so wrong," I said. "Bond or no bond, Logan would have seen Jin and wanted him."

He shook his head. "You're being ridiculously sentimental. Logan was straight before he found out about his mate. If Jin wasn't his reah, he'd have had no chance with Logan."

I would not argue and headed out.

He called after me as I crossed the floor. "That's it? You don't stand and fight for what you want? The semel-aten doesn't know how to do that anymore?"

"You have nothing I want," I threw out. "So why would we fight?"

"I don't believe you."

I stopped at the door and glanced back. "Why are you going through these motions? It's not like you actually want to win."

"But I do," he professed. "And I will."

I crossed my arms. "What happened? What scared you so bad that you came running halfway around the world to see me?"

"What?"

Oh, *very* defensive. I tipped my head. "Let me guess, some nice lady panther wants to have your cubs?"

He pointed at me. "Tell me you don't remember us in bed and what that was like."

I did remember. I had loved it, having him under me, but even more, I remembered how volatile it had all been, and now I had a new definition of what could go on under the covers.

Now I ate in bed with Yuri stretched out beside me. We debated laws and decisions I had made, but... we also had long, drawn-out, intense conversations about why he liked reality shows and I didn't, about why he thought watching *Grey's Anatomy* would rot my brain and why I was refusing to watch the series *Firefly*, which he owned on DVD along with some movie that went with it. I was upset when my shows from the History Channel got erased in favor of some miniseries on the Syfy channel, and he said that satellite TV storage only had room for so much stuff.

I had called him on it, and he had gotten lost in seeing how indignant I got. "You're full of crap!"

"You're so cute when you're pissed off," Yuri had said, pushing out his bottom lip. "Come here, baby."

My huff had sent him into hysterics.

The point was, us in bed was not something I had ever experienced with anyone else.

We talked, we played, we wrestled, we made plans for vacations to cold places, we argued. He chatted on the phone with his mother, Rosetta, who was so proud of him and happy and who always wanted to say good-bye to me. He started teaching me Russian, important things like *moi lyubov*, which meant "my darling," and I grumbled that if I could only use that with him, how was that helping? But the heavy-lidded eyes, so love-soaked, made my stomach flutter, so that, too, was a gift. We laughed so much, out of bed but in it, too, and basically, I had a whole different appreciation of the place I slept these days that had nothing whatsoever to do with sex.

"Domin?"

"Sorry," I said, realizing I was grinning like an idiot, before I walked out the door.

"Domin!"

I groaned as I stopped, and he came quickly around me, close, into my personal space.

"For whatever reason, you're not seeing me right now, so I'm going to hang out until you do, all right?"

Standing there I realized again, for the thousandth time, that truly: Koren Church was a stunning man. He was also completely not what I needed.

It hit me. "Oh. Maybe not a woman. Maybe a man."

"What are you talking about?" he yelled.

"Who are you sleeping with at home that scared you to death?"

"I-I, you, I… no."

"Oh, Koren," I said, chuckling. "Come on. I hit the nail on the head. Tell me all about it."

He walked away without another word. My laughter followed him.

"My lord?"

I found Kabore walking toward me. "Yes?"

"Who was that?"

I met his stare. "An ex-lover."

"Which accounts for his complete and utter lack of respect for your station. Did he have your permission to walk away?"

"No, he did not."

"I should have him flogged."

"No, come take a walk with me through the market instead."

"Let me alert your khatyu."

"No," I said. "Let's just go, me and you."

He shook his head like he always did because I was just so trying. "My lord," he began, so long-suffering. "Let me explain to you what—"

"Just come with me," I pleaded, bumping his shoulder and then walking away.

He called after me to wait.

Chapter Four

I ENJOYED strolling through the marketplace at dusk and even more at night. The tents, the lantern light and braziers, small groups of people milling about, the smell of meat cooking over wood stoves, the tang of incense, the scent of desert flowers and lingering spices served to soothe and delight me. It wasn't busy, but I still got the feeling of movement before it went from night to early morning.

The people who greeted me, who waved, who came forward to touch me or hug me as I walked with five of my guards, all had the same awe on their faces. They were glad to see me, and I knew why. I was not, as played out, the rich man's leader. I was instead more about improving the quality of life for my entire tribe. I was not interested just in the elite; I was interested in the everyman.

I had opened the main floor of the villa to everyone. Guards stood at the bottom of the stairs inside, not at the front gates. The library, the countless reading rooms, the stacks, all of it was available to whoever wanted to do research or learn more about werepanther history. I had all the texts moved from the priest's temple at Satis to the villa. When I had made the journey out to see the new priest, Asdiel Kovo, he was horrified that I was there to take what he considered sacred tomes from vaults that had not been opened in years. But Mikhail had come with me, and armed with his own knowledge as well as that of his new mentors—the former council of Ennead—it became clear that there was nothing Asdiel could do about it. The library itself could be anywhere; there was no law that said it had to reside in the priest's residence at Satis. So Asdiel had to watch helplessly as I removed it all from the rooms beneath his home.

As I walked with Kabore, I thought about the time I had been to Satis before that. It had been two months before the day I put Asdiel in his place. I had gone to see Hamid Shamon, the former priest of Chae Rophon. He had called me to his deathbed, and no one had been more surprised than me. I'd taken a seat in the chair beside him, and I had been pleased when he reached for my hand.

"The road to change is perilous," he advised. "Cleave to your path. To keep traditions alive, they must be that which people can use in their daily lives, accept and take in."

I realized then that I would miss his disapproving scowls as well as his gentle words and the pats on my shoulder whenever he saw me.

"You are trying to make change for the better. You must realize that the man after me will want power. Be ready."

I'd had no idea how right he was at the time.

Asdiel was Hamid's successor, and he hated me with a passion born of a fanaticism with the law. It was beyond me. He was the one who labeled me as kadish. He was the one who said that Elham El Masry should be semel-aten, not me.

I was not from the tribe of Rahotep. I was not Egyptian. I didn't speak Farsi or Arabic. I didn't wear the traditional dress, and my views on education, the homeless, the role of women, and same-sex unions were all heretical. He considered me a threat to the tribe and a liability to the entire werepanther world. I was unholy, unclean, simply an abomination. There was an understanding between us from the day he assumed his new role. We were enemies.

Over time, it became apparent that though I was new, I had some great people around me, incorruptible people, and that I knew what I was doing. When he realized he could not shame me or outmaneuver me, Asdiel resorted to the old-fashioned way of winning: he tried to kill me.

Members of the Shu came for me in the night. They should have been able to kill me, but Taj, my sheseru, had been a member of their number, and he knew what to watch out for. When we took three of the men alive and reunited them later with their phocal—their leader, Jamal Hassan—he begged me for the lives of his men. That I had them in my possession said all that was needed about their crime.

I stood with my guard in the temple of Satis, waiting for the priest, and when Asdiel finally appeared before me, I made it known that his phocal had already pleaded with me to spare his men. I simply needed a confession from Asdiel to keep me from killing them. I was not surprised that he would not give one, but Jamal was. I watched the phocal realign his loyalty right then and there as I made a point about who would do whatever was needed, even grovel for the lives of those beneath them, and who would not.

"And would you beg a stranger for my life, my lord?" Jamal had questioned me.

"I would," I let him know, locking my eyes on his, before telling his men to rise and go stand by him.

I allowed them to live even though, if they'd had their way, I would have had my heart torn out. Yuri didn't have the same compulsion to forgive. He had forbidden Jamal from ever being in my presence alone. For a phocal to be so sanctioned was a grave insult.

Jamal had rounded on Yuri, grabbed the robe he wore over his clothes, and driven him back into the wall. But before I could even open my mouth, Yuri's voice boomed out.

"How dare you put your hands on me? I'm the mate of the semel-aten... I could have you killed for this insult."

I saw Jamal shrink down into himself, his stance deflating, shoulders drooping, hands unclenching. Whatever Asdiel's thoughts on me and Yuri, I had announced to the entire werepanther world that Yuri belonged to me, was claimed by me, and was considered sekhem, "arm of the semel" in some texts, and in others, "heart." I had no idea that such a term existed until I complained to Mikhail that I didn't want to call Yuri "consort," the expected term.

It was because of Jin.

All reahs were required by law to be brought before the semel-aten on their sixteenth birthday to see if first, before anyone else, the leader of the werepanther world was their mate. The thing was—I didn't want to know. If I had a female mate out there somewhere, and she was brought before me as a child, what was I supposed to do? The lure of a true-mate—I knew from watching Logan go through it—was impossible to resist. I would not take that chance. I didn't want to ever find my reah. I was perfectly happy to live without the supposed other half of me. I outlawed the practice of the semel-aten seeing a reah first, because even though the first part of the law frightened me, the second part was truly horrifying for the poor reah.

If the semel-aten decided he wanted to keep the reah in his house, he could. It was his right. Under his roof, she was his to do with as he pleased, and her eventual mate would be thankful that the semel-aten had sheltered her. If the reah never found her mate, she would remain forever in the semel-aten's household as wosret—consort.

At the Feast of the Valley every year, he could parade her out and let her search for her mate in the sea of amazed eyes. Of course, the chances of anyone, much less the semel-aten, ever seeing a reah were a million to one. This was the story we had all been told, about the impossibility, and yet... I had already seen two reahs in my lifetime. One was mated to Logan, and the other had been wosret to my predecessor, Ammon El Masry. Amirah Fehr had run from him, and in the end she had been so consumed with never again falling into his clutches that she had fixated on the idea and gone mad. She had lost all reason before he was killed. Even though there was no other choice but for her to die, the decision was regrettable and unneeded. I remembered her as she had last been, unhinged and vengeful. What those of my household remembered was that Amirah had been the last consort in the house. I would not allow Yuri to be called by her title. Mikhail had found the word sekhem and affirmed what it meant. I announced to everyone that it was how my mate was to be addressed.

Jamal had been disgraced because of Asdiel, and when he arrived at the villa secretly two weeks later, I met him with Yuri, Mikhail, and Taj, and I accepted Jamal's vow of fealty. He pledged himself and his men to the service of the semel-aten. Yuri removed the ban against Jamal being in my presence alone and welcomed him as a brother. Jamal was more touched than I thought he would be, as evidenced by the way he nodded quickly, held Yuri's wrist very hard, and didn't speak.

It had been fun to watch.

Taj, too, had been overwhelmed, stunned but ecstatic to have the support of the Shu. No semel-aten had ever taken the priest's elite guard from him. It was a coup, and I knew Asdiel felt the loss and blamed me. I was simply waiting for the other shoe to fall.

It seemed as though I spent my life in anticipation of what would come next, and not simply from a man with murderous intentions toward me. It hit me as I walked with Kabore at my side, passing street vendors and restaurants, the aromas mixing with the sticky summer air, heavy and humid, that I was always waiting for someone to leave me, fail me, or question me. It made me second-guess myself constantly.

Even Koren, who had apparently come to woo me, thought I was not in my right mind. It was tiring, hearing about your failings from those closest to you and then hearing praise from strangers. The only one who didn't do it, who didn't second-guess me or treat me like an idiot, was Yuri. And I loved him for it.

"My lord!"

I twisted around and Jamal was there, his face ashen, his eyes dark and worried as he strode toward me with five of his men in tow.

"Are you kidding? I haven't even been gone a half an hour, what could have possibly happened?"

"We have received word that Elham El Masry has arrived, and he has the semel of the tribe of Wepwawet with him, Rahab Bahur."

I waited.

"My lord?"

He had obviously expected a reaction. "I'm sorry. Who is Rahab whatever and why should I care?"

"You don't know who Rahab Bahur is?" Kabore demanded from my left.

My attention was now on him, as Jamal had thrown his arms up, apparently defeated by my overwhelming lack of knowledge.

Kabore was stunned.

"Spit it out," I ordered.

"My lord, the tribe of Wepwawet deals in oil and natural gas, and those are the legal riches of the tribe. Rahab also has many pursuits that are not...."

"Legal," I finished for him.

"Yes."

"So he's a thug."

"No, he's the head of crime syndicate that deals in drugs and people—"

"You mean prostitution."

"Yes. He also moves guns and—"

"He's a criminal."

"Well, yes, but—"

"And what was the role of the semel-aten in his life?"

He cleared his throat. "He and Ammon had an understanding that as long as his interests did not bring any human interaction or interest, Rahab could do as he pleased."

"But? I feel a 'but' coming on."

"Now he is here with a champion to challenge Crane in the pit for his place of maahes. His tribe is the smallest of all, but it is the only one I know of that is not based in a town or region but more as a syndicate. Members of the tribe of Wepwawet live in every country of the world and work as operatives, nothing more."

The fact of the matter was that he was not a true semel, not a leader, but the head of a crime family. His was a conglomerate; it was not a tribe, not a family in any sense. They didn't hunt together or ever gather. They swore allegiance to a warlord, not a king who would protect them, lead them, guide and nurture them. I was right—he was a thug.

"My lord," Kabore almost pleaded. "You must take this challenge seriously. Why would a man like Rahab Bahur align himself with Elham El Masry? Why does he want to claim Ebere for his new friend? By killing Crane Adams, what does the man gain?"

"Access to me," I confirmed. "Obviously your crime lord wants Elham to first be maahes, and then semel-aten."

"Yes," Jamal agreed. "That's exactly what he wants."

"At least we know now." I shrugged.

"And you're not afraid of this?" Kabore grilled me.

"Have you met Rahab's man? Do you think he can beat Crane's?"

"I don't know. I have yet to meet Crane's man," he said. "Have you met his champion?"

"I have not, and when I ask, he only asserts that he has everything under control. Perhaps I should go talk to him now."

"I don't know how you will accomplish this, as he has gone to Cairo," Jamal inserted.

"Cairo? What for?"

He exhaled sharply, obviously irritable. "Your guess is as good as mine."

"Is Rahab in the villa with Elham now?"

"No, but his arrival is imminent, as well as the men he brings with him, his sylvan and sheseru," Kabore replied.

I let out a deep breath, suddenly tired. "We better go welcome them, then."

"Yes, my lord. I must caution you to be very careful in your dealings with—"

"I will be."

"My lord," Jamal interrupted. "You must understand that these are two very powerful men who—"

"I think I understand about power," I insisted.

He was quiet for a moment, apparently realizing what he'd said, before he bowed deeply.

SILENCE NEVER failed me. When Elham El Masry stood in front of me with Rahab Bahur on his left, I waited.

"We announce our challenge of your maahes," Elham said to me, Mikhail, Taj, Jamal, and Kabore. He was talking about Crane, who was glaringly absent. "And call for it at midday tomorrow."

I waited.

They were silent.

My eyebrow arched slowly. "Is there more?"

Elham glowered. "I would think that would be enough."

I cleared my throat. "My maahes, Crane Adams, accepts your challenge and will meet your champion in the forum at—"

"We will need the main coliseum, my lord, as riding is a requirement."

I had no idea what that meant. "Of course," I said, and I motioned for Taj. "Please see these men to their quarters and place members of the Shu on their balconies and doors."

Rahab cackled. "I had heard that you had acquired the Shu from the priest. When Elham is semel-aten, we will restore those men to Asdiel Kovo."

And there it was, out on the table.

"You wish Elham El Masry to be semel-aten?"

"I do," he professed before Elham could grab his arm and stop him. "You're an infidel and your reign is sacrilege. You are kadish and you make a mockery of all of us."

I took a moment to let that sink in, to let it fill the space around us, be absorbed by my contingent and his, so no one could ever claim he hadn't uttered his treasonous words.

"Did you hear me?"

"I did," I said, meeting his eyes. "And for those words, when Elham's champion is defeated, I will send you into exile and make your heir semel."

Rahab scoffed, obviously very sure of Elham's champion. "You do that, semel-aten."

I shrugged, letting him see I wasn't worried before I flicked my gaze to Elham. "As for you, when Crane's man defeats yours, you will renounce all claim to my mastaba, and Ebere and her children will never see or hear from you again."

His anger exploded out of him. "I'm her brother-in-law and an uncle to those—"

"The children are mine," I roared. "They are claimed by me, acknowledged by me, and are as much mine as they were their father's. I—"

"They are Ammon's, you son of a whore! You would not even know what to do in a woman's bed! You're a sodomite and—"

"Silence!" Mikhail hissed. "This is the semel-aten you speak to so freely. He could have you—"

"Your words seal your fate," I interrupted, taking a step forward. "Tomorrow, when the champion of my maahes takes the field and wins, both of your lives are forfeit along with your man."

"And when my man wins," Elham crowed, "am I allowed to claim yours, my lord?"

He was really so sure of himself. "If you win and become maahes," I said with a cold smirk, "then surely my days are numbered, are they not?"

I saw his hatred gleaming in his dark eyes. "Indeed they are, my lord."

AFTER MIDNIGHT, closer to one, I myself commanded a flurry of activity in Ebere's chambers.

The lady herself was irritated with me. "What will this accomplish?" Maids flew around us, packing her up quickly, readying her for imminent departure. "If Crane loses, I will belong to Elham regardless of where I am. I prefer to meet my fate at your side."

"Fuck no," I growled. "You go back to Cairo, you get your girls, and if Crane loses, Kabore will call you and you get on a plane and you go to Logan. He'll protect you."

"Yes, but—"

"No *but*. There are laws and then there's Logan. He does what's right, and he and his mate will protect you and your girls from Elham El Masry."

"But, Domin—"

"Let's face it; no one wants to tangle with the nekhene cat. Period."

"You'll get no argument there," she teased.

I rushed forward, grabbed her tight, wrapped her in my arms, and squeezed until she caught her breath. "Just do what I say, my mastaba."

She coiled her arms around my neck and buried her face in my shoulder. "You have shown me more respect and love as your mastaba than I was ever afforded as yareah. I am so proud to belong to you, Domin Thorne."

"When I claimed you, I was doing it to protect myself from having to take a female mate to reproduce, but now I would do it again even if you had no children. I sort of like you."

"I sort of like you too."

I bent my head and kissed her cheek. "Please go and do what I'm telling you."

"I will."

"Okay," I sighed, but I didn't let her go and she didn't pull away.

I lost track of how long we stood there.

Chapter Five

I DIDN'T sleep at all. Everything hung on a challenge I had no control over.

Crane was nowhere to be found, and no one could report having seen him. His rooms were empty, his bed was not slept in, and I could not reach him by phone. I didn't think I could be any more worried until Kabore came to see me in my private suite on the second floor, in one of the smaller sitting rooms.

"Where is Lilitha?" I asked, because in the morning I normally saw the same serving woman. She always brought me my tea.

He was nervous and his coloring was off. "I'm sorry, my lord, but she's dead."

Crossing my arms, I stared into his eyes. "Why?"

"This morning I observed her putting honey in your morning tea."

I squinted at him. "But I don't like honey."

"As I am well aware, my lord." He sounded sad. "It is only goat's milk that you like, and only ever at night."

"Yes," I agreed.

"So you understand my concern when I saw her adding it."

"And?" I pried, even though I understood the outcome already.

"And so I confronted her, and when she tried to tell me that she had simply made a mistake, I had her drink the tea for me," Kabore rasped, his eyes searching mine. "She apologized, insisted that she liked you, but that, really, Elham El Masry was the one and only true ruler of Sobek."

"Sure."

"It was quick and painless," he asserted gently. "She was gone in seconds. It would have been the same for you. She didn't want you to suffer."

I took a breath, walked across the space to the edge of the roof, and there gazed out over the balcony. It hurt to learn of her betrayal, but it was also terrifying. My first thought was: what if Yuri had been home? My second was: what if Kabore were not so vigilant and the tea had come through to my chamber? Yuri actually took honey in his tea. He could have been.... For a moment I could barely breathe.

"My lord?"

I had liked Lilitha. Her sweet face, her laugh, and the way she made sure that if there were pomegranates in the kitchen, one was always set aside for me. She had cared, or so I thought. Apparently I was a terrible judge of character.

It took me a moment to pull myself together.

"Thank you for saving my life," I finally said, not ready to look at him. "It seems that every day I understand why you were first Ammon El Masry's steward and now mine."

"Pardon, my lord, but I was not Ammon's steward."

This was news. I glanced at him over my shoulder.

"I came to this household with Ebere from Cairo. I was merely one of many, and when she went back home, I stayed on."

"I didn't know that," I said.

"So when you came, they all inquired who wanted to run the house of the infidel, and I said that I, Kabore Nour... I would. I think it was fate."

I frowned slightly.

"As I am of Ebere's household, from the tribe of Khepri, and not from the tribe of Rahotep, there would never be another semel whose trust I could gain."

It made sense.

"But you, the maverick semel from America—"

"Maverick?" I teased.

"It's true, my lord," he said, gesturing at me. "You are a sin, are you not?"

"I'm a sin?" That was new.

"You are impure, you are not of the first tribe, and they say your reign is heretical, but I think not."

"Oh no?"

"You seem to me like a man who has been through a test of faith, but your fate was to be semel-aten. How else could you be here?"

There was a valid argument to be made.

"You came from around the world, you killed Ammon El Masry in Mongolia, a place—I would lay you odds—that he never saw himself being. So many paths had to intersect to bring you to the place you had to be to take his life. I find it all fascinating, but for me, when the question was posed, I answered."

"I'm glad."

"I am quite proud to be your steward, my lord."

"Thank you."

"And I will stand with you and the others until things change."

We stared at each other for long moments.

"Didn't you ever want your own life, your own family?"

"Not all men are meant to be mated, my lord, and some, like yourself, sire no children, but that is service in some of its many forms, is it not?"

It was.

"I am here to serve you, my lord, and your sekhem."

I had to ask. "And you see no abomination in my mate being another man?"

"Who am I to question the workings of fate, my lord?"

Indeed. "Thank you for saving my life." It bore repeating.

"Thank you for making it easy," he said hoarsely. "If you actually liked honey in your tea, things would all be quite different at this moment."

"Perhaps you are my guardian."

"Perhaps."

As I related the story to Jamal in the throne room half an hour later, I puffed out some air. "It seems that I can trust no one but those in my closest circle."

"No, my lord, you can trust me," he said firmly. "I, too, like Kabore, can be trusted. I am your man."

But how could I take his word?

Jamal seemed pained. "I have news, and it is not good."

I twisted around against the stone edge of the patio off to one side of my room. "How? What's worse than hearing that the woman in charge of bringing me my meals just tried to kill me?"

"Shahid Alon is Elham El Masry's champion."

The former second in command of the Shu. Shahid had resigned his position instead of choosing to protect me, he was the one going up against Crane's champion. It took a long moment for that to sink in. "So that's where he went when you all swore allegiance to me."

"Yes. I told you he had resigned his position, but I had no idea where he went."

"Why would you? He was no longer your concern."

"I simply want there to be no misunderstanding between us. I had no correspondence from him, and so was not aware that he had sworn his life and loyalty to Elham."

"I know," I said softly. "Had you known, you would have alerted me."

"Yes, I would have."

"I didn't know that Elham could bind men to him, as he is not a semel."

"Even though he has no tribe of his own, he is, in fact, a member of your tribe, the tribe of Rahotep. He can still bond men to him as he is the heir to the semel."

"The man is not my heir," I corrected.

"But by law he is, and as you have not put forth a new heir, if you were to die...."

"Then he would be semel-aten."

"Yes."

I had to laugh. "I will announce an heir tonight."

"Excellent, my lord, but about Shahid—"

"What about him?"

"You're not concerned?"

"Of course I am," I said brusquely, "but what would you have me do?"

"My lord," Jamal came closer. "I've tried to speak to Shahid, and so has Taj, but he won't—he seems very set on his course and—"

"I'm sure he is."

He moved closer still. "Perhaps if you were to—"

"Even if he liked being in bed with me, even if he remembered, that does nothing to help my cause," I said, going back to gazing out at the valley and across to the mountains. "He thinks I'm unclean, and perhaps he knows that better than anyone."

There was only silence behind me, so I assumed Jamal had nothing more to say. I could shock anyone if I put my mind to it.

IT WAS hot, but it always was. There were different degrees of heat. But it was never cool except in the shade or sometimes at night. So on the dais at one end of the coliseum, even under the canopy of silk stretched over the throne, I was cooking in my robes. The layers suffocated though the material itself was lightweight. But it was the least of my problems. The worst was the scene before me.

Crane reappeared when they called for the challenge, walking in from the courtyard, matching the stride of his man. I received no explanation; he didn't even acknowledge me as he strode by, intent only on reaching the forum as quickly as possible. I couldn't stop the contest even to have a word with him, with my absent maahes. It was not permitted. As I followed after him, I started devising all the creative ways I was going to kill him.

I held my breath. The trial was like nothing I had ever seen. It was called Warriors of the Sun-God, or Khatyu of Ra—and it would not be bloody but was instead fast. Every challenge I had ever seen in the pit was beast against beast or semel against semel, shifted werepanthers trying to carve out each other's hearts. I had never been witness to a race.

The challenge was simple: Elham's best man against Crane's.

I sat on the throne, Mikhail on one side of me, Jamal on the other, knowing that once Elham won, he would demand Crane's head and then take his place in my circle, thereby able to spread venom and claim Ebere, by law, as his mate. Rahab would have access to everything I did, and between he and Elham, they would slowly siphon off my power a little at a time until I was left a prisoner in my own home. Worst of all, they would, eventually, come for Yuri after they stripped me of everyone else.

I was sick.

I was furious with Crane for allowing his pride to make a path not only to his destruction but mine. I could taste the bile in my throat.

Jin would never forgive me if Crane died, and even worse than that, there was Logan.

I shivered even though the sun scorched me from overhead. "You swore you had an answer for this challenge," I called down the steps to Crane.

He was silent as the two riders entered the packed arena, each seated atop a stunning Arabian stallion. I had never seen such beautiful horses, one black, one white, as was fitting.

Crane stood five steps below me on my right, Elham on my left. He glanced over his shoulder at me and smirked.

"Domin."

Head up, I found myself swallowed in the dark green gaze of Koren Church.

"May I stand by you through this challenge, my lord?"

I nodded, the lifeline so very needed.

"Good." He stood at my side and put his hand on my shoulder.

The priest of Chae Rophon, Asdiel Kovo, stood up three seats away from me as trumpets sounded. The riders quieted their mounts and then moved them to the starting line. There was a second blast as both animals flew forward. It was beautiful to watch such a gorgeous display of strength, the fluid movement of man and beast becoming one.

No one spoke, no one made a sound, and only the breath of the horses, the thunder of their hooves striking packed earth and the urgent cries of the men were heard.

Everyone watched as the horses thundered toward the turn. The riders were supposed to dismount, strip, shift, and then race back to the steps where their "master" stood. The first one back won. The Khatyu of Ra, in legend, were supposed to have been able to fight in either form—man or panther—at a second's notice. Only the Shu were thought to be capable of such a display of shifting prowess in this the modern age, and Elham had been lucky enough to find a former member of the Shu to stand in the challenge for him.

Watching Crane, I realized how proud he was as he lifted the robe that was supposed to receive his rider. Elham did as well, his sneer of contempt as he regarded Crane easy to see.

"Here's the shift," Koren whispered.

Both men steered their mounts, and both leaped from the back of the horse, but that was where the similarity ended.

Crane's rider hit the ground already shifted and burst free of the flowing robes, the turban, and all other articles of clothing, sliding out from under the flutter of white to reveal the sleek, muscular lines of the only black werepanther in the world.

The crowd came to their feet as one and the roar was deafening as Elham's rider shifted almost instantly. It would have been impressive if the other—the change of the nekhene cat—had not been on display. He moved in a blur, streaming up the steps as the other panther raced in futile attempt to catch him.

He was already cocooned in the robe, had it cinched at his waist, and was facing the crowd, his long, thick black hair whipping back from his face by the time Shahid reached the bottom step and lifted his eyes to Elham.

Everyone screamed as Jin Church, reah of the tribe of Mafdet, mate of the semel-netjer, turned to me and, along with Crane, bowed low.

"The claim of Elham El Masry is denied," Asdiel, the priest of Chae Rophon announced loudly to the assembled crowd. Even I could hear the regret in his voice. The man had wanted Crane dead and me in peril, but it was not to be. "What say you, semel-aten? Do you claim his rider as your own?"

He posed the question out of ritual; he did not actually expect an answer.

I glanced over at Shahid, shifted now back to human, and saw the terror on his face. "I claim him again for the Shu," I said as I rose to my feet. "And if he's mated, I claim his mate and any and all offspring of that union."

I was always thorough.

The man closed his eyes, and I saw him breathing again.

Son of a bitch.

Shahid had left the Shu and married and sired a child. Of course he would do anything to protect that, and God only knew where Elham and Rahab were keeping his family. Perhaps Shahid had not sought them out, but instead, perhaps my enemies had gone hunting for him, searching for the ringer, a former member of the Shu to win with.

Sometimes I missed things, but other times I had to go with my gut. I had thought, no matter what, that Shahid didn't hate me, and lo and behold, I was right. He was protecting people I didn't even know belonged to him.

"You cannot!" Elham roared.

"He can do as he pleases," Asdiel spoke before I could. "He is the semel-aten."

I had never imagined hearing thousands of voices roaring my name at the same time. "Domin Thorne" sounded like thunder in the arena.

When I noticed Elham, I saw him think about striking Shahid, the panther who had failed him only because there was no cat in the world faster than Jin. But then Jamal was there, the phocal of the priest, leader of the Shu, to step between the two men and deliver his threat.

"As the semel-aten has demanded, I expect this man's family here in no less than three days, and should any of them be harmed in any way, the Shu will come for your head."

It was never to be forgotten that while the Shu protected me, they were also assassins, the deadliest in the werepanther world.

"I told you." Crane smirked, and I flicked my eyes to his. "I always have an answer."

It took every shred of self-control I possessed not to walk over and throttle him. Instead, I patted Koren's hand before rising and walking over to Jin.

He was beautiful. I had noticed that the first time I ever laid eyes on him. From the blue-black hair that fell glossy and straight to the middle of his back, the large almond-shaped gray eyes, and his delicate, sharply angled features, he was simply breathtaking. But what made him exquisite to me, to everyone who knew him, was his heart. Jin was the embodiment of the reah—he nurtured, he counseled, and he stood devotedly beside his mate.

He could also be absolutely *terrifying*.

"My lord." Jin bowed low, and I reached under his chin and lifted his gorgeous gaze to me. His eyes were so much like liquid jewels that sometimes, for a moment, I became lost in them.

"He went to you when he should have come to me, talked to me."

Jin straightened and took a breath. "Yes. I made it clear that it was wrong. I yelled at him."

But even though he'd admonished Crane, telling him that it was indeed wrong, Jin had done his bidding in a heartbeat anyway. I wondered for a moment what that must feel like, that safety net, to know that the most powerful werepanther in the world would cross an ocean to stand at your side.

"I, too, was a maahes," I said softly but seriously. "And I never let my semel sweat, no matter how much I wanted to prove a point."

Jin's power rose, and I felt it reach out, curl around me like a cat, rub against my skin, roll through me with a gentle vibration before it receded and there was only Jin once more. The reason was easy to understand.

Yes, he was agreeing with me, and yes, Crane had been wrong, but still, deep down, Crane was first Jin's beset, the companion of a reah, and I was taking him to task. Even more so, I had allowed Crane to be placed in danger.

"Jin—"

"I made a mistake," he confessed, and there was a slight blush to his cheeks.

We had both made one where Crane was concerned.

Wheeling around, I had the Shu arrest both Elham and Rahab. As they were led away, the cheers became deafening.

RAHAB BAHUR wanted to kill me. It was there in his eyes though he gave no voice to it. He trembled with fury. To his right, shackled to a bar, stood Elham El Masry.

"We beg mercy for them, my lord," the priest of Chae Rophon had the balls to say to me.

The sheseru, sylvan, and maahes of the tribe of Wepwawet were all there on their knees in front of me. Elham had no one to stand for him since his tribe was his brother's old tribe, which was now mine. Anyone who had planned to challenge me had backed down once the surefire solution had been annihilated in front of everyone. To those who were not there, everywhere else in the world, it would be reported that the maahes of the semel-aten had easily dealt with a challenge to his seat. Had Crane lost, had anyone but Jin been in the pit for him, for me, it would have meant a coup. Not within a day or a week, but surely within the month, I would have been dead. My reign would have come to an end. I would have been overthrown, and a new semel-aten would have been crowned. As it was, as events had transpired, my position of power had been upheld, and really, another attempt was unlikely. This had been their best chance; they had been so certain that they had tipped their hand with sedition. It had been a mistake.

Everyone waited hours for me. I sequestered myself in my quarters, in what I called my office but was honestly a large receiving room. Had Yuri been there, I would not have had to make calls. As he was not, there was only one place to go for counsel.

"Hello?"

She sounded good even on the satellite phone. "Delphine."

"Domin." She sighed and then squeaked. "Oh no, I mean, my lord—I mean—"

"Please just let me be Domin," I directed. "Please."

I heard a soft chuckle from her, then, "Yes."

"May I speak to Logan?"

"Oh, Domin, I'm so sorry, but we're frantic here and it's the middle of the night and—"

"Please."

Silence and then muffled voices and sounds before Logan answered with his usual charm. "What the hell do you want?"

I grunted. "I have your mate, semel-netjer."

Long silence, and I knew, because I'd grown up with the man, that Logan was calming himself down before he said another word. It took a lot to get an explosion out of him.

"I'm sorry?" he rasped.

"You heard me. Crane needed Jin, he called Jin, and Jin came, because we both know he honest to God thinks that you don't need him there right now."

Deep breath. "I'm going to choke him to death with my bare hands."

"Are you?"

"I swear to God, yes," he muttered irritably.

"Will that be before or after you fall down at his feet and worship him?"

He growled. "I don't worship my—"

"Yes, you do. We all do. He's like some Egyptian god made real. For all we know, the stories about the gods are instances of sightings of werepanthers. Jin is the only link to our divinity, and even more so… he's your mate, my friend. He's the other half of you."

"The other half of me is being ridiculous."

"But that's because he has no clue about true parent/child relationships. Jin actually believes that there can only be one primary love; he doesn't know that nothing changes between you and he. He doesn't get that you can add your son to your heart and how you feel about him doesn't diminish in the slightest." He started chuckling, and I was annoyed because I thought mine had been a very sage observation. "Fuck you, Logan."

"Jin knows all about the love between a parent and a child, Domin. He's just got his feelings hurt because, like you said, he thinks I don't need him here right now. He thinks that my son and I are fine."

"And are you?"

"What do you think?" he snarled. "My mate should be in my bed every night. I can't be me if he's not right here."

"What about your son?"

"My son is now past the imprinting stage and needs to feel a power greater than his own to soothe him, to basically make him."

"Make him do what?"

"Submit. He's an infant, his power rises, and he knows that whoever is holding him is weaker. He pulled Markel through his shift yesterday."

I was stunned. "You're serious?"

"Very."

That was terrifying. "Markel was my sheseru."

"I know."

"What are you going to do?"

"I guess I'll get on a plane and come fetch my reah and the beset of my reah."

There was no way to hold back the huff. "And if I will not release Crane?"

"You will. You must."

He couldn't just be allowed to tell me what—

"Please, Domin," he sighed. "I can't be the only one to talk sense into my reah. Jin only actually listens to me and Crane. That's it, on the whole damn planet."

"Come claim your mate and his annoying friend," I said, using Logan's own term of endearment for Crane. "I want them both out of my home, semel-netjer."

"Thank you, my semel."

"Knock it off." I couldn't help smiling, I felt too good. "You know, you can just stay there. I swear I'll send them both home as soon as—"

"I need him *now*," Logan said, and his voice was deep and dark. He was being strong, it was how he was, but Jin's absence was already wearing. I understood, finally, what that was like.

"Then I'll expect you."

"Yes."

"Should I tell him you're coming?"

"He knows."

I hung up without a good-bye because it was our way. No endearments went back and forth between us.

After I talked to Logan, I called Orso Bataar, semel of the tribe of Khertet, in Mongolia. He was very pleased to hear from me, and I was glad since I was asking him for a favor.

When I finally emerged from my room, everyone was still waiting, clustered in the main hall, every semel and his retinue visiting at the time, along with as many as could push and shove themselves within the walls. It was standing room only; I was the only one who took a seat, there on my throne.

"I will now pass sentence," I shared with the crowd, my voice, because of the acoustics, carrying to every corner.

The silence was thundering.

"I have been called an infidel more times than I can count," I declared to the assembled throng. "And now I will finally act like it."

Not a sound anywhere.

I glanced at Jin, who stood beside Crane; at Mikhail, holding hands with Samani; at Asdiel, sneering at me from where he stood beside my prisoners; and over at Taj as he stood with Jamal and the rest of the members of the Shu flanking him.

"I hereby banish Elham El Masry and Rahab Bahur to the tribe of Khertet, there to become khatyu of Orso Bataar. May they be blessed by Ra in their new life."

There were gasps and whispers, shock and outrage as Rahab's sheseru and sylvan surged to their feet. His sylvan was able to find his voice first. "My lord, you cannot believe that we will allow such a—"

"You will allow it," I said as I stood up. "Or I will take them to the pit now, one after the other, and have my sheseru remove their heads. The choice is yours."

"But, my lord—"

"They are traitors to my rule," I stated flatly. "I am the semel-aten, whether any of you like it or not. The Shu answer to me, you *all*... answer... to me. I will *not* have treason. By the law, I can kill them both outright. In Mongolia, they have a chance to rebuild their lives, start fresh. If they choose not to do this, if anyone attempts to interfere while they are in transit or once they are there, they will be killed at once. This is my mandate and has been agreed to by Orso Bataar."

"My lord—"

"You are the sylvan of the tribe of Wepwawet, are you not?"

"Yes, my lord."

"Who is the heir to your semel?"

He seemed on the verge of hyperventilating. "His brother, Zaki."

"Send word to him that he is now semel of the tribe of Wepwawet."

"But, my lord, you—"

"You think I don't know all about your tribe?" I asked him pointedly. "Maybe it's time that your gang finally became one."

"One what, my lord?"

"A true tribe."

He was shaking. "You know nothing of—"

"I know all about the difference between a mob and tribe, between which one gives and which one only takes. I was the semel of a tribe once that was just like that."

It should have been strange for me to have every eye on me, everyone silent and staring. But somewhere in the past six months, I had gotten used to it.

"Perhaps Zaki Bahur can achieve what his brother could not."

The sheseru and the sylvan of the tribe of Wepwawet both waited.

"I know that your tribe prides itself on money and power, but you must understand, that's the world of men," I said softly, letting my words sink into them. "And I know that we all have to live in that world, but for us there's more. There's always the tribe, always our family. We're talking about that—about you as panthers, about the law and your semel. We're speaking of your semel and Elham El Masry thinking that they were both above the law, that they would be judged as men and not as panthers and as members of the whole."

That was the real point and what so many people missed.

"The judgment of the semel-aten will always be about what is best for the panther, not necessarily what is best for the man."

"Yes, my lord."

It wasn't what they wanted to hear, but it least it made sense. I wasn't some insane, power-mad despot; I was a semel disciplining the members of his tribe. There was a cause and effect to the panther world that was absolute, and people had just been reminded.

"I will expect Zaki Bahur to stand before me and swear his fealty within a month. Do you hear me, sheseru? Do you hear me, sylvan?"

"Yes, my lord," they echoed.

When I checked, I saw how wild Rahab appeared. His eyes, which had been murderous and seething with hate, now projected terror. And it was all because I was making sense. His people understood—they would not try and free him. He had gambled and lost, and it was time to pay up. Just as in nature, when the leader was challenged, the defeated challenger was banished.

Jamal came forward to take control of the prisoners, but before he could issue orders, I stopped him.

"Give the job to Shahid," I said, tipping my head toward the man who had been blackmailed into the nefarious plot to overthrow me. "He will see it done."

Shahid's gaze met mine a moment before he bent at the waist. "Thank you for your faith, my lord. I will never disappoint."

"I know. And when your wife and child arrive, my sheseru, Taj Chalthoum, will receive them and protect them until your return."

Taj hadn't known he was on guard duty, but he moved forward fast, put his hand over his heart, and promised Shahid that he would slaughter anyone who dared hurt them.

The relief, the appreciation, the swell of emotion visibly rushed over Shahid, and he could only nod, clearly overcome.

"Go," I commanded.

He pivoted, signaled the other members of the Shu, and they took the two men out, the crowd quickly parting for them.

"And as for you," I said, stopping Asdiel before he could say a word. "I wanted Jamal here, because I am naming him as heir to my throne, heir to be semel-aten."

No amount of me standing there with lifted hands was going to shut everybody up. I sat down instead, as Taj called for the heralds.

As a rule, the horns gave me a headache, but there were times when I understood why we had them.

Jin walked to the side of my throne and bent down next to my ear.

"Yes, my reah?"

His eyes gleamed with worry. "Have you spoken to Logan?"

"I have."

"And?"

"You think Logan and your son don't need you," I said bluntly, turning my head so I could stare into his gorgeous dark gray eyes. "You needed to be away, and Crane's crisis gave you the reason. You ran without notifying Logan, and now you're here."

He straightened up abruptly, ready to step away from me.

I grabbed hold of his wrist, keeping him close.

"Let go."

"Logan was where, at a gathering?"

"Yes."

"You didn't want to go?"

Jin cleared his throat. "I'm not allowed to attend gatherings anymore. Yusuke went with him."

I rolled my eyes. "Really? You think your maahen can take your place at his side?"

He was silent.

"Or Danny? If Logan's sylvan went with him as well, perhaps your cousin can be switched out for you?"

He tugged, but I was stronger. In his nekhene form, Jin could eviscerate me. If he released his power, he might even be able to make me shift.

Maybe.

I had felt it before and withstood it, but it had never been directed fully at me.

"Don't raise your power, you brat," I said under my breath.

Jin's gaze flicked to mine then, and his eyes were all pupil. I was seeing a wild thing, unstable because his mate was not with him.

"You are the only nekhene cat in the world, and your mate and your son need you desperately."

"So you say," he said, and then his eyelids fluttered and I was once again, that quickly, in the presence of a reah. The difference was like night and day—he could be feral one moment and the epitome of hearth and home the next. I had no idea how Logan rode that wave on a daily basis. My own mate was simply the one who wanted to keep me and love me and be my sanctuary.

"You miss Yuri."

I didn't answer as he straightened up and smiled down at me.

"Don't deny it. I see it all over your face, feel it beating between us."

"I have no idea what you're talking about."

"What's Koren doing here?"

"I thought he must have come with you." I was indignant as the sound of horns filled the hall, and the silence that came afterward was instantaneous.

All eyes trained back on me as I stood once more, walked to the edge of the dais, and stared down at Asdiel, who started to object.

"You have lost your reason if you think I would allow a man not—"

"Silence!" I said, my voice rolling through the room. "I make the decision. Only me. You have no say, as you are no more divine than I am. And if you like, I can separate your head from your body and show everyone the color of your blood."

The color drained from his face, and I could tell that he was smart enough to know what was about to happen.

"The temple of Satis will no longer house the priest of Chae Rophon, because from this day forward, there will no longer *be* a priest of Chae Rophon. I strip you of your title and station and banish you to the tribe of Mafdet, there to serve the semel-netjer. You will understand real power when you stand before him."

"I—"

"Satis will become a school," I said, my voice rising. "Where anyone may go to learn and live as they study the law. All the vaults and rooms there will be opened and the contents catalogued. No mystery will remain—all artwork and treasure found there will be shared, and any wealth hidden in Satis will be restored to the tribe of Rahotep."

The roar of approval made the priest shudder.

"All staff will remain, as they will all report to Jamal Hassan, who will take the position of guardian of the law of Satis."

I was smiling as I did a quick spin on my heel and found Jamal staring up at me like he had seen a ghost.

"You are worthy of the title of menthu," I proclaimed, enjoying myself, "and the Shu will guard you and no longer serve me, the semel-aten. My sheseru and my private guard will see to my protection. They perhaps both thought I have lost faith in them, which I have not."

I didn't even have to see Taj to know he would be struck by my faith in him and his khatyu.

Almost.

I had almost made the mistake of distancing myself from my own house, putting faith in assassins instead of those loyal to me. But now the Shu had their own commander to protect, and that would please them, as there was no longer a divided loyalty. I had reclaimed my own sheseru and my khatyu, and they would swell with pride. It took me a while sometimes, but I could make everything work.

"I will no longer be the semel-aten, but as our beloved priest, Hamid Shamon, baptized me, will now truly be akhen-aten. I will change the direction of my reign and will bring about great change. The new era for Sobek will be Harmakhet, the new dawn."

The hall exploded with cheering.

"We will sweep away the old Sobek and create a new modern city that will rise from the ashes of the old and be a mecca of prosperity. The outside world will be allowed in Sobek, industry will thrive, and nothing will be as it has been."

No one could hear a thing over the din of hundreds of voices raised together.

There would be resistance, I knew, but the old Sobek was over and a new one was coming. It would take me years, I knew, but the building would start immediately.

I needed werepanthers from all over the world to come and make their homes in Sobek. I wanted diversity and change, and because the city and all the land belonged to me (it was deeded to each and every semel-aten), I could make that happen. I would find the best people, the smartest, the most ingenious from every tribe in the world, and together we would build our new state.

Of course, I had just put a giant bull's-eye on my back, but change was scary. I would just have to be careful. The Shu themselves had tried to kill me and been unsuccessful; standing against anyone or anything else would be easy. I hoped.

I descended to the floor and moved until I stood in front of Asdiel, only my khatyu and Taj keeping the crowd out of the small circle of men.

"My lord, you—"

"No." I stepped in close so he could hear me over the joyous noise of the gathered throng. "Your time is past. We don't need a priest of Chae Rophon anymore; we don't need the same rules and penalties. The tribe of Rahotep is still just a tribe. It can't function in this bubble anymore. Instead it will be like every other family headed by a semel the world over."

"You—"

"We need someone to lead us out of the darkness, not keep us inside."

"You would annihilate every tradition! You—"

"It's over, it's done. All of this that you and some of the others hope to keep alive does no one any good. If people were prospering, if everyone in the community was thriving, I'd say yes, keep it like it is, but that's not the case. We have poverty and crime and homelessness. That is not acceptable, and I won't have it."

"You won't?" he roared. "And who are you to make these new laws for the rest of us? You are nothing! You are no one!"

"I was the semel-aten, and now I am akhen-aten, who will lead us into our new day."

"You're mad with power!"

"I want what is best for my tribe."

"These people are not your tribe!"

"They are more mine than yours," I enlightened him.

He moved close to me. "You may call yourself by this new title, by this 'akhen-aten,' but you will not be able to deliver this city from—"

"I will." I signaled for Taj, who was there with a few of his khatyu immediately. "The priest has no family, that was the law, so you will go to Logan Church and—"

"Did you think I missed the coming of this overthrow of my power, Domin Thorne?" he snarled. "Are you under some mistaken belief that I thought you an honorable man?"

I frowned.

"And while it's true that I do not have the legions of followers that you do, there is still one I can count on, still one who will do my bidding."

"Tell me, please, who is this lost soul, so that I may go and save him or her from your mad delusion."

"You will know soon enough," he confirmed. "When what you love most is taken from you, remember that it was on my order that it was done. I took him from you. I ended his life."

Yuri.

"He's already dead," Asdiel hissed.

I never saw the knife.

Chapter Six

MY VISION went white. Everything hurt, and there was screaming and yelling and something hot flecked over my face before I collapsed. I couldn't breathe; my heart was in a vise because all I could think of was Yuri.

My mate.

The city of Ipis, the tribe of Feran… Hakkan Tarek… he had my mate. He had Yuri. Men loyal to the priest, or at least to an antiquated law, had my mate. I had to get him back.

The thought consumed me even as my body convulsed in pain.

I had to shift. My body wanted me to shift.

But if I changed into a panther, there would be nothing of me left. I was an animal. I needed to retain my faculties and….

Werepanther.

I could shift into my half-man/half-panther form, but that would take so much energy and I didn't seem to have any, and….

My vision changed, the angle dropped, and then there was only the sweet coppery smell of blood and the ripple of fear. I charged forward to kill it, whatever was weak and injured and ready to die.

I was pushed down to the floor so hard that all the air rushed from my lungs and I was left gasping, choking, like a fish out of water.

"Domin!"

I was drowning and rolled to my stomach and vomited up blood.

"Domin, you must shift!"

But I could tell I had done it once already and I didn't want to do it again. There was something wrong with my body. I was hurt, and I wanted to lie down even as I needed to get to Yuri.

I had to save Yuri.

"Domin! Shift!"

It was a command from my maahes, and I bristled at his hubris. How dare he tell me what to do?

"You're going to bleed to death if you don't shift!"

The heaving continued and became retching that I could not control.

"No, Jin!"

Crane sounded frantic, which meant that to get me to shift Jin would not simply let his power rise as he'd probably done once already, but would this time use his power as a call. In my weakened state, I would respond to his pheromones, and the moment I desired him, I would be sucked through my shift and yanked inside out in a violent, painful rush.

I would not. I was the semel-aten and had just finally baptized myself anew, as I had been considering for the past month. My only regret was that Yuri had not been there to hear what I'd announced. Just imagining the glow in his eyes....

For the life of me, I could not pinpoint the exact moment when I had fallen in love with Yuri Kosa. I had said I loved him in Mongolia because those were the words he needed to hear for him to go with me. But I hadn't really loved him, not then.

But now... if he was there, if he was with me....

"Domin, please!"

Koren's voice, as though that would—but I had to thank him and I'd almost forgotten. I needed everything balanced between us.

"Koren," I coughed because it was all I could get out.

"Domin," he said softly, and I felt his hands on my chest, on my throat, in my hair. "Oh, please."

"Thank you for standing beside me at the challenge," I said, and then it was like my body was set on fire and my bones were melting under my skin.

MY EYES blinked open, and I found Jin, Crane, and Jamal.

They were stunned.

I scowled, which made Jin's face light up.

"I had to remind the disbelievers that they were in the presence of a semel, not a regular cat. You do not shift enough; they have all forgotten about your power."

"Of course," I said, clenching my jaw as I swatted at their hands and moved fast, much too fast, rolling to my feet in one fluid movement. "Did you call Yuri? Did he answer his phone?"

I would have fallen if Koren hadn't been there suddenly to catch my shoulder and brace me.

"*Domin*," he said. My name was infused with more feeling than I thought the man capable of. "Be careful, you lost so much blood."

"Did he answer?"

"No, my lord," Jamal responded. "We have tried. There is no answer."

I realized then that I was naked from the waist up, splattered in blood, with an enormous puffy barely healed red scar extending from my abdomen to my left pectoral.

My eyes lifted to Koren's clear olive ones.

"The priest had a dagger," he said. "You would be dead if it hadn't been for Jin."

I looked over my shoulder at the mate of the semel-netjer. He was in a robe with nothing underneath, I was betting.

"Thank you for saving my life."

Jin's eyes glittered, the light in the clear gray eyes really something to see.

"The wound in your stomach is deep," Koren clarified as I held Jin's gaze. "The knife was only dragged across your chest, the damage merely superficial, just a scratch in comparison. Had Jin not put himself between you and the priest, he would have had your heart."

"And what has happened to the priest?"

"The nekhene cat dismembered him," Jamal chimed in to tell me.

The idea that the delicate man I was seeing—because even at five eleven he was still fragile—being strong enough or fearsome enough to rip through flesh, muscle, and bone was shocking. And there he stood, contained, even demure, staring at me from behind his mask of serene tranquility.

"Did you frighten everyone?" I demanded to know.

"I did, my lord," Jin reported. "But when your wound was shown and the weapon discovered, I was less terrifying and more avenging angel."

"Good." I exhaled slowly, realizing that I was drained and barely able to stand, but having a burning question for Jamal. "When did you start calling Yuri?"

"The second we knew you would live, my lord, the moment we could stop focusing on you, we tried calling him."

"And he hasn't picked up?"

"No, my lord," he slowly uttered. "His phone must be off."

But I knew they were trying to call a regular cell phone, not a satellite unit.

"Koren shared with us that Yuri had taken the wrong phone, as he heard a conversation that you and Ebere had about it."

I had forgotten he had been in the room as well.

"So it could be anything, any interference between here and Ipis, but it could also simply be, as I said, off."

I absorbed that. "Jamal."

"My lord?"

"Keep trying to call Yuri."

"Of course," he said, sounding pained. "Now, would you please go to your room? If you could see the hue of your skin, you—"

"It doesn't matter about me. You have to find Yuri!" I yelled and exerting that much energy made my knees buckle.

Koren pulled me close, bracing me with his slightly taller frame. "Put your arm around my neck."

I did as I was directed.

"Lean on me, for once."

Something sarcastic and barbed lay on the tip of my tongue, but his face, turned into me, behind my ear, flooded me with comfort. It was instinctive, his nuzzling, one cat to another, but it calmed me, the man I was, not simply the animal. "I'll take you to your room," he said, his voice a sultry purr over my skin. "Let me."

I was light-headed.

"We'll be right behind you with water and meat," Crane rasped, pushing Jin forward.

"You'll keep trying Yuri's phone?"

"Of course," Crane gave me his word. "But please, Domin, you have to rest."

"But—"

"Please," Jin insisted.

I tried to pull away from Koren. "I think I can walk on my own," I said, sounding drunk as I accidentally bumped noses with him. "I don't need your help."

"You're going to have to take it," he said, gesturing for Jamal to hook my other arm over his broad shoulders.

Had Yuri been there, I would have been carried.

It was just another reason to miss the man.

IN MY room they placed me gently on the bed and propped pillows behind my back and under my feet. I wanted to move, but there was no way until I ate and drank. Sprawled out, I regarded Koren and Jamal.

"What if he's already dead?"

Jamal shook his head. "No one in their right mind puts their hands on the mate of the semel-aten."

"But that's the point—they're crazy."

"Who, my lord? This threat of the priest's, it could be empty."

"Then why isn't Yuri answering his phone?"

"There could be a million reasons," Jamal said tightly. "You know that as well as I."

"I need to know that he's okay."

"Of course."

"Send men to Ipis now."

"Your sheseru took it upon himself to do that, my lord. Taj is on his way to Ipis as we speak, with fifty men and ten of the Shu."

"Really?"

"Yes, my lord, he left moments ago, when I convinced him that you would live."

"Why was he waiting to—"

"He needed to know first" was all Jamal said.

"Why?"

"Why do you think, idiot?" Koren chided. "Because he's your goddamn sheseru and he's not leaving until he knows that you're okay."

"But if Logan were hurt but Jin was in danger, then—"

"Don't compare Yuri to Jin! One is a true-mate and the other is an infatuation that will soon wane."

"Kor—"

"If you were dying and Yuri was your reah or your yareah, all effort would be immediately made to bring him to the semel. After you and Logan went after each other in the pit that time, Mikhail went immediately to bring Jin to Logan."

"Yes, I—"

"But Yuri is not your mate. Whatever name you want to call him by is fine, but two men, unless you happen to find another male reah somewhere, will never be *maat*."

I shook my head.

"It's not, Domin. Panther law does not recognize—"

"I know what it recognizes, and I will change the law for all panthers, not just me."

"And you can, and you will, I have no doubt of that. But until then, a man like Taj, who places greater importance on you than on Yuri, is going to wait to make sure you're okay before he runs off into the night to check on your boyfriend."

"Whatever you want to say, he is my mate." I coughed hard, which sent a wave of pain through my entire body.

"Please, my semel," Jamal began. "You need to—"

"What if it's Constantine?" The question was directed at Jamal. "What if he's the one who's going to kill Yuri?"

"Constantine is a member of your khatyu, my lord. You must believe in your own men."

I didn't trust anyone at the moment.

"Constantine would lay down his life to protect Yuri. Look somewhere else for betrayal, not at your own house."

"My own house?" I snarled. "Are you fucking kidding? Like my house is so sacred and secure? Like I'm so beloved that no one would try and hurt me? Are you listening to yourself?"

"My lord—"

"Elham El Masry had the nice lady that brought me breakfast, lunch, and dinner try to poison me."

Koren gasped, but I didn't care. Let him be shocked.

"Yes, I—"

"So don't give me the whole 'in my house' bullshit. Anyone could be trying to kill him. Anyone! I trust you, Kabore, my sylvan and my sheseru, my mastaba—oh." I had a sudden thought because my brain was firing all at once and I couldn't keep anything straight. "Did someone call Ebere and tell her that Crane won the challenge?"

"No, my lord."

"Well, for crissakes, she's gonna want to know."

"Yes, my lord." Jamal sounded pained. "But would you please just—"

"Anyone in the tribe of Feran could be trying to kill him."

"My lord, aren't you forgetting who Yuri is?"

"I don't understand what—"

"He's not some weak creature easily overcome; he was a sheseru and one of the strongest panthers I have ever seen. He will not be easily dispatched, my lord."

"Unless he's taken by surprise."

Jamal shook his head. "I'm sorry, but I see him as far too capable."

But I couldn't see him at all; that was the problem. I needed to gaze into his eyes with my own, put my hands on him and feel his heart beating under my ear as I laid it on his chest. "I swear if I we both make it out of this, you are never leaving my side again."

"My lord?"

I had spoken the words between clenched teeth. "Just—okay, if whoever is after him doesn't try and kill him, what else could they do?"

"What are you talking about?" Koren was irritated, but I hadn't been asking him.

One of the best things about Jamal was his willingness to hypothesize with me and think about the worst-case scenario. All the others went on and on about not dwelling on what could happen or on bad things, but Jamal would go with me down the dark and twisty road in a heartbeat. It was a splendid quality.

"I believe the greatest concern would be if, for whatever reason, the tribe of Feran tried to conceal him," Jamal enlightened me.

"Conceal him?"

"Yes." He nodded. "If they were to take him into the catacombs of Abtu to hide him or simply abandon him there, then for us, who are not familiar with the caverns, it would be highly unlikely that we could locate him. The cave is vast. You would have to cover so much ground to secure him—I don't know how we would be successful before he died of starvation or dehydration."

"Why would you say that to him?" Koren was indignant. "That's not helping."

"Yes, it is," Jamal asserted. "My semel prefers to be prepared for every eventuality and to make himself ready, if he can."

My mind was working. "So we would need speed in that instance."

"Yes," he agreed.

Speed.

"Here," Crane said as he walked into my room carrying a huge basin of water, followed closely by Jin, who carried a platter of sliced meat. "Shift, Domin, and let's get this all down you."

"Jin," I said, meeting his gaze. "I need you to come to Ipis with me in case the tribe of Feran hides Yuri in the catacombs of Abtu."

"Of course." He smiled like it was the sanest request in the world.

"I know that Logan will be here soon, but—"

"I wouldn't let you leave the villa without me anyway," Jin stated. "And I couldn't leave here without seeing Yuri. I wouldn't."

Logan was going to kill me.

Chapter Seven

WE WERE still fighting.

"I forbid it."

"Have you lost your mind?"

"You're the semel-aten, for crissakes, Domin!"

"Technically I just named myself akhen-aten," I mentioned drolly, trying to inject some levity into the situation.

"Call yourself what you want, but the world knows you as the semel-aten, and as the semel-aten, it is completely irresponsible and selfish of you to put yourself in danger!"

"We're talking about my mate," I reminded him.

Koren spun around and pointed at me as I lay there on the bed. "Do not start this shit again. No matter what you try to say, Yuri Kosa is not your mate!"

He had no idea about anything.

"You don't just give up on us for... that."

"You lost me."

"Domin," he said softly, soothing. "How do you go from years of us to taking Logan's sheseru into your bed?"

"He wanted to be there, I wanted him there... I'm missing the question."

"Domin—"

"You want me now because I'm the semel-aten."

"No."

"Oh yes." I laughed softly and it hurt, so I tried to stop. "Yuri just wants *me*. We can live in a shack on a beach somewhere, and he would be perfectly content."

"That's because you're beautiful and—"

"It's the chase, the hunt you crave, Koren," I said honestly, for once. "I understand, but I don't want to run anymore."

"How can you give up on us? On me?"

"*You* gave up on *me*!" I yelled, finally sick of his bullshit. "You left me! You have never known what you wanted, and I kept—no." I deflated. "Not again."

He stalked back over to the bed and flopped down beside me, placing a warm hand on my cold chest, still clammy from the shift, my body still trying to regulate itself and heal at the same time. I needed to sleep, but I wanted Yuri more. If anything happened to him....

"Domin!"

I flicked my gaze back to Koren.

"I know that you don't want Yuri to get hurt, but there's a world of difference between that and actually claiming the man for your mate."

How could I make him understand?

"Here's what happened," he said, sliding his hand up over my left pectoral, across my collarbone to my throat. He was gentle as he traced his fingers over my skin, and my eyes drifted closed as he rubbed his thumb over my bottom lip. "I stepped out of the picture, and you finally saw him."

I made a noise of agreement.

"Why do you think you never saw him before then?"

Because I was stupid? Because I was blind? Because I was so infatuated with the idea of having Koren Church that I couldn't at all see what was right in front of me?

"You didn't see him because you never even considered him."

Batting his hand away, I rolled over on my side. "You should go."

Immediately his hand was on my hip.

"It was a brand-new thing, being semel-aten, and you didn't want to start the adventure alone, so you took—"

I cut him off. "No." Because I had not loved Yuri when we arrived in Sobek. But it was so much more than that now.

"Just—"

"No!" I yelled.

"Listen to me! He's not the one for you. He's *not*."

If I had my full strength, I would have thrown him out, but I was exhausted. That didn't mean I was defenseless. I could wield my memories like a whip. "I came home with that piece of key lime pie because it's your favorite," I began. "And I—"

"Oh, for shit's sake, Domin, not this again!" he yelled, leaping off the bed to get away from me. "Why do you always—"

"And I threw open the door, and there you were with *Talon Danvers*."

"I—"

"You knew she was mated—she's a goddamn yareah!" I exclaimed.

"You know as well as I do that Christophe and Talon have an open—"

"But that's not the point," I said, rolling over on my back. "The point was that I had pie in my hand and what did you say?"

He shook his head.

"Koren?"

"I don't remember."

But I did, and that was the problem.

I had come in, flushed with excitement to see him since he had just returned from a business trip. But instead of coming home to me, waiting for me, he had gone immediately out to a club and picked up a woman. And not just any woman, but Talon Danvers, yareah of the tribe of Pakhet. My barging in had not even given him pause.

"Room service!" Koren announced happily as he continued to pump in and out of the woman writhing below him. "Thank God. I'm starving!"

It was hard to even pull oxygen into my lungs, but that was fine— the air in the room was thick with the scent of sex and sweat anyway.

"Come here," he demanded, his hot gaze raking over me. "Talon will suck your dick."

But unlike Koren, it mattered who touched me in bed, and I never wanted a woman to do it. For me it was not a preference, it was simply how I was made.

I took a step back, and my face, I was sure, was his first indication that something was wrong. Instantly, he was defensive.

"Like you haven't fucked anyone since I've been gone," he snarled, all the while still hammering into Talon. "It's not like we're mated, Domin."

And we weren't. Just because I had thought it in my heart, carried myself as though I were special because Koren Church loved me, counted the days until he came home… didn't make what I felt real. It didn't make me matter to him. I was settled; he was still on the prowl. It was crystal clear as I fled the room, dropping the pie on the floor in the doorway.

As I tore down the steps and out the front door, I heard a car. When I checked the driveway, I saw Logan get out of the passenger side of Jin's Jeep Wrangler and Jin draped forward over the steering wheel. It took a second for me to realize he was laughing, not crying, and that Logan was fuming.

"You're a maniac!" Logan roared as he stalked toward the house. "How did you even get a driver's license?"

It hurt to watch them because it was all so normal, Jin climbing out and then running after his mate, Logan yelling at him to stay away because he was mad.

"Baby!" Jin called after him.

"No!"

When Jin finally ran, stepping around in front of him, barring his semel's path, I saw Logan glower before he took Jin's face in his hands.

"Be more careful," he demanded, growling at Jin. "If anything ever happened to you, what the hell am I supposed to do?"

Jin tipped back his head, and Logan bent and kissed him, and it was sweet and hot but mostly it was just them. Mates.

I bolted from the porch, but Logan caught my arm before I could reach my car.

"Are you all right?" he inhaled. "You smell like you're hurt."

It was just my heart, though; I wasn't bleeding.

"Domin?"

I cleared my throat. "Your brother is fucking a yareah in his room. You better take care of that, my semel."

His eyes widened, and I saw the anger and embarrassment flood his face.

"I mean, we both know Talon Danvers is a whore, but still… under your roof?"

Logan ran up the steps into the house, and I was almost free. Except for Jin.

"What's wrong with you?" He sounded worried.

"Koren is screwing Talon Danvers in his bed."

His eyes got huge. "But you were waiting for him to get home."

"I was," I said, and I got in my silver Gran Turismo and drove away.

"Domin!"

Back in the present, I realized, as I had the day I left for the sepat with Logan, that I didn't need to say good-bye to Koren. There was nothing left between us.

"I think someday you're going to find someone who absolutely transfixes you," I said.

"I already have," he said, furrowing his brow as he reached for my face.

My head swiveled as Jin and Crane and Kabore walked into the room, followed by several servants.

"You must eat and drink again, my lord," Kabore announced, snapping his fingers at everyone, directing them. "And you, *ex*, move away from my lord."

Koren clenched his jaw, but he got off the bed as my steward swept forward, his shiny black knee-high boots clicking on the stone tiles as he rushed to my bedside.

"Now, my lord, shift and eat. We're all here, and the moment you regain your strength, we will go and find your mate."

"Yeah," Crane murmured. "What he said."

I took a breath. "I have to get to Yuri."

"Of course you do." Jin's eyes glowed quicksilver. "He's your mate."

Yes, he was.

THEY FELL asleep around me, all piled onto the bed I normally shared only with Yuri. I would have to give orders to have the bed stripped and the linens washed while I was gone. If my mate smelled Koren on the sheets, he would annihilate me. I sighed at the thought. Yuri being possessive of me, when no one else had ever been, never failed to arouse me.

I missed him, I wanted him beside me. I was hurt and I needed to rest, but even more, I needed my mate. His touch on my skin would be so good.

We had fought the night before he left. I had ranted and raved, and when he had defended me, even though I was telling him how horribly I was failing—he was always my staunchest supporter—I had launched myself at him only to be grabbed and thrown up against the wall.

I was strong, but Yuri was stronger, bigger, and had easily fifty pounds of muscle on me in human form. In my werepanther form, I would have had the upper hand, but that was not what I wanted. His might, a display of it, was what I craved.

"You try my patience, my semel," he rumbled in my ear, holding me tight with a hand around the back of my neck, pressing my cheek hard against the stone wall, his knee pushed between my thighs, parting my legs.

I shuddered under his power exerted over me because only Yuri knew, no other lover ever suspecting, even Koren, that my desire to submit was just as strong as my need to dominate. It was absolutely necessary for me to relinquish control so that my mind could finally, just for a moment, rest.

The shirt I wore was torn away, swept to the floor in tatters. He licked up the side of my neck to behind my right ear and made my knees go weak even as I ordered him to get off me.

"You don't want me off you," he taunted, biting down hard into the tender skin. "Do you, my semel?"

I almost came.

When he shoved me forward, my groin forced to the wall as he rubbed against my crease, grinding, pushing, I demanded that he get on the bed and put his ass in the air.

"No, that's not what my mate needs."

The restraints Yuri had hammered into the wall were freed from where they were hooked behind a curtain on the left and another on the right. He had put the bolts into the wall himself, secured heavy silver chains to them, and finished them with thick manacles. He had then covered the shackles from any prying eyes that might ever enter our private rooms. The benign swath of silk that draped over the shackles was dark midnight blue.

He unhooked the first and I heard it, the scrape of metal over stone as he moved it, and then the restraint enclosed my wrist. It stung, as silver always did when it hit werepanther skin. As the change in us was chemical, biological, the shift caused all of us to be born allergic to that particular metal. Normally it was avoided, but Yuri had asked for both the chains and cuffs to be forged from silver for that specific reason. He wanted to make sure I couldn't get free.

I shuddered as my arms stretched wide, the second shackle locking to my right wrist.

"What does the kitty need?"

"Fuck you!" I yelled, fighting and twisting. I tried to bite him, but I had no range of motion, held fast, only able to use my head, hips, and legs. My chest was wedged against the hard, sharp stone wall.

I snarled when he laughed at me, squirmed when his hands went to my belt and trouser stays. My slacks pooled around my ankles, covering my dress shoes, seconds later.

"If you struggle, you'll hurt yourself, so stay still," he ordered, warm breath caressing my ear before he put his open mouth between my shoulder blades.

He took his time, licking, nibbling, sucking, then finally kissing down my spine until he reached the small of my back, and he dragged my briefs down. My hard, dripping cock bounced free, brushing the wall painfully even as I felt him bite down into my right ass cheek.

"Oh, please," I begged, my voice not my own, the whine, the crack, not normal.

Rough hands spread me, opened me wide, and then he dipped in his tongue to taste me, sliding over my puckered hole before pushing inside.

"Yuri!" I yelled, pushing back into his face, wanting him deeper.

He devoured my ass, nibbled and suckled, relaxing my muscles, making everything wet and open and wanting.

I was panting, lips parted, writhing against the wall as he discarded my underwear, shoes, and socks, all of it shoved to the side so I stood chained and naked.

"What do you need?"

But I couldn't say—it would make me weak and I couldn't be, could never be. "Let me go."

He left me, and I was in agony as I stood there and yanked and tugged on the restraints, causing them to cut into my wrists.

"Stop," he ordered, and then he put his hand over my cock, stroking, jacking me off, but shielding tender flesh from sharp edges even as he screwed two lubed fingers deep inside my rectum.

"Yuri!" I howled in anger and pain and bliss.

There was no gentle, because I wasn't having it. I didn't want it, didn't need it, wouldn't have appreciated it even if it had been offered. Instead there was stinging heat as he withdrew his fingers, only to quickly slather my hole before he grasped my hips and pushed his enormous mushroom head against my entrance.

"Beg."

I tried to push back, to lift up, to gain any kind of leverage at all.

"Domin."

This was part of it, the control I had to release.

"Beg," he ordered again.

I was shivering. My entire body had broken out into a cold sweat, and I could feel him inching in, stretching slowly, my muscles fighting so hard, the pain searing through me, my cock so hard it hurt, drooling precome as he wrapped his hand tight around my balls, making sure there was no release for me, just pressure and ache.

"Yuri."

"Yuri what?"

"Please, my mate, please, Yuri, fuck me, take me. I belong to you."

"Yes," he said and thrust hard and deep, breaching me and burying himself to the balls in one violent thrust.

I roared his name, and he pulled out only to plunge back inside, harder, faster, hammering into me, setting a rhythm that was driving and rough, without a hint of tenderness.

Letting my head loll back when he fisted his hand there in my hair, the force painful, I whimpered with happiness.

Everything stopped, everything fell away, and all there was, was the pistoning of his hips pounding my ass, the slide, and the fullness. The pinch subsided, going from sharp, scorching pain to dull ache to tensing, quivering throbbing desire. I could only stretch my fingers along the wall and grip, feel my feet leave the floor from the thrusts, and simply let every whine, moan, and cry flow from my throat.

He stretched his hand over my head and then my right hand was free.

"Grab your cock. I want to see you come on the wall."

"Don't stop," I pleaded, because I was so filled, so stretched, and yet there was still more I needed to have stripped away.

He gripped my chest with one hand, the other bruising my hip as he took me and used me and burned the knowledge of who I was and what I was to him first into my body and then into my brain.

"You're nothing but mine," he snarled, and the sound so dark and fierce it brought the first jolt of release. "If all else is taken, that remains. Always."

I could feel the hard ball of cold and terror start to break apart in my chest. Even if I failed, even if I was no longer semel-aten, he would always be mine. He could never be lost.

"Did you hear me?"

My balls tightened, my muscles locked, and my breath caught in my chest.

"Did you hear me?" he roared.

"Yes," I rasped as my vision went white.

"Yes, who?"

"Yes, my mate," I barely got out.

He drove hard and deep, and the teeth in my shoulder made me gasp. As the orgasm wrung me out, I screamed his name.

He purred mine softly in my ear.

I clamped down around the thick pole impaling me, and his low rumbling purr brought an answering whimper before he convulsed within me and flooded my ass with liquid heat.

"There's my sweet man," he soothed, and I felt hot tears on my cheeks.

He bucked forward as my muscles milked his length, and I was so tight inside that as we stood there, molded together, semen dripped wet and thick between our legs. It felt decadent and intimate, and I shuddered with aftershocks and contractions.

He wrapped his brawny arms around me, plastered his massive chest to my back, and kissed up the side of my neck so slowly, so gently, that I went boneless in his arms.

"There, yes, lean on me so I can unlock your wrist."

I gave him my weight, and he reached up and released me. No longer tethered to the wall, I would have slumped to the floor had he not held me up.

"Domin!"

The muffled yell brought my attention from my memories to the present and to Jin, standing out on the balcony.

"Stop moaning and go to sleep. You will have your mate soon, and I suggest you unburden your heart and tell him everything that you think he doesn't know already."

I scowled.

"Silence heals nothing, fixes nothing, and unlocks nothing. Just because you don't say something doesn't make it any less true."

"Do you speak from experience?"

"My semel knows I love him and I know he loves me. Yuri might know the same, you even declared it once in Mongolia, and I know because I was there. But after this, you have to make him understand his place."

"You realize you're the last person in the world who should be giving me this lecture."

He exhaled slowly. "I do see the irony."

"Logan is going to kill us both, you know—you for going, and me for asking you."

"I suspect so, yes."

"He'll never let you leave his side again."

"And there is comfort in knowing that, as there will be for Yuri. It is a great thing to be needed by another."

Yes, it was.

Chapter Eight

IT WAS what a prince did.

"We both know that I won't be the maahes of this tribe once Jin leaves," Crane argued. "I'm leaving with him."

"I know that," I said, before I made sure to darken my face to a scowl. "But until that time, Crane Adams, you are the maahes of this tribe, and you must remain here and lead."

"I can't do that."

"You can," I asserted, "and you will."

He was wrong to expect support from his best friend. Jin only cackled instead of helping him out.

"Are you insane?" He was incredulous.

"Just quit bitching," Jin said with a yawn.

I tried the logical route to put him at ease. "Mikhail will be here to answer—"

Mikhail spoke up. "I'm going with you."

I watched Samani's eyes go big and round behind him.

"No." I shook my head. "You will stay here and take care of the tribe and advise Crane while I'm gone."

He took a breath as he gestured at Jin. "And you will take the reah of the tribe of Mafdet with you without his sheseru or a dozen or so—"

"You're kidding, right?" Jin half yelled. "Nothing and no one's gonna hurt me, Mikhail. Crane's in charge of the first tribe. Could you just stay here and give him some goddamn backup?"

Mikhail's dark cobalt gaze was a glower.

Even in the midst of chaos that morning, I found the both of them so endearing. Mikhail was trying to do his duty to everyone, and Jin was just being Jin, clearing his own path.

"Logan's going to kill you all," Crane said impassively.

"Probably," I agreed.

Jin waggled his eyebrows.

JIN HAD killed the priest on a Monday; it had taken me the night and all the next day to recover from my injuries. Kabore was still worried, but our physician, Thema Pakhom, said she would let me travel only if I did nothing to exert myself.

"You must be careful, Domin. You haven't healed fully yet, and none of us want to lose you to something as banal as internal bleeding."

I had watched her eyes soften like they did whenever I was around. Apparently more people in my home liked me than I was aware of. So even though I was still weak, we left late Wednesday night to drive ten hours, planning to arrive in Ipis the following morning.

"You're still sore?" Jin was checking as we sat in the back of the monstrous black Hummer.

"The rest of us do not all heal as fast as you, nekhene cat," I grumbled.

"Or as fast as the semel-netjer, apparently."

I growled at him, and he laughed, which was such a nice sound I let my irritation go and used his shoulder for a pillow.

"Sit by me," Koren offered, but Jin's fingers threading though my hair felt too good to move away from. And Yuri would not mind me showing up smelling like Jin.

We took twelve men with us, since Taj, with his sixty, was already there. We had heard from him, but the news was odd. He had been allowed into the city of Ipis, but not into the home of the semel. Without me there, the tribe did not have to, by law, grant him entrance, and so they did not.

He had seen Yuri behind a gate and reported him in good health, though he had seen bruises on his face and his left arm was bandaged from wrist to bicep. But the smirk had been his. When Taj had yelled that I was on my way, he had brightened. I wanted Taj to put Yuri on the phone, but he was not allowed to. It was a mistake, the one this semel was making, keeping me from my mate, and he would know that soon enough.

"IS THAT grass?"

"Yes," Kabore responded, yawning as we arrived at ten the following morning. "Ipis sits over an underground lake. The whole area is lush with plant life."

It was stunning. Sobek was dry, almost everywhere I'd been in Egypt was, but this was gorgeous and brought the classic image of an oasis to mind. When we reached the town itself, we parked close to an outdoor café and got out, my khatyu filing out silently behind me. Instantly there was a contingent of men there to greet us, and I wasn't surprised. They had to have seen us coming for hours; there was only one two-lane road there and back from Sobek. I had spoken to Taj, and he had asked if I wanted him to leave his position outside the semel's home to come greet us. I ordered him to stay; I would be there soon enough.

"Sah'eed nahharkoo."

A man stood in front of twenty men, even though every second more and more people gathered behind them in the square.

I couldn't speak the language, and I wasn't in the mood to try and stumble through it. "I am the semel-aten, Domin Thorne. I want to speak to Hakkan Tarek, the semel of the tribe of Feran."

Everyone went to their knees.

"Who is Hakkan Tarek?" I demanded of the crowd.

No one said a word.

Jin cleared his throat behind me.

"What?" I asked, glaring over my shoulder at him.

He mouthed words.

"What?"

"Give them permission to speak," Kabore muttered out of the side of his mouth.

"Oh." I cleared my throat. "Please, everyone rise, and someone please tell me where I might find the semel."

They all rose quickly, and I tried not to scowl.

"My lord." The man who had first spoken to me stepped closer. "I am Hanif Tarek, son of the semel, Hakkan Tarek. Welcome to Ipis."

"Thank you. I need to speak to your semel at once."

"Of course, he is at the fort, my lord. I will take you to him."

"The fort?"

"Our home, my lord."

"All right."

"I'm sure he will be very pleased that you have come to mediate, my lord, and find a resolution for the newest of our many issues."

I frowned. "Did my sekhem not inform you of the reason for first his visit and then mine?"

"He did, my lord, but my father will not hear that concern, but only that of the catacombs at Abtu."

I was confused. He had to be at least twenty-one, what the hell was going on? Why wasn't he the semel? Why had his father not stepped aside and begun mentoring his son?

"Why are you not the semel, Hanif Tarek?"

He cleared his throat. "My father's as-yet-unborn son will be semel."

I was missing something. "You are your father's son, are you not?"

His eyes went to the ground.

"Hanif?"

Nothing.

"Look at me."

He lifted his chin and met my eyes with his.

"Explain."

"My father has taken a new yareah, and it is with her that he will bring forth the next semel."

"Jin."

He moved up beside me.

"I think I'm missing something," I said and then tipped my head at Hanif. "Repeat what you just said."

It was hard for him to meet Jin's pale gaze. "My father has taken a new yareah, and so the son that he sires with her will be named the new semel of Feran."

"No." Jin shook his head. "Even though your mother has passed away, her—"

"She has not passed, my lord."

Jin was startled and so was I. "Not passed? Your mother lives?"

"Yes." He was really trying to keep his face a mask of civility.

"Then how in the world has your father claimed a new yareah?"

"He simply said that my mother was no longer yareah and pronounced his new consort as his new yareah."

Jin shook his head. "He may take as many women to his bed as he pleases," Jin said tightly. "But only the semel-aten can have a consort, or wosret, and only if she is a reah. Any semel who is not the semel-aten cannot have consorts. He may have whores, diversions, mistresses, whatever he would call them, but they cannot replace your mother as yareah, and he certainly can't have any but his firstborn male child with his yareah be semel. Is he mad?"

Hanif swallowed hard. "Of course not."

"Where is your father?" Jin was scowling.

"He is at our home, as I explained to the semel-aten. Also, the djehu of the peq, Ayaz Suyuti, and the djehu of the shen, Chanzira Adjo, are there with him."

"So your father is counseling them?"

"No," he said softly, "your sekhem, Yuri Kosa, whom you so graciously sent ahead of you, is counseling them, my lord, and trying to help them reach a resolution."

Yuri.

"He is safe and well?"

"He is, my lord," he said oddly, haltingly, and I didn't like it. "He is quite fit."

I wasn't imagining things—his smell changed when he said Yuri's name.

When he widened his eyes suddenly in obvious fear, I had no idea why. "What?"

"You're growling my lord," Kabore said from my left. "Excuse me, but could you tell us, when the sekhem arrived, how many men did he have with him?"

"One."

I felt the rumble start low in my chest.

"There was only one man?" I heard Jin almost gasp. "Are you certain?"

"Yes." He glanced uncertainly at Jin, unsure of how to address him, as he had not been introduced—I could not introduce my party to anyone but the semel first; those were the rules of hospitality. "There were just two of them—Yuri, your sekhem, and the other," he finished fast, and then blushed.

Yuri. My mate had allowed this man to use his first name.

I had the sudden urge to snap the neck of the beautiful young man in front of me. But jealousy was simply another test of faith, wasn't it?

"As I said, he has been doing his very best to help the two djehus come to an amicable resolution, but he as of yet has been unsuccessful."

"I see."

"But he has been successful in keeping Garai Milar safe since his arrival."

"Safe?" I prodded.

"Yes, my lord."

"Safe from what?"

"Deoles, my father's sheseru."

"You lost me. Why would the son of another semel be in danger from your father's sheseru?"

"Is that not the way of it, my lord? A sheseru punishes and makes the panthers of the tribe submit to him?"

"No." I glanced sideways at him. "Is that why my sheseru, Taj Chalthoum, was not allowed within your father's home?"

"Yes, my lord. Had you sent your sylvan, he would have been permitted."

I was so confused. "Please take me to your father and explain to me on the way what the hell is going on."

He shook his head. "My lord, I am not worthy to speak to—"

"Yes, you are," I insisted. "So my sekhem, he allowed you to call him by his first name?"

"Oh, he was not given a choice, my lord. My father decides what rights everyone has once they are here in Ipis. He is the law here."

"Is he?"

"Yes."

"Meaning?" I prodded.

"Meaning that all the laws that you live by in the outside world, my lord, do not apply here in Ipis. Only what my father thinks and wants matter."

"And why is that?"

"He is a divine vessel."

"For who?"

"He is Ra reborn."

"Is he?" I lifted an eyebrow, pivoting to face Jin.

"That's a perversion of the law," Jin announced, staring at the younger man.

"Unless you want to be reported to my father by his khatyu, I would suggest that you keep your voice down," Hanif warned us.

"Why?"

"I have found that questioning my father or drawing his attention through beauty brings about the same result."

"And what is that?" I inquired.

"His interest, my lord."

My stomach was starting to twist into knots. "And Garai Milar, did your father take an interest in him?"

"Yes, my lord."

It was painful to hear, and I had to draw a breath and calm down a second so I could go on without yelling. When my eyes met Hanif's again, when I could, I saw how frightened he was. "Garai Milar was raped?"

"He was taken, yes, my lord."

"Call it what you will. If he didn't ask for it, it's rape."

He suddenly started shivering. "Please don't kill my father, my lord. Swear you won't, or I'll raise the alarm and you will never get inside."

I narrowed my eyes, staring the smaller man down. "I swear that *I* will not kill your father, Hanif Tarek."

"Bless you, my lord."

"But now tell me how my sekhem made Garai Milar safe."

"He is Garai's champion, my lord. He is, in fact, also the champion of my sister Masika and of my cousin Dalila."

I inhaled deeply, willing myself to calm. "Yuri Kosa is the champion of three people?"

"Actually five, my lord," he admitted. "The two djehus are also under his protection."

"This is an outrage," Jin quietly seethed from beside me. "I want to be in that fort *now*."

"And you will," I comforted my best friend's mate under my breath even as I smiled over at Hanif, attempting to put him at ease.

"So tell me, are all visitors to your father's home his to do with as he sees fit?"

"Yes, of course, my lord. As I explained, my father is Ra's vessel on Earth."

"I see, and where is your sylvan?"

"He was cast into the fire for speaking out against my father."

Kabore said something in Latin before crossing himself.

"So your father, he kills those who oppose him, as well."

"Yes, my lord."

"So my mate was given what choice?"

"To fight in the pit or submit."

"Submit to your father?"

"No, my lord, my father does not take men like your mate to his bed. They must be beautiful, delicate." He tipped his head at Jin. "Like your companion."

I noticed how he bit his bottom lip. "Hanif?"

"You should take him back to where your vehicles are my lord. He'll be safe there."

"No." I shook my head. "He'll be fine. So the men that your father does not take to his bed, what is done?"

"He has Deoles Aran, his sheseru, take them on an altar that is brought into the main hall."

I bristled. "So my mate, he could either fight in the pit or submit to this Deoles in front of a crowd?"

"Yes." He beamed at me, like we were having the most normal conversation ever. "It is sport for my father to watch Deoles take big strong men like your mate."

"And when my mate refused?"

"I thought it a frightening choice, my lord, but your mate is extraordinary and though Deoles is bigger, he is not stronger."

I gritted my teeth because it was imperative I stay calm.

"And then when he won and my father's eye fell on my sister… your mate selflessly said that he would champion her and so went again into the pit."

"How many times in one day does he fight?"

"He fights five matches per day, my lord."

Hanif trailed off, and I felt a wave of anger sweep over me. It wasn't mine; it was Jin's. The thing about me was, I cared about Yuri, but as long as he wasn't hurt, this semel could do whatever he wanted with his own family, his own tribe. But Jin... reahs weren't made that way. Preying on the weak was bound to pull righteous anger from the reah, which would, in turn, ignite rage in the nekhene.

"Would you father defile your sister himself?"

"It is not defiling, my lord, it—"

"Would he do it himself?" I repeated, willing my voice to remain level.

"No, my lord," he acknowledged. "He would watch Deoles take her."

It was as though a hot wind skimmed over my skin, prickling like tiny pins, and I realized everything I thought was crap. I shivered with my need to protect and shelter and save. I had to close my eyes for a second, let the surging feelings roll through me so I could hold it together and not scream. The change I hadn't noticed, had told everyone wasn't me, had nevertheless taken hold. I didn't just want to rescue Yuri. I wouldn't be content to liberate just him and Garai Milar. I wanted to free them all.

"May I ask a question?" Jin requested sweetly.

"Of course," Hanif said, and I could tell that Jin had him completely charmed.

"Is the semel-aten's mate fighting in the pit in panther form?"

"No, my father's new yareah likes to see men sweat while they fight, and so they fight in human form in the pit."

"That is not permitted by law," Kabore informed the younger man.

"Yes, I know," he agreed. And I realized then how timid he was, that the curve of his mouth was a reflexive action done out of nervousness. "But that is how we do things in Ipis, in the tribe of Feran."

"Okay." I cleared my throat. "My sekhem, he had a phone with him. We tried from Sobek but were unsuccessful in our attempts to reach him on it. Was it removed by your semel?"

"Yes, my lord."

"His private property was removed?"

"As I said, yes, my lord."

"All right, well, then, please lead us to your fort, Hanif."

"Of course," he said, but he didn't move.

My eyes narrowed.

"Just as you do at home, my lord," Jin said, his voice purposely high, "you must lead. No one moves unless you do."

But I had another question for Hanif. "Your father seems to have no use for propriety and observance of the law. So why do you practice it, along with those with you here, your tribe members and your khatyu?"

"The people that you see before you now are all members of the shen faction, my lord. Their djehu, Chanzira Adjo, is a strict believer in the law. Also, the djehu of the peq, Ayaz Suyuti, he also would show you great deference were you to take a tour of any of the farms outside of town or higher in the hills. The djehus both agree on the law, and this is, I believe, another reason why my father has been unable to have them both sit down together and come to a resolution on the catacombs of Abtu."

"They don't respect him," Jin said.

"No, they do not. They see him as an abomination and complained many times to your predecessor, my lord."

"But Ammon El Masry never responded?"

"No, my lord, he felt it was something my father should deal with."

"Even though it was your father that they were complaining about," I said, disgusted.

"Yes, my lord."

"Okay." I suppressed the urge to snarl. "Lead us. I'll follow you."

"You seem upset, my lord."

"It's fine. Please escort us to your home," I said shakily.

"Yes, my lord," he said, big limpid brown eyes locked on my face.

"Now," I said sharply when there was no movement.

"Greet the people," Kabore coaxed softly.

Twisting around, I lifted my arms, and everyone went down to their knees. "Thank you, tribe of Feran, for the warm welcome into your city. I am honored to be visiting with all of you here." The applause and cheering was instant.

Hanif gestured me forward. "Come, my lord."

We were followed, everyone walking with us, children bringing me flowers, people waving from the shops that lined the route, and young girls strewing petals onto the path.

"My lord, we are so honored to—" Hanif began.

"Tell me about the catacombs of Abtu," I ordered the son of the semel.

He was startled. "Oh, yes, well, the caverns, of course, are here right above Ipis in those hills you see there. The entrance is about 2.4 kilometers away and—"

"I believe my lord would prefer to know why the land is being contested," Kabore advised.

"Oh, of course." Hanif cleared his throat. "The title of the land was granted to the family of Ayaz Suyuti back in the time of the Crusades, which was when the fort that we call our home was built."

"Then what's the question?" I asked, quickening my stride.

"But from that time to now, there has been much mating between the two factions, until the last fifty years, when the lines between the two became quite distinct."

"So there are two people who have equal claim to the land."

"Yes, my lord. Both have equal bloodlines and can trace back to a common ancestor. Brothers, actually."

"Was one of the brothers a semel?"

"No, my lord."

"Does one of the lines link to a yareah?"

"No, my lord."

"So... brothers with equal claim?"

"Yes, which means that both the peq and the shen have equal claim to the land, even though the deed clearly states that the house of Suyuti should inherit."

"But it says heir to the house of Suyuti."

"Yes, not simply the name, but the heir to the bloodline."

I understood the problem. There had been so much intermarriage at this point, that there was no single person who could be singled out as the heir apparent. "And this has been going on for how long?"

"The clashes between the two clans have been escalating over the last ten years, but lately, since Ayaz Suyuti found gold in the caverns, it has reached a—"

"He found gold?"

"Yes, my lord."

It was all clear. "And he wants to mine the gold."

"Yes," Hanif replied.

"And Chanzira wants to keep the catacombs as they are, untouched."

"Yes," he assented. "Exactly."

"Ayaz, because he is a farmer, a man devoted to the land, sees the gold as a way to improve not only his way of life but the life of his family and friends."

"You understand perfectly."

"And Chanzira, as a person already from wealth, wants the land left undisturbed and not dredged and destroyed."

"Exactly. How did you know?"

"It's obvious," I said, even as I wondered how in the world that dispute was going to play itself out. "But the answer isn't."

"No, it's not, and the problem is that my father, if he decides either way, will be hated by one of the groups."

I would have divulged to him that his father was already hated, but Hanif seemed way too fragile, like one more horror and he would break. I had no idea the amount of therapy it was going to take—or if it was even possible—to help him.

"Eventually my father will have to make a decision, but if they refuse to follow him, either side, my father's base of power would be toppled."

"Sure," I agreed.

"I mean, if he is not trusted by the peq, then crops are upset, livestock, and so the wealth of the tribe is affected. If it is the shen who do not follow him, then trade is upset, tourism—and we have a thriving tourist business here in Ipis, as panthers come from all over the world to see the catacombs."

"You have an excellent grasp of the inherent problems."

"I just—it seems to me that whatever choice the semel makes will be wrong."

"Maybe it will, but that's part of being in power, making those hard choices."

"But if you were to choose instead of my father...."

"Then I would be the bad guy in that scenario."

"Yes."

"But in Ipis your father is the law; no one would believe that he granted me this power."

"Unless he gave it to you."

"Yes."

"I'll speak to him."

But it didn't matter if he did or didn't. My path was set. "How much further?" I inquired of Hanif.

"Right up ahead, my lord."

I saw Taj emerge from the side of the building when we got closer and saw the men with him fan out along other walls, close, but not obviously so. They were doing their damndest not to resemble an occupational force.

"My lord, I still can't allow your sheseru inside."

"Of course," I agreed. "Will you excuse me for a moment while I tell him?"

He breathed a sigh of relief that I was going along. "Yes, my lord."

Darting over to Taj, I questioned him about the Shu.

"Rahim is in charge, and he and the other nine men are already inside. He's in position; he says that he can see Yuri and the two djehus. He is concerned with how you will extricate everyone without loss of life."

"Taj," I said, staring into his eyes. "Tell him not to do anything, just to wait for you. I don't want to lose anyone. It sounds as though they've lost enough."

"Are you certain? That's not like you."

"I know."

"What's your thought, then?"

"I have to either make Hanif Tarek the semel here or end the line and Mikhail will be here permanently. I don't know yet. How Hanif reacts when I kill his father will make the decision for me."

"Okay. So we have the okay on the semel and his sheseru?"

"Yes."

"All right, then, as soon as we breach the walls, we'll take them."

"If you can get to them before Jin." I was concerned. "This was a hasty decision, and I'm going to regret it, but for right now, I suspect that Jin will eviscerate the semel on sight. We'll have to wait and see on the sheseru."

Taj cleared his throat. "If, or when, I guess, Jin's power rises—without Logan here, what is your plan to calm him back down?"

"I don't have one."

"Okay, so we'll hope for the best."

"Send word back to Crane. Have him send Logan here."

He was shaking his head.

"What else would you have me do?"

"Nothing. I'll see it done. How long after you go in do you want me?"

"Does he have a lot of khatyu?"

"What does that have to do with anything?" Taj sounded annoyed.

"I don't want any of my men hurt."

"Your men will not be hurt, Domin," he groused, like I was trying his patience. "But to answer your question, from what Rahim can see, there are barracks for a hundred men. He and his men released gas canisters inside already. They have all of his khatyu immobilized."

I was surprised. "There were no soldiers inside?"

"There are maybe ten in the main room with the semel."

"I thought this would be difficult."

He shrugged. "I did maintain that none of us would be hurt, if you recall."

"Okay, then, I'll see you inside."

"When?" he inquired. "I want to know precisely when you want me."

"Ten minutes after I go in."

"Okay, good."

"Does Rahim know where Constantine is?"

"No, I had them check everywhere, and there's no sign. You'll have to ask Yuri what happened, and I don't know how many men he took with him. I don't know who else is missing, because I think I've accounted for everyone."

"No, Hanif advised me. It was just Yuri and Constantine."

"You're kidding."

I shook my head.

"You need to talk to him about that."

I put it on him. "That's your job, sheseru. The protection of the mate is a duty of your station."

He studied me. "And will you relinquish it to me?"

"Yes."

"Consider it done," Taj said forcefully, and I realized that even right there on the street, I had learned something. Instead of doing everything, I had to let others help me. I couldn't be everywhere at once. I needed the support.

"Thank you."

"Of course."

"Okay," I said, squeezing his shoulder. "Be careful when you come in."

"You be careful. If Jin's power rises and it's unstable, the Shu will run instead of being caught in it. They won't allow themselves to ever be pulled through a shift."

"All right," I said before I walked back to Kabore, Jin, Koren, and Hanif.

"He won't come in with us," I notified the semel's son.

"Thank you, my lord."

"Will you show us inside?"

"Yes, follow me."

I was expecting a palace, a villa, something. I thought when Hanif had said "fort" that he meant just not as artful as other homes. But it was truly a fortification and seemed like many of the others the crusaders had built that I had seen in Egypt.

The walls were twenty feet high, made of white limestone, and when we walked through the open doors, I noted they were easily three feet thick. I would have posted armed sentries on the outer wall and men carrying high-powered rifles with pistols in holsters on their hips. But there was no one. When we passed though the iron gates of the inner wall, there were no armed guards anywhere in the courtyard. It felt medieval, the interior no more lavish than the exterior until you reached the archway that led from the rest of the common areas into the home of the semel.

The enormous pillars were all carved with different Egyptian gods, beautifully rendered.

"Come, my lord," Hanif called, leading me deeper into Hakkan's home.

The floor was laid in brightly colored mosaic tile that formed an enormous sun. The scattered gilded chaises added to the sumptuous surroundings, and the entryway opened up to a marble floor with a deep pit of steadily rising flames. At the other end of the room stood an enormous throne on a raised dais much larger and more lavishly decorated than mine back at the villa.

A man sat there, flanked on his right by a stunning woman and on his left by just as beautiful a man. The woman was draped in dark blue silk that contrasted perfectly with her alabaster complexion. The man was barely covered, but what there was of his outfit was gold silk. Both were awash in sparkling jewels. In front of the dais stood an older woman, another younger woman, and a man about the same age. There was also another man with such defined, grotesquely carved musculature that it seemed as though he'd been carved from stone, the heavy muscles in his chest, arms, and legs all taut and defined. If I had to hazard a guess, I would have suspected he was the sheseru.

"Here is my father," Hanif said proudly, stepping into the room. "May I present the semel of the tribe of Feran, Hakkan Tarek."

"Welcome to Ipis!" the man on the throne called out.

He was sort of lounging on the throne, one leg draped over the arm of one side, reclining back into the corner of the ornate piece of furniture. He was dressed in a red silk galabeya with a matching abaya over the top, and he could not have been any more at ease in my presence.

"Thank you," I called back.

As I stood there, unsure how to proceed, I noticed the smell, a sweet almost citrusy scent with undertones of smoke and sandalwood.

"What is the odor?" I posed the question to Hanif, something I would have normally never done, ignoring a semel to speak to someone else.

"Semel-aten, please address any questions to me," Hakkan said from his throne.

I ignored him, kept my attention on his son. "Hanif."

"You should speak to my father," he said, trying to redirect me.

"Your father will not be semel after this day, Hanif Tarek. It will be you. So I am speaking to the man I should be."

I was not a stickler for the law. I allowed challenges, was making changes in it myself, but still, as I watched Hakkan Tarek rise when he heard my words to his son, I understood that there was no saving him. He had hurt too many, done too much damage. We would start again.

I turned my head to Jin and found him surveying the room. "What?"

"I think it's a drug," Jin said. He walked up the dais and everyone gasped, but he did it like it was not an enormous breach of law. He felt like I did—there were no rules in the home of Hakkan Tarek, so why even attempt to follow customs that were so engrained in both of us?

Striding over to the woman, he pointed at her face and then returned his gaze to me. "There's a stench in here. Her pupils are huge, look at them, and everything feels coated," he said, touching the throne the woman was on. "It's like there's oil on everything."

"Where's it coming from?"

He tipped his head at the open fire pit in the center of the room.

"Smother it?"

"Yes," he agreed. "Pouring water over it will just create a huge gust of steam. Just get people in here to fill it with sand."

"How dare you come into my home and—"

"Silence!" Jin roared, and everyone froze because the sound could not have come from him, but it had.

Hakkan rose fast and charged toward Logan Church's mate.

I had not seen Jin in six months, so I wasn't prepared for the increase in his power.

Vaguely I was aware of shouting, boots pounding across the floor, a wave of people coming into the throne room, all of it. I knew Taj was there, but my eyes were on Jin.

It was physically painful, and because I was already weak, the pain was acute but only for a moment. I felt a scalding wave hit and then break around me, slip by, and move on. It only touched me for a moment, but it was enough to drive me to the marble floor on my knees. Hakkan was not so fortunate. The burning, devouring heat was all aimed at him.

He was sucked instantly through his shift, and it was horrible to see. Bones cracked and muscles twisted, like turning something inside out, but not gently—viciously.

The screaming was instant and deafening. Hanif fainted in Kabore's arms. The woman who had been sitting beside Hakkan scurried behind her throne, screaming as she moved.

"You will not attack my semel!"

It was Deoles Aran, the sheseru, who roared out his warning before charging up the stairs toward Jin.

I watched him slam into what appeared to be an invisible wall, freeze, and then, as though he were grabbed in a claw, get thrown back down off the platform to the floor below. His body spasmed, shuddered, and then began jerking violently, faster and faster. I wondered how his heart could take it before there was a final bending, an obscene contortion, and he was wrenched into his panther form.

It was horrible, but he deserved every moment of excruciating agony. Jin was an avenging angel, and they were lucky he was not a sadist. If Jin ever learned to delight in the pain of others, holding someone in the limbo of the shift would drive them insane.

I'd seen him pull others through the change at the sepat in Mongolia, witnessed the morph firsthand. It used to appear painful, but it was fast, so I wasn't sure how much the brain processed before it was over. But now the shift Jin controlled in others hurt, there was no doubt in my mind. There was blood and other fluid—it was like they were being skinned alive though I knew this was not the case. In moments I saw muscle and bone appear and then the panther shape I recognized quickly reformed.

I shouldn't have worried that the rest of us would have felt it for more than a brief moment. He had fine-tuned his power, could focus it like a laser now. Jin, who had always been a force of nature, was now even scarier.

Once I lifted my head, I saw him standing near the fire pit. He was there with two panthers lying sprawled at his feet, both heaving for breath. They weren't dead, and I knew they would not be. If Jin was in control, as he was now, there was pain and punishment, but not death. Evidence of the judgment the nekhene cat had dealt was in the shredded clothes strewn about the dais and the floor. A low howl came from the woman, and the man, behind the throne.

"Everyone," I said, walking up to the dais beside Jin. "May I have your attention!"

Yes, I was fearful, but I reminded myself this was still the man I knew. I took hold of Jin's hand when I was close enough, and when he tried to pull free, I tightened my grip.

"No, Domin, I'm unclean right now, I—"

"You are my reah," I soothed him. "And this display, though frightening, does not diminish you in my eyes, nor does it compare to the crimes of the men who you pulled through their shifts."

He studied my face, and I lifted his hand and kissed the back of it before my gaze flickered to the still shrieking woman. The young man with her, whom she was holding on to for dear life, just stared at us in mute shock.

I felt for them, the debauched semel's two chief playthings, his sacrilegious new yareah and his male consort. They were both so young, had been drugged and heaven knew what else in their time there. The man could pay with his life for that sin alone, but there were, I already knew, so many more crimes for him to answer for.

"Stop," I said to the woman when I couldn't take the shrieking anymore, "or I'll make you."

Instant silence, and I faced all those in front of me.

"I am the semel-aten, Domin Thorne, and *my* word is law here, and no one else's."

I wasn't prepared for the immediate gasps and then crying, or for everyone in the hall falling to their knees, or to see an older woman come rushing up the stairs with her arms wide and tears streaming down her face.

Jin stepped around me, and only then did I understand. She didn't want me, she wanted him.

She flung herself at Jin, wrapped her arms around his neck, and sobbed. Her words were a mantra of blessings, and in the midst of it, I heard the word "angel" over and over and over.

I was stunned, I had no—

"Domin!"

My head swiveled sharply and I saw Yuri rushing across the floor to reach the dais. I bolted down the steps and met him halfway, my heart hammering as I took his face in my hands.

"I missed you."

"And I—are you hurt?" His voice rose as his gaze took me in.

He was the one who was hurt. There were bruises on his face and neck, his lip was split, and there was blood seeping through the bandage on his left arm.

"I'm fine," I said, lifting my chin, my eyes fluttering closed. "Kiss me."

"In front of—"

"Please."

I was crushed in his arms, held to his heart, and could feel the drum that lived in his chest as his lips sealed over mine. I shivered as he slid his tongue into my mouth and mated it with mine. He claimed what was his and I melted against him. When he finally lifted his lips away, just enough to speak, not enough for our skin not to brush, I was trembling.

"You missed me?"

"Yes, too much."

His rumble of laughter made me smile in spite of everything else. "Say it now. Tell me the truth, not for any other reason than because it simply is."

I groaned.

"Domin," he whispered, and I gave up.

"I love you."

"Yeah?"

"Yes. More than I should."

"And?"

"You are my mate."

"Are you sure? I see Koren standing over there."

I licked up his throat and felt a shiver tear through him. "Yes, Yuri Kosa, I am sure. You are mine."

"And?"

"I'm yours."

"Always."

"Always," I echoed.

I had never been hugged so tight.

Chapter Nine

OUTSIDE IN the main courtyard of town, where there was a huge limestone fountain, the smells of food cooking, and a warm summer breeze, I felt better than I had when I was inside the home of the semel of Feran. I would never set foot in the fort again, and I didn't want anyone else in there either. It was cursed and I couldn't wipe the feeling away. I also wanted to know what precisely had gone on, but Yuri was being difficult.

"I'll tell you later," he said, tugging me after him.

"You'll tell me now!" I roared.

"We have too much to do right now, Domin," he insisted, moving me because he could, because he was stronger than me.

I planted my feet and he jerked to a stop. Yes, he was strong, but I was still six two to his six five, and though I didn't have his muscle-bulked body, I was not a small man. "What the fuck happened to Constantine? Tell me now," I commanded, trying not to lose it.

He didn't speak.

"Was it just you and him?"

"Yes."

My hands curled into fists. "Never, ever, do you go anywhere without me again. Do you understand?"

"I—"

"Do you understand?" I heaved out the words.

His nod was quick, and his grin was small, just curling his lip, but the flush under his eyes, on his cheeks, and how pleased he was, annihilated my anger.

"You were worried."

"I was terrified!"

He was amused.

"Don't be so smug."

"Okay," he teased.

I found myself growling at him a lot.

After a moment, when I was calmer, he spoke. "So we'll never be apart again?"

"I don't know," I said thoughtfully. "Maybe you can visit Logan. I'll see. If I let you go, it could only be to a place I implicitly trust or with people I—"

"Why?"

"What do you mean 'why'?"

"Why is it so important to you?"

"What? Your safety?"

"Yes."

"Because you're mine."

"Is that all?"

"Is that all?" I was indignant as he pivoted to face me, stepping into my personal space, right there, all I could see. "*Is that all*? What else is there?"

"Why, Domin?"

"You're my mate, you're my... my...."

"Domin," he said, his voice husky and low, slipping his fingers over my jaw and then cupping my cheek. "Tell me."

"I just bared my soul a few minutes ago and—"

"Domin."

"What do you want to hear? What... I don't—"

"You're all flustered." He purred as he slid his hand around the back of my neck, hauling me close to kiss me.

People always asked permission. Even Koren, even as in love with me as he said he was, always requested permission. Yuri didn't ask, never had. He went with the premise that I wanted his hands all over me and didn't second-guess. He didn't treat me like I was special beyond being the man he loved. I had no idea I would so love being mauled outside my bedroom.

"My semel," he said, and his breath was warm on my face.

"Don't go where I can't follow, all right?"

"Yes, my lord."

I gave him a superior grunt and watched his eyes sparkle in amusement.

"You know anybody can see that you love me."

"Good," I said, happier than I thought I would be just to have him there with me. After a moment I cleared my throat and took a different tack. "So where is Constantine presently?"

"Really?"

"I command you to tell me!"

"He didn't have a choice."

Oh, I couldn't even wait to hear this.

He raked his fingers through his thick dark brown hair. It was long on top, there were pieces that fell into his eyes sometimes, but it was buzzed short above the nape of his neck and on the sides. I teased him often that he had the hair of a manga character. "Hakkan gave him the choice to fight me in the pit or to be put on the road back to Sobek with no food or water."

I nodded slowly.

"It's a choice for a semel or a reah or a sylvan or sheseru, but for a normal cat, he—"

"He could have run back here to town, he could have gone on to Sobek, he could have traveled at night, but we're talking ten hours by car. There were other options than fighting you in the pit."

"I don't think so."

"I do. Where is he now?"

"He has to be in the fort somewhere. We fought yesterday. He was either my third or fourth match. It got fuzzy after Deoles opened up my side."

I felt cold inside, hollow, and I felt the anger rise fast. "Constantine fought you while you were bleeding?"

"Yes."

"Why were you bleeding?"

"Because Hakkan allowed weapons into the pit," he said gently, moving forward, and only then did I notice that he was moving more stiffly than normal.

He bent and our foreheads touched, both of us standing there together, quiet and still for a moment before Kabore came up beside me.

"My lord."

Breaking my communion with my mate was hard, but Kabore needed to speak to me. "Yes?"

"Apparently, Yuri had communicated to Ehivet Milar, Garai's father, that you were sending him here to see Hakkan, and now he has arrived."

"Why?"

"It seems he had a communication from someone here this morning that you had taken Hakkan into your custody."

"Okay." I took a breath. "Find Constantine for me."

"Is he here somewhere?"

"He fought Yuri in the pit yesterday."

"I'm sorry?"

"I want him," I said softly. "Now."

"At once, my lord," Kabore said, and he was gone before Yuri could turn me back around to face him.

"It's not his fault. Please don't punish him for—"

"I'm not going to punish him. I'm going to kill him."

"Domin," Yuri inhaled sharply. "You—"

"Everyone should always be most afraid of me," I announced. "Now, come with me to speak to Ehivet and tell him what's happened to his son."

"Oh God," he groaned. "I became his champion when I got here, but there was nothing I could do about what went on before I arrived."

"No, there wasn't," I soothed. "Where is Garai now?"

"There." Yuri pointed, and I saw him running.

Garai Milar was beautiful and lithe with flawless skin and dark emerald-green eyes. I had seen him inside, standing close to the dais, before we evacuated the fort. Once we were all walking out, he had clung to Yuri's arm, not wanting to be far from him until Jin had spoken to him and sworn that no one would ever touch him again without his permission. When Jin Church looked you in the eye and promised, there was never any doubt that whatever he said was gospel.

Now Garai was flying toward a group of people, and I saw an older man emerge, throw open his arms, and receive the younger man who hurtled into them. Tears were instant in both men, and it was obvious I was looking at father and son. I watched Ehivet tighten his arms around his son, stroke his hair, and speak into his ear.

"Shit," I groaned, stopping, not wanting to intrude.

"Come on." Yuri put a hand on my shoulder, squeezed gently to get me moving.

When we were close, Garai noticed us.

"Oh, Father, the semel-aten."

The delegation from the tribe of Tegeret all went to their knees at the same time.

"No, please," I said, moving in close to them and putting a hand on Ehivet's shoulder to get him to stand.

He didn't move, and because the semel did not, no other member of his tribe did.

"Please, Ehivet Milar, rise."

He did so, taking his son's hand immediately and then lifting his eyes to mine. "I can never repay what you've done, my lord."

"I was late," I confessed.

"No, my lord," he said sincerely. "As soon as you were settled, those in your household sought to help you in your reign. Each took the duty of their station to heart. Your mate, your maahes, your sylvan, and your sheseru all resolved to help their tribe and then those beyond. You acted on the advice of your mate; you became involved when no one else would have. I have no idea how you are supposed to police the whole world, but you started here, at home, with me. It was my fault that I waited to contact you; I know now you would have moved just as expediently. You understand the law and Tarek's breach of it, and so came here with the intent to free my son. You are a man of principle and I will be loyal from now until the end of your reign, my lord."

"Thank you."

"Know that my house will always stand behind you, ready to protect you and be counted as your humble servants."

"Your words honor me."

"I am in your debt, my lord, for all time, and know that the tribe of Wepwawet will also fall in line and support you."

"Wepwawet? That is—was—Rahab Bahur's tribe."

"And it is now Zaki Bahur's, his younger brother's. My sister is godmother to my son and mated to Zaki Bahur. I reported what you did, and now Garai has conveyed the enormity of your mate's service to him." He broke off, reaching for Yuri's hand.

My mate clasped forearms with the older man, and Ehivet's face hardened, the man stoically refusing to cry. "You have a place at my table and even in my tribe if you were ever to need one, Yuri Kosa," he addressed my mate solemnly. "You are always welcome, you are free to come and go in my territory, at any time, at your leisure. You are krates of my tribe."

Yuri was shaken, and I would have been too. Krates—"brother" or "sister" of the tribe—meant you were adopted into another tribe but swore no allegiance to a new semel. It was never done, the practice considered dangerous for the leader and the tribe, as you could be inviting a viper into your home. But there was no greater gift, no greater honor to bestow.

"Semel—"

"Ehivet," he corrected me, having trouble pulling his gaze from Yuri but finally shifting it to see me. "Please, always address me as though we are the oldest of friends."

"Ehivet, the tribe of Wepwawet wants me dead or—"

"No, my lord, they—"

"Please." I interrupted. "Always address me as though we are the oldest of friends."

He nodded.

"You were saying?"

He cleared his throat and eased his son closer, tucking his arm around him even as Garai rubbed his chin over his father's shoulder. "My gift to you is the loyalty of the tribe of Wepwawet. Rahab was a bully; his brother is not as fierce but is kinder and more honorable. My sister is stronger than both Rahab and Zaki, and she already has plans for change. Both tribes deal in commodities that it is better you do not concern yourself with, Domin Thorne, but for all the power we thought we had, only you and your house were able to accomplish this goal. I could have retrieved a body; you have restored my son. Both tribes stand in your debt, and my sister sends her regards and her oath as well as that of her mate."

I bowed. "Thank you."

"No, Domin Thorne, thank you," he said and bowed lower.

We were silent a moment.

"Will Tarek die?"

"Either here or in Sobek," I said frankly.

"I know there is no fault that lies with his daughter, Masika," he declared. "But I will have no mating between my son and the house of Tarek. The covenant bond is rescinded."

"Record it in your tribal record as having my blessing."

"Thank you, my lord," he rasped and then released his son's hand to step in and hug me. It was the tight, hard clench men give each other, but I understood it was so far out of his comfort zone that I needed to accept it for the gift it was.

I hugged him back, and then he stepped free and hugged Yuri as well. Garai hugged Yuri, too, and I realized, as he stared up into Yuri's face like he was God, that at eighteen I would have thought the same if he had saved me. Yuri was as close to a guardian angel as the boy was ever going to get.

"Thank you for protecting me, sekhem," he said, shivering. "What was done was a horror, what was threatened before you arrived.... I would have killed myself first."

"No, never." Yuri put his hand on the soft cheek. "Hurting yourself is never an option. And you did nothing wrong in any way. Always remember that."

Garai teared up, and then they were gone, all of them walking back toward a waiting helicopter that appeared military. It wasn't noisy; it sounded more like a jet. As we watched them lift off, Yuri was smiling at me.

"What?"

"You have your first ally."

"Because of you."

"Because you allowed me to go, Domin."

"It won't happen again," I vowed. "Now, come on, I want a word with Constantine."

"You know, we should get helicopters," he said, his hand on the back of my neck.

"I was thinking the exact same thing."

I HAD no idea what had been burned in the fire pit that had created the smell in the fort, but I was too afraid that it was some kind of drug to chance it. I decided to demolish the building, level it, and then rebuild.

In the meantime, a home would be built in Ipis for the new semel, Hanif Tarek, and his family.

Ayaz Suyuti said that if he would be permitted to leave, he would bring bulldozers and earthmovers back with him.

"You may come and go as you like, djehu. I simply need you to sit down with Chanzira to talk about the catacombs before I leave."

"Yes, my lord." He beamed as he grabbed my hand and held it tight. "Whatever you want, simply ask and I will see it done."

He moved next to Yuri, who was standing beside me.

"Thank you, sekhem. I can never repay the debt owed you."

Yuri seemed pleased, but his eyes were not as warm as they would have been if Koren hadn't been there.

In the midst of everything else, Yuri was openly hostile and ridiculously jealous.

I was delighted.

The way he stood beside me, the press of his chin to my shoulder, the scent marking, a continual action, his hands on me, the crowding—it was just so obvious.

"I will be back with what we need to fill in the fire pit, my lord. I will also bring enough for a feast to welcome you to Ipis. Your coming has saved our tribe, and the peq cannot wait to show you the welcome you should have received when you arrived."

"Thank you."

"I will thank the reah when I come back."

I glanced over at the line twenty feet away from me.

Jin stood under a makeshift tent beside the fountain in the center of town. He was now dressed all in white, the contrast to his dark hair and eyes quite striking as he greeted people one by one.

The line to see him stretched for hours, and it wasn't moving quickly because everyone wanted to hug him, touch his hair, shake his hand, and tell him how thankful they were that he had come. They then walked over to me, thanked me for bringing him, and went down on one knee and swore lifelong allegiance to the law and to me. It had been hours already, and again, I was being kept from the only thing I wanted to do, which was to take Yuri back to the Hummer with me and put him over the seat behind tinted glass. I wanted to have his skin between my teeth so bad I trembled every time he brushed against me.

"You are wound very tight." He rubbed his chin on my shoulder.

I swallowed hard as I held the hand of a little girl before patting it and telling her to get up.

"Thank you," she said, lifting her arms for me. I knelt and took her into my arms. She put her little head down on my shoulder. "Thank you, semel, for saving us. Now my brother and sister can come home."

"Where are they now?"

"In Giza, with my aunt."

"Yes, call them home."

"We have already," a woman said from behind the little girl. She was shaking, and her husband was watchful, making sure she stayed vertical, his arm around her waist. "You have delivered us from a madman, my lord. You will be forever in our prayers."

I hugged the woman, and she clung to me like she was drowning and then took her husband's hand and let him hold tight.

I checked on Jin after that, just glanced over at him, and got the wave. Completely in his element with the meet and greet, the action so ingrained in a reah. He had a new question for every person, noticed something and commented. And the people loved him, stared like he was the second coming, and waited patiently for their turn.

He was flanked by Taj on his right and Koren on his left, with Kabore moving people along, gesturing for them to step aside or come close. I had five members of the Shu there close-by, and ten khatyu keeping vigil over him.

"Domin," Yuri rumbled, "Hakkan's family is here."

Seeing Hanif in tears was unexpected. He rushed forward and went to his knees along with his mother and sister.

"Rise," I ordered.

They all stood, and Hanif's huge wet eyes were locked on mine. "My lord, you did as you said and did not kill my father."

I shook my head. "I lied to you."

"My lord?"

"Your father is in breach in the law, Hanif, so that means that I will, in fact, execute him."

He took a faltering breath.

"I don't usually perform the act myself, but it will be done on my command. Either way, your father won't live another three days."

"But," he sputtered. "My lord, I—"

"You must understand," I sighed. "The moment he abused any guest in his house, disregarding all rules of hospitality, he was, at that moment, forsaking his life."

"My lord, I—"

"He abused another semel's son, he took another yareah and forced your mother to see her children and her house defiled, he—"

"My lord, we have caught your quarry," Rahim Dewidar, Jamal's second, called out, interrupting as he came striding forward in front of two other of the Shu. They were walking Constantine Ordos between them. They shoved him to his knees down in front of me.

He gazed up at me, and I saw he was hurt. He was bruised and scratched, and his left eye was almost swollen shut.

"You fought Yuri in the pit," I said, holding out my hand to Rahim.

He passed me a pistol.

"No," Yuri said quickly, pleading.

I saw Constantine shiver.

"You have a new choice. You may shift and fight Taj to the death in the pit, or you may remain here and become a servant of the house of Tarek and be a member of the tribe of Feran."

He gulped, and I saw tears welling. "You would banish me here? You would strip me of my tribe that I was born into; I would no longer be of the first tribe, but part of the tribe that made me fight the mate of my semel in the pit?"

"Yes," I said, my voice level and hard, holding out the gun for him. "Or you can put a bullet in your head now; I don't care which. But from this day forward, I will never see you again, because if I ever do, even when I visit here, I'll have you hung. Do you understand?"

"Please, my semel. I—"

"Choose now!" I roared.

"Here!" he cried out before his face crumpled. "I will remain here."

I had the almost overwhelming urge to strangle him to death.

"My semel... please...."

"Remove him from my sight, and if he says another word, take out his tongue as well. He can speak when we're gone."

"Yes, my lord," Rahim said, taking the gun from me, studying my face as he did so.

"You have my leave. I want Deoles up here next."

"Yes, my lord," he said before he had Constantine dragged away. "Domin."

My eyes moved to Yuri.

"Thank you for sparing his life."

"He's dead to me," I advised my mate. "And I will kill him if I ever lay eyes on him again. Do you understand?"

Quick nod.

I gave my attention back to Hanif and his mother. There were two other women behind them. "Your sister and your cousin?"

"Yes, my lord."

I greeted both women, who thanked me profusely and then gushed all over Yuri. Hanif's mother, Hakkan's yareah, Alana Tarek, was next in front of me.

"Will we be given the body of our semel to bury in the crypt of his fathers, my lord?"

I studied her face. "I would think it would defile the others, yareah. What say you?"

"I would like to tell you that because once he was a good man, only later bewitched by a belief in his own power, he could be forgiven."

"But he cannot," I empathized.

"No, my lord, he cannot. He turned on his own children."

I took her hand gently in mine. "There are no perfect men, but most try to make the right choices for their tribes. You must help guide your son on his new path."

"I will."

"You should return with me to Sobek until—"

"With your permission, my lord, we will remain here and oversee the building of our new home. It will be built for a family, to receive friends and shelter travelers. You must visit often and check our progress."

"I will."

She thanked me again.

"The woman he made his new yareah, was she a puppet or a villain?" I inquired.

"She's a child, my lord, and was given power over life and death. Please remove her from my sight when you leave. She was a laundress before she was elevated; perhaps she might find redemption in serving others." The yareah of Feran was an amazing woman.

"And the boy?"

"He was forced as the girl was not. Please send him back to his mother."

"I will have it done."

She was close to tears.

"I understand that if it weren't for my mate, your daughter was to be a conquest of your mate's sheseru."

"She was." Alana shuddered, squeezing my hand tight.

"He raped many of the young men and women, did he not?"

Her eyes were turbulent, and I saw it then, that even Hakkan's yareah had not been safe.

"He let horrors befall his own house."

"Yes, my lord."

"He dies today."

"Bless you, my lord."

My eyes flicked to Yuri, and he, understanding, called over to Taj. "You are needed, sheseru!"

Hanif caught his mother when she fainted.

DEOLES COULD barely stand, still exhausted from the shift Jin had pulled him through that morning. But he was defiant when he was led up to the bench he had put both men and women across when he raped them in front of the assembly on the order of his semel. It sat now atop tarps, and he shuddered when he saw it as understanding washed through him. The area was covered in plastic for a very practical reason.

"You would really kill me for following orders?" he railed as Taj pushed his head down onto the polished wooden bench.

"If I were a madman, my sheseru would protect my tribe from me," I reasoned as Taj lifted the heavy cudgel.

"You're a coward," he hissed, his voice full of trembling fear and boiling rage at the same time. "You should perform the execution if you believe so much in what you're doing."

"No," Taj said, hefting the weapon to the height needed for the killing stroke. "A true sheseru protects his semel from filth."

The giant ax was heavy and it fell fast. There was a gasp as Deoles's head dropped into the waiting basket, and then the body and the bench were wrapped in tarps and removed from the dais. I had my men take both a mile away into the desert and burn them.

As I was walking over to check on Jin and Yuri, I stumbled, my knees nearly buckling.

"My lord," Kabore said, catching me under the arm and making sure I stayed on my feet.

"I'm fine."

"You are not fine," he clipped his words. "You are barely risen from your deathbed and have spent the day doling out punishment while standing under the hot sun in scalding heat. It's a wonder you're still vertical."

I felt a little faint, but I figured I just needed some water. "Stop, you're fussing."

He walked me under an awning, and even the slight change in temperature was welcome.

"Thank you."

"Water," he barked at some of the servants, who rushed over.

"I probably need to eat something before I see Hakkan Tarek."

He didn't answer, and I waited.

"I didn't think it would be you," Kabore said suddenly.

"What are you talking about?" I grumbled.

"It's remarkable, really."

"What's that?"

"You interfere all the time."

He'd lost me. "I'm sorry?"

"For a man who says that he believes in fate, you don't allow it to play itself out very often."

"I have no idea what you're talking about."

"The Shu."

"Do *you* know what you're talking about?" I squinted. "Maybe *you* need some water."

"Even before the Shu became yours, my semel, they were still yours to command. The Shu were the first line of defense of the priest, but they are also the most deadly assassins in the werepanther world, and at the discretion of the semel-aten, they are dispatched."

"Water for my steward," I called out.

He snorted out a laugh. "You have only been in power for six months, my semel, and you have dispatched the Shu four times. Did you know that?"

I shrugged. "People needed help with their semels. I should have dispatched the Shu here, but because of Yuri, I had to come."

"But first you sent your mate."

"I allowed him to come," I insisted.

Kabore shook his head. "The truth of the matter, Domin Thorne, is that today you blew into this city like the Day of Judgment, and you saved Ipis from a madman."

"I wish I had known earlier."

"You're not worried about the decisions you made here today. You know what is right and you were not afraid to make them."

"What decisions?" I said irritably. "I simply carried out the law."

"And how many semels before you have done that?"

"I know Ammon didn't." I winced as the scar on my belly and chest throbbed with pressure. "But surely his father…."

He shook his head as he tugged gently on my bicep, urging me over to a table. "Sit down on the bench."

I dropped down onto it faster than I would have liked, not steady at all. "How would you know?"

"I'm sorry?"

"How would you know if Ammon's father had or had not carried out the law here?"

"I lived through his time as semel-aten."

I studied Kabore. "How old are you?"

"Sixty-five."

I was stunned. "Are you kidding?"

His eyes glowed warmly. "How old did you think I was, my lord?"

"Maybe forty."

"That is very flattering." He seemed pleased as I dropped my head down onto my crossed arms. "You appear to be flushed. Do you feel all right?"

"I'm fine."

"May I touch you?"

I was going to give him a sarcastic remark, but instead I just said okay. His hand was freezing, and I complained when he touched his palm to my forehead.

"You're burning up."

My eyes fluttered shut. "Just let me rest a minute."

"No, I will not come this close and—" His hands were on my back, and they were all that was keeping me vertical. "I will not lose you, my semel."

I felt my body getting heavy.

"Go fetch me the sekhem!" Kabore barked at someone.

That was the last I heard before I fell to the ground.

"MY LORD."

"I'm fine," I assured my doctor, because I knew her voice and she was turning into such a— Wait.

I popped my eyes open and saw five people in white coats shuttling around me before I found the face I knew, the one the nagging voice belonged to. I was confused. "Dr. Pakhom."

"What did I say?" Her tone was razor sharp.

"Not to exert myself," I parroted, what she had said the day before. "What are you doing here?"

"I was flown here to take care of you, my semel," she said simply.

"Flown here?" I snapped. "By who?"

"I don't know. I was informed that I was needed and I was put onto a helicopter, and here I am."

"Are you insane?" I berated her. "You could have been killed! What if someone was trying to kidnap you or—"

"I was escorted to the flight by Jamal, spoke to Taj by radio for the entirety of the journey, and was met by him and Rahim the moment we landed. So, no, my lord, I didn't feel as though I was in danger even for a moment."

"But—"

"And I was needed. I am your physician. I came immediately when I was called and would do so again."

I shook my head. "Don't ever just—"

"I will come whenever I am needed, wherever," she professed before chuckling, her eyes softening and the laugh lines around them deepening. "I find you very charming, did you know that, my semel?"

Everyone had lost their mind.

"Where's Yuri?"

"Here, my lord."

When she stepped sideways, I saw my mate. He was stretched out on the bed beside me, with IV tubes in both arms and one of those heart monitors attached to his middle finger.

"What's wrong with him?"

"His body is fighting an infection," she let me know. "He was not allowed to shift after his fights, and the wound on his arm was hot to the touch. When I removed the bandage, I found it oozing puss and inflamed."

"I didn't even bother to—"

"No." She shook her head. "You're not a doctor, and I'm sure he was so happy to see you that his endorphins disrupted the pain."

"Is he"—he appeared very pale, more so than usual—"going to be okay?"

"Yes. I have fluids going into him, and an antibiotic, and I've cleaned and dressed all the other wounds I could find."

"All the others?"

"His body is covered in scrapes and bruises and gouges. When he's stronger, I'll have him shift and most of it will be gone after the first time. You know our ancestors were a very smart lot. They knew that fighting in the pit should only be done in panther form, otherwise we could lose a lot of perfectly good men, like the Romans lost gladiators. Blood sport is just that. The pit was supposed to be used to settle disputes, not for pleasure."

I rolled sideways and reached out to put my hand on his left cheek. "He's cold."

"That's good, because he was burning with fever a few hours ago. He'll regulate his own body temperature shortly."

"But he'll be fine?"

"Yes," she cooed.

Why did she sound like that? When I checked, her face was all blotchy. "What?"

"He had the same concerned questions about you," she said, making a noise like I was adorable.

"Stop that," I commanded to no avail.

"He was so worried."

"Whatever for?"

"Apparently you fainted, and when he saw Kabore carrying you... he came a little undone."

"I just needed some water."

"No," she scoffed. "You needed *a lot* of fluids. None of you realize that you're in a bloody desert. The only smart one I've seen is that reah out there."

"He's drinking a lot of water, is he?"

"Gallons, yes. He's also standing in the shade."

I grunted. "That's because Jin's perfect."

She laughed. "Well, along with needing hydration, your blood sugar was upset as well, so I gave you some glucose. You should feel better soon, but you'll need to eat, all right?"

"Yes."

"Again, that knife wound would have killed a normal cat. Only because you're a semel, only because he stabbed in and up and not down did he miss your heart. You need to heal. You need to lie in bed and not move."

I pointed at Yuri. "If I lay still, can he—" I coughed. "—you know."

She shook her head. "Gay or straight, it really is the only thing you think about, isn't it?"

I scowled. "Do you know how long we've been separated?"

"Yes, you can go to bed with him as long as there is no pressure on your abdomen. Do you understand me?"

"Yeah, all right," I muttered, finally surveying the room. "Where the hell am I?"

"It's a field hospital."

"There's only two beds in here."

"Okay, it's a mini–field hospital." She laughed lightly.

"When did I miss that you were such a smartass?"

She beamed. "You allow so much freedom in our presence that all of us are ourselves, my lord. It's a rare gift."

I grunted. "I should quit being like that."

"No," she crooned. "Never."

"I'm not a nice man," I said flatly.

"Of course, my lord."

My focus moved away from her again, mapping the entire area. It looked like a hospital out of every war movie I had ever seen. The difference was that it was sealed in plastic and cool air was being pumped in from two enormous generators I could see in the corner of the room. There were five people there, counting the doctor, and I saw one of the men walk over to Yuri and give him a shot.

"What was that?"

"Tetanus," Dr. Pakhom disclosed. "I'm not taking any chances."

"How long was I out?"

Her brow furrowed. "For six hours, my lord. You gave me quite a scare."

"And you said Jin is outside and he's safe?"

"With Taj and Rahim, nine members of the Shu, and fifty or more of your khatyu milling around," she teased. "I suspect so, my semel."

"Where's Kabore?"

"Here, my lord," he said from close beside my bed.

"Tell me where Hakkan Tarek is."

"When Dr. Pakhom and her team were delivered, an eight by eight by eight steel cage was delivered as well, from Jamal. We placed it outside under a tarp, and he has shifted to his panther form and is in it."

"He's like a zoo animal."

"Yes, my lord."

"How was a cage delivered plus five people?"

"Eleven, my lord," he corrected me. "Jamal sent six more of the Shu."

"How?"

"By carrier helicopter, my lord."

"We don't have a carrier—"

"There are others that do, my lord."

"I want answers now," I said, starting to sit up.

"No, no," Kabore ordered, placing a hand gently on my collarbone and then pressing me down into the bed. "You must be careful with yourself. We need you."

"What the hell is going on?"

"What's going on is that we have been waiting for a semel to trust for a hundred years, and it turns out to be you, Domin Thorne."

"Who's we?"

"If you clear the tent, I can tell you."

"I don't understand."

He just waited on me.

"Clear the tent, then."

He faced the others. "Would you excuse us a moment, Doctor?"

"Of course," she said and herded her team out through the plastic flaps to another zippered door before we were alone.

I could see them outside, but between the hum of the generators and the distance, no one could overhear us.

"Now," Kabore said, turning back to me. "Ask me anything."

"Who is 'we'? Who has a carrier chopper to lend me?"

"The Iusaaset, my lord."

"What is the Iusaaset? Aset is throne, but what's the rest?"

"Throne of all, of the atum, of your ancestors, those who protect you," Kabore revealed. "We are the ones who police the world, Domin Thorne."

The words hung in the air between us a moment before I slowly sat up. He let me, even though he seemed worried and moved one hand close in case he had to steady me.

"I knew it." I swallowed hard. "It's not the job of one man."

"No, it's not."

"So you, what, are all over the world in every city, every—God, just everywhere?"

"Yes," he affirmed. "Werepanthers would never remain hidden from the world if there was no greater organization at work. And while most semels govern their tribes well, and most fall into line and follow tribal law, there is still a criminal element as well as those who would expose us and make people aware of our existence."

"I remember once when I was young, going to a magic show off the strip in Vegas, and there was this guy, and his assistant changed magically into a panther. I mean, I knew they were both panthers, and I thought, that's fantastic. I never even thought to do that, but then when I talked Logan into going with me the next night, they were gone."

"Yes, I'm sure that was the Iusaaset."

"Did they kill them?"

"No, that is still for their semel to decide. They would have been sent back to their tribes and disciplined there. And sometimes, depending on the crime, death is an option. But you know as well as I do, imprisoning panthers leads quickly to madness, and they can never go to human jails because of the shift. So that's where the Iusaaset comes in."

It was hard to wrap my brain around. "And who commands the Iusaaset?"

"Omar Turog, a strong military man, a great sheseru, if you will, and his partner, Hsin Suen, more a sylvan, if you think of it like that. The Iusaaset is always led by two, one that commands the military component and one the civilian side. There are also the seven laws, as they are called, or simply the seven, who advise them. Now, both Omar and Hsin will report to you as well as their teams."

I shook my head. "No, it's too big a responsibility for one man. It—"

"As I said, just like here, you have a sheseru and a sylvan who will offer you counsel, as well as the seven. You may also bring one man to be your private counsel."

"You lied to me."

"Yes."

"You didn't come with Ebere."

"No."

"You've been in the villa since the time of Ammon's father, waiting to see when a semel that deserved to be recognized by the Iusaaset would come."

He nodded. "Omar Turog has been waiting for my report on you."

"And I passed?"

"Yes, my lord. Before we left Sobek, I left word that you were to be trusted and invited them to come. I sent word through Rahim, who has a completely different contact than me, that they needed to come now and make contact with you. They are on their way."

"Who, this Omar or Hsin?"

"Oh no, my lord, their agents will come in their stead. If the top ones show up, then that will be Dov Yadin and Wickham Morris. I see them most, as they are both field operatives. Dov was with Israeli intelligence, and Wickham MI5 before they were both recruited to work for Iusaaset. As they are both werepanthers, they could not turn down the offer. And so you know, all members of the Iusaaset are made members of the tribe of Rahotep, and so you are their semel."

I was reeling. "No one can expect me to rule over men who know more about everything than I do."

"You were born to be a semel, my lord. None of these men were. You must always remember that."

"Why me?"

"Because you are changing everything, my lord," Kabore said bluntly. "Your plan is to remake Sobek; no one has gazed outward in over a hundred years. They become semel-aten and look inward at what they can have, and much like Hakkan Tarek, their greed and gluttony and depravity eats them from the inside out."

I searched his face for some sign that this was all a huge joke.

"But you, you who appear to be floundering, every day you change something. Every moment you are semel-aten, and now akhen-aten, you alter a law or enforce another. You have dispatched the Shu, as I said before, four times already in only six months. You want to help everyone, make certain that everyone is safe, and now, with our resources, you can."

"I doubt that these men are going to listen to me."

"They want nothing more. Right now they simply react. You will allow them to be proactive as they put your new laws and plans into action," Kabore explained. "All of them want to be directed by you, and the seven-man tribunal is there to convene or not. They would only offer advice, my lord, much like the old council of Ennead now advises your sylvan. It's a new day, my lord, but everyone knows that it is your rule and that you will lead us to the future."

"I feel like I'm gonna pass out."

"Please, no, you've scared me enough for one day."

"Who else knows about the Iusaaset?"

"No one except those that work for us and the tribunal."

"And how do you get a place on the tribunal?"

"You're invited."

"How many are on it now?"

"Six. Since Hamid Shamon died, his seat has not been filled."

"The priest," I said.

"It was why he wanted Logan Church to be semel-aten; he felt that Logan would be the kind of man that the Iusaaset could follow."

"And he would."

Kabore shook his head. "I respect the semel-netjer, but Jin Church is far too unpredictable a mate for a semel-aten. Had Ammon been a different sort of man, with Ebere El Masry as his mate, he would have been an excellent candidate. And this is what happens, you understand? Good semel, questionable mate, or vice versa."

"Why would the mate matter?"

"A good mate is key for the health and well-being of the semel. They are the person who you first seek counsel from, the person with whom secrets are shared in the bedroom, either on purpose or unwittingly. And they are the one who simply sleeps beside you at night."

"Jin is the best mate Logan could ever have."

"You'll get no argument from me. We've watched the semel-netjer and his mate, seen trials of separation that we could have prevented or ended but had to watch play out. We have seen the growth in both, but again, while there is no better mate for a semel than his destined reah, the nekhene that Jin is, is not a good mate for a semel-aten. The nekhene cat is safest in that small town up on that mountain, away from prying eyes. To have Jin here for an extended amount of time invites danger," he said ruefully. "I once listened to Ammon rant and rave about how dangerous Jin is. And while I disagreed with what he thought should be done, I couldn't fault his logic. As Jin's power grows, how combustible will it become?"

"Jin will never hurt anyone as long as he has Logan there beside him."

"Precisely," he agreed. "So the semel-netjer can do only that for the rest of his life. He will lead his tribe and love his mate. The fact is, that's all he wants to do—he has no desire for power. It's a great blessing that the nekhene cat wound up with a mate like Logan and not a madman. Think of the horror that could have been."

"Now I understand why the priest wanted Logan."

"Did want." Kabore exhaled. "In the end, he agreed with me that fate had stepped in and given us the gift of you. You must know that he truly embraced your reign before he passed."

"Yes, I know."

"When I suggested to him that we reveal ourselves to you, he agreed that it was for the best. And he also proposed that we offer his seat on the tribunal to the semel-netjer."

I could have Logan with me? My safety net intact? "Is that an option?"

"Yes, it is. We've all agreed that he would make a fine addition."

"As my counsel, I would want you."

He was surprised. "My lord, I am only a steward. Simply a vehicle to help you reach your destiny and no—"

"It's you, Kabore. Tell them."

He was nodding. "Thank you, my lord. The trust and faith is—" He was touched, it was evident in his tone. "You honor me."

But I didn't have time to wallow in sentiment; my mind was racing. "If you police the world, how was Jin ever kidnapped? How was the sepat allowed to go on? How was Ammon El Masry allowed to abuse Ebere? How was the travesty I just interrupted allowed to continue? I don't understand."

He shook his head. "Just like any military operation. I mean, are soldiers sent to stop domestic violence? Are they sent to punish corrupt politicians or find missing children? This is what we're talking about. We prevent someone from going on the news to out themselves on live TV as a werepanther, but we don't investigate a semel using his power to defile young girls."

"That's why the priest had to call the sepat, the honor challenge, against Ammon El Masry, when all those parents came to him for justice after what Ammon did to their daughters?"

"Yes. We could do nothing. Not then. But if you will take the reins, then we will do as we do now and serve you and your cause of change and rebuilding. There are so many things that need to be ratified, but there are also laws that are set in stone, and both must be upheld."

I was starting to get it. "You want to be like Yuri, an extension of me, so panthers the world over will see the office of the semel-aten and truly believe I am the most powerful werepanther in the world. It won't just be in name, it will be because if I say something, it will happen, because I have the muscle to back it up."

"Yes."

"And what if the power goes to my head and I go nuts?"

He tipped his head to one side. "It seems to me that you've already had your epiphany, have you not, my lord?"

"In having my original tribe ended, you mean?"

"Yes. Your original line, your original house, was ended by a man who you call brother. The tribe of Menhit can never rise again. If you were to fall into darkness, would it not have happened then?"

I shrugged. "Maybe."

"Your mother died when you were still an infant. Your father was abusive, he controlled his tribe through rage and jealousy, and when you came to power, all you had to try to hold it together with was a feud with your friend's tribe. You were different then, vengeful and mean, bitter and full of self-loathing. That you are now able to still think selfish thoughts or tell yourself you don't care and then act in a completely opposite way, in a way that has been—from the time Logan Church pronounced you maahes to now—one of thoughtful introspection and faith, is to me a miraculous thing. You lifted yourself from—"

I cut him off. "Stop, I'm gonna throw up. I am not that good. I do a lot of stupid crap, and you know I do. But I have Yuri, I have you and Taj and Mikhail and Ebere to keep me on track."

He cleared his throat. "Do you know how many men who lead listen to those around them every single time, my lord?"

"All of them?"

"None of them. Most men in power listen but don't hear and do what they want anyway. You actually listen, mull things over, and sometimes you do what you think is best anyway, but a lot of times you change what you thought or you temper your response based on what one of us in your inner circles has recommended. It is a rare and excellent quality in a leader, to know his own mind but to allow counsel. Don't ever second-guess your true quality, Domin Thorne. You are remarkable."

I was quiet and so was he.

"I think you would need to travel."

We both focused on Yuri, who was awake and listening in.

I was so happy to see his eyes open. "How long have you been awake?"

"Since Kabore asked the doctor to step out."

"You're such a jerk," I said softly, reaching for him and sliding my hand into his hair, then pushing it away from his dark eyes. "So you heard all that stuff about a good mate, huh?"

"I did," he murmured, so very pleased.

"And?"

"And could you have picked better?" He scoffed. "I don't think so. Man, did you hit the jackpot with me. You couldn't ask for steadier or more loyal."

I had to smile. "No, I couldn't."

He winked at me and I groaned.

"Okay, so, where the hell am I going?" I checked with Kabore.

"You have to travel the world. Instead of there being a Feast of the Valley, it should be you—Egypt—going to them."

Obviously he was having some sort of psychotic break. "What?"

"You need to name a new maahes and leave that person in Sobek to lead, with Mikhail and Jamal and Taj. Then you, Yuri, and I hit the road with Dr. Pakhom and her team, and maybe twenty-five of your khatyu, and we go and visit every tribe in the world."

It took a second for what he'd said to sink in. "Do you have any idea what you're talking about?"

"I think he does." Yuri was nodding. "You would never be at home, not in your lifetime. You would be meeting people, bonding with them, bringing together the whole world of werepanthers. If there was a problem, you would be there to handle it, and if it was more than you could handle, you'd call in the Iusaaset. You can talk with the tribunal, check in all the time with your new maahes, and visit your own tribe once a year. But if you did this, if you traveled—Domin, just think of all you could accomplish."

"What would I accomplish?"

"You could bring everyone together. I've always said that there are a lot of lost panthers out there, like Jin used to be, like Crane, and we could make sure that everyone knows that the akhen-aten is there for them."

"Yuri—"

"I think it's what we're supposed to do."

"What about all my changes for Sobek?"

"That's for your maahes to do."

It was, and I needed a new one. I needed a second-in-command who would be with me going forward, and the answer had been right in front of me the entire time. "Yes, it is Kabore."

"Oh," I heard Yuri say. "That's brilliant."

"Pardon?" Kabore's attention went to my mate. "What is brilliant, sekhem?"

"Your semel's mind."

"Every now and then," I agreed.

"My lord?" He was confused.

I cleared my throat, which brought my steward's attention back to me. "Sometimes I miss things that are right in front of me."

His face was so easy to read; I saw the exact moment of understanding. "Oh no." Kabore stood up and put up his hands. "I am far too old to—"

"You know everything I know." I waggled my eyebrows. "You speak every language that is spoken in Sobek, and you know about me and about the Iusaaset, and you'll be my counsel and my maahes. You'll be wonderful, Kabore Nour, and you will have Mikhail and Taj there to back you up, plus Jamal and Ebere."

"My lord, I would need to accompany—"

"We all have to step up." I smirked at him.

"It's gonna be great." Yuri grinned at him, sealing the deal.

"He really does complement you well," Kabore snapped, giving up, scowling at me and then tipping his head at my mate.

"I know."

Chapter Ten

IT WAS late, but I was on a roll. Outside the medical tent in the courtyard of Ipis, I sat down with the others to eat while I called Jamal. The newly appointed menthu agreed wholeheartedly with me appointing Kabore to be maahes and then warned me that Logan Church had not been happy to arrive and find his mate absent from the villa.

"On a scale of one to ten?"

"He was a fifteen, my lord," Jamal deadpanned.

I groaned. "Did he leave already?"

"Yes, my lord."

"Who was with him?"

"He has his sylvan with him."

"His maahen was not with him?"

"She arrived with him, yes, but she remained behind to stay with Crane."

"Narae Yusuke, the princess of the tribe of Mafdet, is there with my maahes?"

"Yes."

"I'm going to name Kabore as my new maahes when I return."

"That is excellent news, my lord, as from the way the lady greeted Crane, I suspect that she will be taking him with her."

"She was all over him, huh?"

He coughed. "She was, my lord."

I hit the End button on the satellite phone and leaned sideways against Yuri, now sitting beside me. We could see across the courtyard to where Jin and Koren were meeting with the djehus of the two factions, the peq and the shen. Of course it made sense that they would be sitting with the reah, and that he would be mediating their conversation. I had planned to have a seat with them myself, but Alana had brought me and Yuri food, and when the yareah of a tribe served you, you ate.

Taj was dozing with his head on his folded arms. Rahim was beside him, resting his head on his fist as he picked at his food, and Kabore sat next to him.

"Rahim."

"My lord?" He sounded exhausted; they all were.

"I apprised Jamal, and he agreed that you will be the new phocal of the Shu."

"Thank you, my lord, for that honor."

"Good job, buddy," Taj yawned, not lifting his head.

"When I'm gone, you will have to protect Jamal as well as the others."

"Yes, of course, my—where are you going?"

"Yuri and I are going to visit every tribe in the world."

"I'm sorry?"

"Probably more than one at once, obviously. Like, in the US, we'll do state by state or something. I don't know. There's a planning component to this."

Yuri chuckled and moved his hand off the table down onto my thigh.

He was hurt, I was hurt, but we were both more battered than broken, and I just wanted to find someplace quiet to kiss him.

"What are you talking about?" Taj grumbled, lifting his head.

"I'll tell you later. Why don't you all start turning in for the night?"

There was instant complaining with everyone, even Rahim, who had never met him before that morning, all pointing at Jin.

"So no one's worried about me," I groused at the table.

"You're the semel-aten, the akhen-aten," Rahim said, "but he's a reah."

Jin would always be more special than me, and I was tired enough for it to matter.

An hour later, I was still watching Jin talk to the two djehus and found myself staring at Koren, sitting there beside him.

"Every time he sees your eyes are on him, it makes him think that you're interested in him," Yuri said, his breath in my ear.

I shivered, which drew a chuckle from him before he pressed his lips to the side of my neck. "I was only thinking that, from a distance, you could imagine you were seeing Logan sitting there with his mate."

Yuri grunted. "People say that they look so much alike, my previous semel and his younger brother, but I, for one, have never seen it."

"You don't want to see it," I mumbled.

"What?"

"Nothing," I said quietly, studying my gorgeous mate. "But so you know, Koren doesn't think I have any interest in him, because I don't and because we talked about it already and he knows better."

"You talked about it?" That was the part he heard? "What did you talk about?"

"Don't be an idiot," I said huskily, my voice deeper than usual and scratchy because I was tired.

"So you made it clear to him that it was me."

"Of course!" I huffed. "But he doesn't really want me anyway, not really."

"No?" he fished as he stood up and patted my shoulder to get me to follow.

"No, I think something happened back at home and he got scared and came to see me."

"Why?"

"Because if he chose me, even though I'm a man," I said as I rose and followed him away from the table, "no one would question him. I'm the semel-aten, right?"

"But what? If he finally chose to be gay, others would question him?"

"Maybe."

"But if he is the mate of the semel-aten, it would be okay?"

"Yeah." I shrugged as he took hold of my bicep and walked me under the canopy of a shop, around a display of some kind and then out into an alley.

"Why is he questioning now? What's with the timing?"

"That's what I asked," I almost purred, very content to be manhandled behind my mate, led to wherever he was taking me. "Where are we going?"

"So what did he say?" He ignored me, leading me around the side of a building to a door he opened and pulled me through.

"He didn't answer," I said, glancing around at the tiny room, hung with runners of gold and dark blue silk. There was a table with a pitcher of water on it and one glass, a dark bowl of glistening, scented oil, and a freshly made cot. "What are—you know I still have to talk to the semel and—Yuri!"

He shoved me back against a wall, not hard, but firmly, and then kissed me. It wasn't his usual claiming, devouring kiss; this one was gentler than normal, slower.

"What's—" I kissed him back, dragged my tongue over his. "—with you?"

"It's done, I see that now," he answered, putting his hands on the sides of my neck as he opened my mouth wider, suckling, nibbling, then pressing into me gently, drawing each kiss out. "I'm not worried about Koren Church anymore."

"Why—" I pushed my tongue deeper into his hot mouth, tasting, the whimper in the back of my throat making him smile against my lips. "Why would you ever worry about Koren? I already—"

"I know," he said, moving his hands to my hips as one languid, drugging kiss became another and then another, each one building, each one making me need a little more. "It's done."

When he parted my thighs, the whine was involuntary and much hungrier than I would have liked. "What's done?" I was trying to catch my breath.

"You and me," he answered, fusing his mouth to mine. He unbuckled my belt and undid the button on my pants before shoving them, along with my briefs, to the floor.

Him and me? "Yuri, what—"

"Shut up or someone will hear us," he said, and I realized his pants were already down, puddled around his ankles as he reached for me.

"What—oh." I bucked forward into his big, strong hand, now slicking up my cock with the oil from the table. It smelled like citrus and musk all rolled together.

"We're not done," I gasped as he stroked me from balls to head, pulling hard, how he knew I liked it.

"Not with each other, but with worry or uncertainty, we sure are. From right this second, I know you choose me."

I felt my stomach flutter at the sound of his voice, the faith in it, and the possessiveness. His eyes, locked on mine, were hot, his pupils blown with desire.

"I missed you."

"I know you did." He smiled suddenly, and it was beautiful, full of trust and heat and surrender. "Now just fuckin' have me."

It was his yearning, his submission that flipped a switch inside me. I spun him around and bent him over the bed.

He trembled and moaned, and the animal inside of me recognized prey.

"You take it," I demanded, snarling. "Spread your legs."

He obeyed quickly, and his moan was sweet as I grabbed hold of his big beautiful ass and parted his cheeks, revealing the pink puckered hole.

"Grab your cock."

The second his hand moved, I positioned myself and thrust. There was no gentle pressing, no slow breach. I shoved inside of him, the oil allowing for an easy glide even though his body tightened around me like a fist.

"Domin!"

I waited, even though I wanted to slam into him over and over. I held still until he got used to me filling him, stretching him, until I could feel his muscles rippling around me.

"I have to move," I said, my voice cracking with the aching, consuming need.

"Then move," he purred under me.

I grabbed hold of his hips, my hands scrambling on his sweat-slicked skin, and hammered into him. He clenched his muscles with each plunge, and I was lost in the sensation of pounding inside of him, of the tightness and the heat. But it was more, because it was Yuri, my mate, my love, and I had never wanted anyone like this.

I had the overwhelming desire to claim and be claimed, to have his hand where mine was now, pressed against his chest and then traveling higher to his throat to turn his head, lift it, so I could kiss him and have his taste in my mouth as I fucked him.

"Domin, please." The breathless, panted request tore a river of feral want right through me. "Harder, faster...."

But my body wasn't strong enough to ravage him, so I slowed instead, changing my angle, lying over his broad, muscular back, sliding my arms under his armpits and up over his shoulders. I ground into him, writhing behind him, the press and retreat making him shiver as the angle dragged me over his gland again and again.

"I'm gonna come," he almost cried. "You feel so fuckin' good— you're fuckin' killing me."

"Good," I whispered, my fangs lengthening, too big for my mouth before I shifted.

"Oh, not fa-air." His voice cracked, because that fast, I was a werepanther.

I was the half-man/half-beast form and my claws were cutting into his flesh, pinning him to the bed, holding him down as I continued the slow drag in and out of his ass. When I curled my body over his and buried my fangs in the soft flesh where shoulder met neck, he jolted under me, driving me down deeper into his body.

"Domin!" he screamed.

I felt his muscles clamp down on my shaft, felt the squeeze, the pressure, and heard his breath catch as his body convulsed.

I was right behind him, pumping hot and wet inside of him before finally collapsing, shivering with cold as I shifted back, just a man lying sprawled and sated on top of his lover.

Yuri's rumbling laughter made me smile in spite of my exhaustion. "What?"

"There's blood and spunk and sweat all over this bed."

"So what? I'll buy whoever a new one."

"No," he whined. "I just meant that I don't wanna leave here. I want all of it all over me. I love having your marks on me, your come leaking out of my ass, and my blood on your lips. I love knowing that you bit me because you fuckin' *had* to." He sucked in air. "I love that I drive you so nuts that you have to show everyone that I belong just to you."

"Do you?"

"It's so fuckin' hot."

I kissed his back. "Don't move, okay?"

"I can't move—your dick is still buried in my ass."

"I like it there."

"I like it there too."

My eyes kept trying to drift closed.

"You're getting heavy, love."

Love.

I whimpered, stupidly happy, spent and just wanting to lie draped over him for the rest of my life.

"I love you."

"And I love you back."

His long sigh of happiness was a gift.

I WOKE up hard and aching, and when I lifted my head, I found my mate sucking me off.

It was later. I smelled food and my stomach rumbled.

"Oh," he moaned, and he slid his lips off my shaft. I was entranced by the saliva left on the head of my penis and by him swallowing. "You're hungry. I should—"

"Do not stop." I bucked against his chin. "Suck me."

His gaze was scorching, his eyes full of devouring need before he bent and took me down the back of his throat again.

"Oh fuck, Yuri," I whined, loving that his hands weren't idle; instead, one fondled my balls while the other moved under me, sliding over my crease until I moved to allow better access.

I lifted up, bent my knees, put my feet down on the cot, and let my thighs fall apart. The invitation could not have been made any clearer.

He slid oily fingers, two of them together, inside of me.

"Yuri," I croaked.

"Who else has ever fucked you?"

"No one."

"Only me."

"Only you."

His smug male rumble made me shiver even as he scissored his fingers inside of me, stroking, pressing, sliding over my gland, making me vibrate with fresh need.

"You're all slick and hot. Gonna ride me so I don't hurt you."

"No. I want you to fuck me hard."

He chuckled and I would have yelled, but he pulled out his fingers and I gasped at the change, at the loss.

The man was so big, so strong. He was on his back down on the cot and had settled me on top of him in seconds.

"And now what?" I grumbled, straddling his thighs.

"Fuck yourself on me."

I reached behind and took hold of his thick pole, lifting up at the same time. "I swear I have no idea how anyone can take all this." I shivered, lining up the huge flared head with my entrance, letting it slip between my cheeks, feeling how slick he was, how hot.

"You can take it," he rasped, his breath catching as I began to press down on him.

"Yes, I can." I ground out the words as he fisted my shaft in his slippery grip.

"So tight," he groaned, and it hurt, but the burn was what I liked, the pain was part of what I craved, at times, and Yuri knew that.

Sinking steadily down, I impaled myself on his enormous leaking cock, shivering with desperate need.

"Domin," he whispered, and the sound was sexy with an edge of demand. "Ride me."

I was panting and sweating, chills rolling through me, my body overly sensitized, on the fence between pleasure and pain.

"Oh fuck." He trembled, and I put my hands down over his hard pectorals and lifted up before levering back down, fully seating him inside me. "This was—I don't wanna hurt you."

"You won't hurt me if you don't crush me," I said, reacting to how full and stuffed I was. Yuri was so strong, so powerfully built, and even though he did not have the definition and the washboard abs, the man was massive. I was addicted to him, to his barrel chest, to how hard his body was, how solid.

He rolled us over, but before he could crush me, he lifted his weight and then pulled my legs up and draped them over his forearms as he drove down into me, rubbing over my prostate and making me howl.

"Damn, you're loud." He laughed softly, very pleased with my reaction as he pulled out only to slam back into me even harder the second time.

"You like me loud," I said, not sounding like me at all, my voice deep, guttural, and raw.

His gaze locked on mine, and I reached up and framed his face with my hands. I watched his lashes flutter, saw how dilated his pupils were, and saw him bite down on his lower lip so he wouldn't make any noise.

"I like to hear you too. I love all the sounds you make."

"Domin," he breathed, and I could see how hard he was concentrating not to come.

"I feel good?"

"Better than—your body is holding me so tight, I can feel every clench, every ripple, every… you need to not move at all."

I pulled him down to me instead, lifting up for his kiss, wrapping my legs around his waist and grinding my erection into his stomach, craving the friction.

"You should come all over me, mark me, show me who I belong to."

The words were enough.

I threw my head back and yelled his name as I spurted come over his chest and abdomen. He fucked me through the aftershocks, thrusting deep, his rhythm never faltering until the end, when he came inside of me and then froze.

"I feel too good to move."

I started chuckling.

"Stop it, oh God," he moaned, arms around my knees, holding me against him, trying to keep me immobile.

I stayed still, gazing up at him, delighting in his lazy grin, his hooded eyes, and the red marks covering his pale skin. No one could miss what we had been doing while we were gone.

He eased free of my spasming channel and warm liquid ran down the insides of my thighs as he collapsed onto the narrow space of bed beside me.

"I love you," he said, kissing my temple, apparently not caring that I was sticky and sweaty, instead inhaling the smell of us together. "And that won't ever change."

"How do you know?"

"Because you're mine," he sighed, using my words from earlier.

I folded myself against him, my arm around his neck, thigh over his hip, and nuzzled into the hollow of his throat, under his jaw, inhaling his delicious, masculine scent.

"Yeah, you like belonging to me."

"Yes, I do," I agreed as I closed my eyes and relaxed.

"No, no, no." He laughed softly, massaging the back of my head. "You gotta get up."

I loved him, but he wasn't in charge. "All you're doing is holding me."

"No, you must get up," he entreated, even as he wrapped his burly arms around me.

I snuggled in tighter and then let out a deep, contented sigh.

"Are you listening to me?"

Obviously not.

Chapter Eleven

IT WAS even later, and there weren't many people milling around the square when Yuri and I joined Jin at the table. He appeared tired but happy. Taj was sitting beside him, fast asleep, head on his arms, and Koren was on the other side in the exact same position.

He was visibly pleased when we sat down.

"How are you up?"

"I don't need as much sleep as the others," Jin said, lifting his hand and giving a small wave.

A woman immediately brought a pitcher of water for us, and some eish—Egyptian bread—along with some koshari and sliced lamb. I wasn't sure what kind of small roasted bird she delivered to the table until Jin said that it was pigeon. She also brought sliced cucumbers and tomatoes and fresh hummus with olive oil, then dates, figs, and plums along with plates and napkins and a decanter of thick red wine.

Koren twisted on the bench and stretched out, putting his head in Jin's lap.

"Logan would kill him for that," Yuri said as Jin stretched out a hand and rested it on Koren's shoulder.

"No," Jin said softly. "Logan's much more concerned about his son these days."

"How can you be so smart and so stupid at the same time?"

Jin dismissed me with a wave. "Kabore is sleeping in one of the vehicles and Rahim is in the other. The rest of your khatyu are in different homes around town, and Taj is obviously here with me and Koren."

"And the djehus?"

"They're coming back first thing in the morning to see you. Oh, Dr. Pakhom and her people are in the medical tent, sleeping. She has Hanif Tarek in there with her because she had to give him a tranquilizer to calm him down."

I looked over at the cage where his father was penned. "He was given food and water, wasn't he?"

"He was," Jin said as his face scrunched up.

"What's with you?"

"Something troubling."

"Would you like to share?"

Jin was worried, I could tell. "Dr. Pakhom also tranquilized him and gave him a lot of intravenous fluid. She made a very interesting diagnosis."

"For fuck's sake, Jin."

"Okay, so, apparently the semel has stage four syphilis."

"Why did you say that like I should care?"

"Because it probably explains everything."

"It would explain the change in him?"

"It would, yes."

"And so what? I'm supposed to just let him off the hook because he's sick? Let him make amends?"

"That would be the right thing to do, wouldn't it?"

I checked with Yuri. "Your thoughts?"

"I think everyone who had sexual contact with him should be checked out. I have to call Ehivet Milar and have his son tested. I know that Deoles was the one who raped Garai, but we don't know that he didn't have it too."

"You're evading."

He locked his gaze on mine. "I think you want to kill him and you always do what you want."

"If I always did what I wanted, you would have never come out here alone."

Yuri's eyes locked on mine. "That just says that you were concerned that you might have appeared weak if you made me stay. You let me do whatever I wanted, so it seemed like you didn't care one way or another."

I held his gaze.

"It's true. You know it is."

"It was, but not anymore."

He kissed my cheek. "I'm glad."

Jin scoffed, and my focus shifted to him.

"And you?"

"And me what?"

"What do you think?"

"You're so different from him."

"From who?" And then I got it. "Logan."

He nodded. "Logan never asks for advice from anyone."

"I've been trying really hard to be just like him, you know," I confessed.

"Why?"

"Because he's the perfect semel," I said petulantly. "He always knows what to do. I wanted to be the kind of leader he is."

"You can't," Jin said. "Logan doesn't depend on anyone. You don't have that luxury."

"He depends on you," I reminded him.

He shook his head. "Not really. Logan can make decisions and not have to count on anyone. You're more thoughtful than he is."

"You mean weaker."

"No, I mean what I said." His voice rose a little as his beautiful eyes softened. "Logan never had his line ended, never had to overcome what you did. Logan has always been the law. There's never been any interruption in that."

"Yeah, but second-guessing yourself isn't a good thing."

"But you don't, not as far as I can see. You ask for the opinions of people you trust and then you make an informed decision. I don't see anything wrong with that."

"Yeah, but if Logan were semel-aten, Hakkan would already be dead and the question of why would have died with him."

"And how is that fair to a man who by all accounts was a good semel up until a year ago?"

"I don't—"

"So thirty plus years of being a good leader is washed away by a year of horror?"

"Yes," Yuri chimed in. "I know you're about life and forgiveness, my reah, but what was done, what might have been done, has to carry the most weight."

"Plus," Taj said, yawning before he shared his perspective, "if you allow him to live, then he has to have that horrible realization of what he did to his family. It's actually the greater mercy to simply put him out of his misery."

"It's not a question of any of that," Kabore said as he sat down.

"I thought you were asleep," I said.

"I received word that Logan Church is on his way here from Sobek and came to let you know."

"Oh," I said, turning. "Kabore heard… I wonder how?"

Yuri rolled his eyes.

"Could it possibly be that brand-new invention—a phone?"

"It was an accident. I took the wrong one," he reasoned.

"Perhaps to make sure it never happens again, the one you have should be destroyed."

"I think Hakkan beat you to that."

"And you see," I said to Jin, "yet another reminder of his indiscretions. You cannot simply disregard the law. It's there for a reason. No semel is above it."

He was biting his bottom lip.

"What's wrong with you?"

He furrowed his brow and gave a slight shake of his head.

"Don't be a pussy," I instructed.

He flipped me off. Kabore was flabbergasted.

I stretched my arms wide. "Here it is: no matter where any of us go, no matter what any of us ever do, you are all my family and there will never be the law between us. So speak your mind."

"Even me?"

I took in Koren as he sat up sleepily beside Jin. "Especially you, idiot."

He smiled that smile I had always loved: unguarded, genuine, all shining eyes and warmth. I leaned across the table and reached for him. He put his hand in mine and squeezed tight. Yuri grunted beside me, and Koren laughed, let my hand go, and reached for my mate.

"Try not to bury the hatchet in my back, all right?"

Yuri got up and walked around the table. Koren was up before he reached him, and I watched Jin tear up as the two men hugged.

"God, you're a soft touch." I swallowed around the lump in my own throat.

I got flipped off again and then gave my attention back to Kabore. "Yeah, I'm different. Everything about me is. Are you sure I'm the guy you want to put up for the job you and I were talking about earlier?"

"Oh yes. You're who we've been waiting for, Domin Thorne."

"Okay," I said as Yuri took a seat beside me. "What were you going to say?"

"I was going to say that you have to take in all the factors of the life of Hakkan Tarek. You must have a trial so that everyone may speak," Kabore answered.

"Eat something," Yuri prodded. "You need to keep your strength up."

"Yes," Jin said softly, his voice smooth and rich, like it always was. "Please eat, Domin."

"Everyone sit down with me."

It was nice that they all did.

WE SAW the lights first and then finally heard the sound of the Hummer coming up the two-lane road into Ipis. It stopped outside the square, and they came walking in, ten men in all.

They had taken care, as my khatyu did, to make sure Logan didn't stand out. He was dressed as they were, but the problem was that even in black cargo pants, black combat boots, a long-sleeved black shirt, a Kevlar vest, and a hat that reminded me of the ones the German army wore in the Second World War, I could still pick Logan out from the rest of them. His stride was longer and more fluid; he wasn't used to moving in a formation with others but instead walking out front. He carried himself like royalty.

It took me a minute to realize who the smaller man walking behind the others was. He was dressed in traditional Egyptian clothes, and I knew why. Nothing in the barracks of my khatyu or the Shu would fit him. At five nine, a fragile porcelain doll, he simply could not be outfitted for combat.

"Fuck, what was Logan thinking?"

It came to me then as I saw Jin's cousin, Danny Rayne, a vision of what the reah would have resembled if he were smaller and his eyes were brown. Danny was so sweet, so cute, it made my teeth hurt.

I wanted to see what Koren was going to do, but Jin was the real attraction. I saw him close his eyes and take a breath. He didn't even have to see Logan to know that his mate was there.

"Don't have a pissing contest," I coaxed. "Just get up and go to him."

His eyes closed, and I saw tears slip from under the thick black lashes.

"Jin, don't you miss him? Don't you miss your son?"

"It's not that easy, Domin. I—"

"Yes, it is. That's the only man in the world who can deal with all your bullshit."

His eyes met mine.

"Hurry."

He rose fast, turned, and ran.

Logan stopped and had just enough time to open his arms before Jin flew into them.

The instant they touched, we were all hit by a blast of air that smelled like freshly cut grass, jasmine, burning wood, and a crisp fall breeze all wrapped up together. A feeling of happiness and contentment rushed through me, and I had to grip the edge of the table not to fall forward.

"Jesus, how does he do that?" Taj asked.

"Who?" I teased.

"Seriously!" He scowled at me. "What kind of power do you have to have that it feels like that when you're happy?"

It was like being caught in a sonic boom, and we were all reeling from the power of the reah reaching his mate.

"It is scary to contemplate the nekhene cat unleashed in anger," Taj said.

"Yes, it is," Yuri agreed.

"Is it safe to allow him to leave Sobek?" Kabore was concerned.

"Yes," I said as I observed the semel and his reah. "As long as Logan is with him, Jin is contained."

"He should scare you, my lord."

"Never," I murmured. "Look at them."

Logan had one hand on Jin's right hip and he had wrapped the other in his mate's long glossy hair. He yanked his head back and then bent and kissed him. It was possessive and dominant, and I saw Jin tremble and clutch at Logan.

"My brother never cares who sees him claim what belongs to him," Koren commented. "I envy that ability to just not fuckin' care."

I checked faces, eyes, the way people stood and watched, and how they suddenly had to clutch a loved one to them. Love, so clearly on display, affected everyone staring at the semel-netjer and his nekhene cat. I had never seen so much obvious adoration and complete acceptance. When Logan lifted his mouth from Jin's, Jin's eyes slowly drifted open. Logan took his chin in his hand and studied his face before he bent and touched his forehead against Jin's and began talking. I was glad to see Jin nodding.

"I don't understand why you aren't frightened," Kabore said suddenly, sounding confused.

"Because," I replied as Logan gazed down at his mate a moment longer before taking his hand and walking toward the table. "You don't understand all the things he is."

"My lord—"

"Jin is a complicated mess," I maintained. "And only Logan understands him."

"Speaking of complicated...." Yuri cleared his throat.

"What?" Koren groused.

"Oh, for heaven's sake." I gestured at the younger man. "God, Koren, you're such a prick."

He was fighting getting up, and the indecision was annoying me and killing Danny.

"If you make him cry, I'll end you," Yuri warned Koren.

"I thought he had the hots for Mikhail?" Taj inquired about Danny.

"It changed," Koren muttered as he got up. "He changed, I changed—it's all different now."

We could all see that adorable, doe-eyed, luscious little Danny was almost vibrating with need as he stood by the fountain, worrying his bottom lip. He could not have been gazing at Koren with more heartbreaking longing if he'd tried.

"Oh, come on, Church," I prodded my ex. "Time to step up, huh?"

"It's not that easy to—"

"So you're gonna do what?" Yuri chortled. "Let another man have that?"

"Fuck no," Koren growled, and I liked the sound. It suited him, some commitment, finally.

We all watched him rise and then saw Danny tremble even as he lifted his chin and squared his shoulders.

"That sort of makes sense," I said, yawning. "Both Church men have mates who are Raynes."

"Jin's not a Rayne anymore, he's a Church," Yuri reminded me.

"Oh, that's right," I agreed, watching Koren reach Danny.

Danny hesitated, hooded eyes missing nothing, but when Koren gestured for him to come closer, he didn't hesitate. He leaped at Koren.

I had never seen that particular expression on Koren's face before as Danny wrapped his arms and legs around the bigger man. He was wiggling and whining, and Koren engulfed him in his arms before he slid one hand down over Danny's ass.

"You didn't tell us." Yuri chuckled as Logan reached the table.

Kabore took a breath when the semel of the tribe of Mafdet caught him in his stare. Gold eyes swallowed him, and my steward was momentarily speechless.

"I wasn't sure what Koren was going to do. It's hard to know with him," Logan said point-blank, never anything but directness coming out of the man.

"I don't know," I said, watching him carry Danny out of the square, rubbing circles on his back as Danny kissed along the length of his jaw. "I think this might be it."

"Me too," Logan agreed. "And I like it. Danny's actually very good for him. He's smart and knows what he's worth to the tribe. He won't let Koren get away with anything."

"On the flip side," Jin offered, "Koren makes Danny feel very confident and protected, and they simply fit. I hope Koren keeps him."

"Maybe it will be Danny who leaves," I said.

Jin thought that was funny.

I rolled my head back so I could see Logan, gaze up into the gold eyes I knew so well. "And?"

"I want Crane," Logan said without fanfare.

"Yes, I know. He's yours."

"Good." He scowled. "You look like hell."

"I was stabbed."

"So I understand," he said coolly.

"No, no, that wasn't my fault," I said defensively. "I had no idea that Jin killed the priest."

Logan said nothing, just let go of Jin's hand and put his arm around his mate, eased Jin against his side. "Will you be able to leave here tomorrow? I'd like you to see my son before I leave for home."

"Of course."

His attention was back on Kabore. "I'm Logan Church, semel-netjer of the tribe of Mafdet."

"This is an honor, semel."

Logan nodded, like, of course it was, before he let go of Jin and walked around the table to Yuri, who stood to greet him.

I enjoyed seeing the two men hug tight and hard before Logan let him go, and I stood so he could grab me. "It's good to see you."

"And you," Logan said into my shoulder before he let go. "Tell me what's going on here."

We all sat down, and Logan kept Jin's hand in both of his as Jin leaned on his shoulder. They really should have been on billboards together, Jin was so beautiful and Logan was all strength and heat. But what I noticed more than anything was the change in Jin. The sort of thrumming energy present since he had arrived had dissipated. Everyone had been a little on edge with him. Kabore was right—the power, though fascinating, seemed unstable. The nekhene cat was like a bottle of nitroglycerin; you didn't know when a slight jostle might set him off.

With Logan beside him, though, it was like a switch had been flipped, and he was just him. Just Jin.

"Domin."

I came out of my thoughts to find Logan staring at me. "Yes?"

"My advice would be to transport the semel from here. Take him back to Sobek, read the charges, and then execute him."

"Logan, he's sick," Yuri said. "We're talking about the law and that's all."

"Yeah, but—"

"A semel who is sick has his mate to depend on, his maahes if he has one, and barring that, his sheseru and sylvan. There is a sacred bond between a semel and his house, and if the semel breaks it, then it is up to those who support him either to take control or allow him to run amok."

"But a semel's word is law," Yuri argued. "When you were hurt in the pit the time you fought with Domin, you forbade anyone from helping you or—"

"And would that have continued until I died?" he demanded sharply. "Didn't Mikhail go get Jin the following day, even though I forbade anyone from acting?"

Silence.

"It sounds like the sylvan was the voice of reason and he was killed. The sheseru allowed himself to be corrupted, and his mate and his family did nothing."

"Logan, they were powerless," I said. "The son is—"

"Weak, I suspect," Logan said, passing judgment. "You should make these djehus both sylvan and sheseru to help him and bring the whole tribe back together."

Everybody went silent.

It was brilliant.

"Which do—"

"The djehu of the shen should be sylvan," Jin began, "because she knows the law. The djehu of the peq, as he is familiar with what it takes to keep control of people who are spread out, knows how to instill authority, should be sheseru. I implied that this would probably be what you would do."

I stared at the two of them.

Logan squinted at me. "What? Something wrong?"

"You two are so in sync now that you share a brain?"

Logan met his mate's eyes for long, quiet moments before his attention was back on me. "Yeah, something like that."

"The djehus still have yet to agree on the dispensation of the catacombs."

"What's to agree on?" Logan remarked as Jin rubbed his chin over his mate's shoulder, scent-marking him as Yuri had done to me earlier in the day. "The money it would take to mine for gold in the catacombs is, I'm sure, cost-prohibitive. And if the djehu gets outside investors, he'd have to prove who own the catacombs first. It's not going to happen. They need to simply get behind the tribe, and they will if they're invested."

"And if Hanif Tarek doesn't like who I pick for him?"

"He's already shown himself to not be strong, Domin. I don't think you worry about what he thinks."

"You just know what's best, huh?"

"Always," he assured me. "But it's up to you to sell it."

Rahim came to the table and bent to speak to Yuri. "Alana Tarek would like a quick word with you, sekhem."

"It's late. She's still awake?"

"Would you be able to sleep?"

"No," he answered as he got up, squeezing my shoulder as he left the table.

"I'll talk to the djehus in the morning," I advised Logan. "Or, in a few hours, I guess."

After several minutes, Jin got up. "I want to say a word to Alana as well, since she's awake. She had wanted to talk to me but I didn't get a chance today, and maybe I can give her some comfort."

"I'll go with you," Logan said, getting ready to follow.

"No, stay here," he soothed his mate. "Yuri's already there."

Logan scowled, ignoring me. "Taj, would you escort Jin?"

"'Course." Taj yawned tiredly. "C'mon, reah, let's go."

Jin bent and kissed Logan's cheek. "You worry too much."

"I don't worry enough, and I need to take you back to your son in one piece. He's probably wondering where we both are now since he's never seen Crane before."

Jin was startled. "You brought Ilia with you? He's here?"

"Of course," Logan replied. "When I was asking Domin when he was going to leave because I wanted him to see Ilia... did you not hear any of that at all?"

"I guess not, I— And you left him alone with Crane?"

"With my maahen and Domin's maahes, yes."

"Yusuke's here?"

"Yes," he said nonchalantly. "She wanted to see Crane, and Danny's been inconsolable since Koren left. I really need to put my house in order."

So did I, I thought, but said nothing.

"Logan, we need to get back to our son," Jin said, sounding flustered suddenly.

"And we will." He gentled his mate. "Tomorrow. You've been gone a week already."

"Thank you for reminding me," Jin said curtly. His brows furrowed, and he left quickly enough that Taj had to jog to catch up with him.

"Was that smart?" I asked my friend. "You seem worried, semel."

He shook his head. "Tell me about Mikhail's girl. I've never seen him act like that. I didn't know he actually *could* look like that."

I laughed softly, then recounted everything about Samani and what she wanted and what Mikhail wanted and who I thought was going to end up caving.

We talked and it was nice, and Kabore had interesting asides to add, and I had Logan riveted when I recounted Jin winning the challenge.

"Speaking of Jin," Logan said, catching my gaze, "how long does it take to talk to the yareah?"

I was ready to pass out myself. "Kabore, would you please go tell them all that we need to get some sleep?"

"Of course, my lord." He tipped his head before he got up to fetch our absent mates.

"It was a good choice to promote Jamal," Logan remarked. "He's a very honorable man."

"Oh, I agree. I think that…." I turned to look after Kabore.

"What?"

"Why didn't Taj come back?"

Logan frowned. "Because I ordered him to escort Jin."

"Escort him, but not stay. Why would he need to stay if Yuri was there?"

"Taj wouldn't leave Jin," Logan assured me.

"He would," I argued, getting up. "Because Yuri was there."

"What're you—" Logan tensed. "I assumed this town was secure, Domin."

I bolted after Kabore, tracking him, and Logan was right behind me with Koren following fast.

"My lord!"

I heard the yell and ran around the corner. Kabore was there, down on one knee over one of my khatyu who was dead, his throat torn out, and the thick pool of blood he lay in appeared black in the moonlight.

"Oh no," I cried out, slowing as I reached him, seeing his pistol in his hand.

"Jin!" Logan screamed, flying by me, charging down the alley that opened out into a smaller courtyard of the home where the new semel, his mother, and sister were staying. "Domin!"

I rose and Kabore followed me, and we ran through the darkness to find them. Instead we found Rahim, eyes closed, head back, sprawled on the ground with a bullet in his side and one in his shoulder.

"Kabore, get Dr. Pakhom now, and wake up fucking everybody."

"Yes, my lord," he said before scrambling to carry out my orders.

"Domin!" Logan rounded on me, and instantly I knew it wasn't him. The man I knew was gone, replaced by a panicked, frantic animal.

"No!" I barked, changing my stance, readying myself for the blow. "Don't turn on me. There was no reason to think I had dissenters. There was no one here but the semel and his family, and only the semel was not pleased that I was here. He was the one the priest commanded to kill Yuri, and I stopped him. I killed his sheseru today—there was no other power here, Logan."

"You missed something," he snarled.

"I couldn't have. I didn't." I shook my head. "Everyone wanted me here. There was no one but the semel."

"Then the treachery is there!" Logan shouted. "Which one is the house?"

I bolted, and Logan was right behind me as we ran. Almost to the house, we both stopped midstride when the door jerked open and Alana flew out toward us, screaming.

She was covered in blood.

"Oh God," I gasped as she flung herself into my arms, sobbing.

"Yareah," I said, trying to calm her. "Speak to me."

"They're all dead!" she shrieked, shock and terror overwhelming her as she passed out cold.

I sank with her to the ground as Logan ran by me into the house.

"My lord!" Kabore yelled as he reappeared at my side with several of my khatyu.

I grabbed his wrist, yanking him to his knees and shoving Alana into his arms as I leaped up. "Have someone guard her and then meet me in the house."

"I need to come with—"

"Watch her!" I roared and then ran after Logan into the house.

I nearly fell over a woman as soon as I went through the door. She, like the first man we had found, had her throat slashed open. Whirling around, panicked, I saw Logan sitting on the stairs leading to the second floor, hands covered in blood.

I reached him fast, almost falling into him, grabbed his face and tilted it to me.

"There's no one here. I think they took Yuri and Jin up and out through the roof," he reported.

I shook my head, letting him go. "There's no way. This is Jin. Nobody sneaks up on Jin, there's no way his power doesn't rise and—Logan!"

"There's so much blood upstairs." He was trembling and it was scary to see him do it. Logan coming apart was disconcerting. "And Jin's robes are there… he must have shifted and… if they had Yuri, Jin would have gone if someone said they would kill him if he didn't. Jin wouldn't leave Yuri and vice versa."

"Logan—"

"Where the fuck are your khatyu?"

I heard my name yelled, which answered his question, and then men pounded up the stairs, and Kabore was with them, directing, shouting orders, sending them all in separate directions.

I grabbed Logan's shoulder and dragged him from the house, back out into the courtyard. Koren was there to meet us, along with a disheveled-looking Danny, and he pulled Logan after him to a bench. They sank down onto it, and I watched the area flood with my guards and lights as they roused people from nearby homes and carried lanterns and flashlights into the area.

Kabore came running and stopped close, checking me over before he touched me, something he never did. Gently, he pushed me down on the bench beside Koren before he knelt in front of me.

"You must stay, my lord, both you and the semel-netjer. Everyone's up. Dr. Pakhom is with Rahim. I have men here around you to see to your safety. Please remain here."

I nodded, and he rose and was gone.

Everything was whirling. I'd just gotten Yuri back—I couldn't lose him. It simply wasn't possible. What was I supposed to do?

There was yelling suddenly, two of my men had joined me, and the sound almost shattered me.

"My lord, we found your sheseru."

I was up and running again, and Logan was right behind me. Taj had been discovered and taken to the makeshift hospital. When we arrived, Dr. Pakhom was working frantically to stop the bleeding as Taj fought to keep an oxygen mask off his face.

I reached him and got around the doctor trying to cover his mouth. He grabbed my hand, and they squished together with blood.

"Hanif Tarek has ten men," he rasped. I saw his pallid skin; he was ready to pass out. "They shot Jin when we came up to the house. I didn't see them. I wasn't ready. And then Jin went down and Yuri got in between a machete and Jin, and—oh God, Domin, he's dead... I'm so sorry. He's dead."

My knees went out and I sank to the ground beside the bed. The same bed Yuri had been in earlier in the day.

"But you have to save Jin. Jin... save...."

"Get out!" Dr. Pakhom screamed. "I can't save men if you don't— get out!"

Everything spun, and I was grabbed and lifted and yanked. I realized Logan had me and I was being dragged after him. Then we were back outside in the hot, sticky night air.

"Where?" Logan demanded. "Tell me where they would be!"

"I—I don't—"

"Domin!"

Jamal's words came back to me then, our conversation about the tribe of Feran.

"Conceal him?"

"Yes." Jamal nodded. "If they were to take him into the catacombs of Abtu to hide him or simply abandon him there, then for us, who are not familiar with the cavern, it would be highly unlikely that we could locate him...."

"Domin!" he yelled again.

"They took them to the catacombs," I apprised him. "Hanif wouldn't think we'd ever go there because we don't know them. That's where they are."

"You're certain?"

"I am."

"Okay," he said, and that quickly, I saw his reason return, saw the frenzy leave him, and watched him take a breath and settle.

"Kabore!" I yelled over at my steward. "I need you to get keys to a car and meet me at the catacombs now! Right now!"

"At once, my lord!"

He never second-guessed me, so by the time we reached the Hummers, he was there with five men. Logan and I got in the back of the one Kabore pointed at, and Koren followed, scrambling in after us as Kabore got in the passenger seat and one of my men slid behind the wheel, ready to drive.

"Where are we going?" Kabore shouted.

"To the catacombs," Logan roared. "Domin knows that's where they went."

"How do you know?" Koren yelled as the engine roared to life and four other men climbed in before we lurched forward.

"I just do," I said, lowering my voice so everyone else would, ordering the driver to hurry.

"Logan, we should wait to speak to the yareah or see if Rahim or Taj will wake—"

"No, Domin knows," Logan assured his brother.

"This is crazy," Koren chided. "You don't know and—"

"Domin," Logan cut off his brother, his tone solid. "Yuri's no more dead than I am," he announced, and I when I gazed into his golden eyes, he was him again, all strength and power. "Do you have any idea what you would actually need to do to kill Yuri Kosa?"

"It just takes a gun, Logan, which they have."

"Yeah, but that makes no sense," he said thoughtfully. "If they were going to kill Yuri, they could have shot him like they did Rahim and Taj. It's not logical."

I closed my eyes and breathed in and out and tried to think with my head and not my heart.

The Hummer made it to the top of the hill, and the headlights found a black panther in the darkness.

"My lord!"

Logan was out of the car before it even stopped, running fast, legs flying, arms pumping, covering the ground and then falling down beside Jin. I was right behind him, glancing around for Yuri and seeing nothing.

"Check everywhere!" I ordered the men fanning out around us.

"Jin!" Logan howled, and I watched him wrap his arms around his mate and bury his face in his fur. "No, no, no... please."

I had never seen Jin so still, and it was hard to watch Logan lift the large head of the panther into his lap.

"I need you! Your son needs you!"

Nothing happened, and I noticed Logan's shirt smeared with fresh blood.

"Logan, he's bleeding."

"I know he's fucking bleeding," he choked out, his voice as I had never heard it before, utterly fractured.

"Anything?" I called over to the others.

"There's blood, my lord… so much blood."

I wasn't ready to lose Yuri. Maybe in another fifty years. Possibly. But not yet, not now….

Logan roared and the air suddenly reeked of sex.

"What did you—" I went down on one knee, not because I was fighting and wanted my friend, but because of the energy it drained from me to have the heat and desire wash over me. His pheromones simply annihilated me.

Koren went to his knees beside me. "Domin, Yuri's—"

"No," I said, my hands in the dirt in front of me, head down, trying to draw air into my lungs when it was too thick and wet.

All my men, even Kabore, were frozen. It was overwhelming, the power rolling off Logan. It should have mattered, it was chemical, my body should have responded, but it didn't. I was a semel, and so I was as strong as he was. Logan and I were different on the outside, but inside, where it counted, we were the same.

"What the hell is that?" someone gasped.

"Shit." Koren caught his breath, and his hands, clutching at me, hurt. "Domin, watch out."

I glanced up in time to see Jin's body contort, lift, and bow into a semicircle before snapping in half the other way.

Scrambling to my feet, I dragged Koren back, then grabbed Kabore's arm and yanked him after me. I didn't want to be close.

There was a fine mist of blood, then a hotter spray as Jin screamed, and wings—huge giant dragon wings—erupted from his back.

My men were smart and fell to the ground, faces down in the dirt, so no one was disemboweled by the force of the appendages as they cut through the air.

"Oh Logan," I moaned, terrified for him.

The creature that rose was not Jin. All I saw were the huge green eyes of a bird, almost a hawk's head, something resembling a beak, reptilian black skin, and claws, but longer and hooked, like talons. I should have been horrified. Everyone else was except Logan, who was rising slowly and holding out his hand.

There was something… familiar.

"Come to me," Logan said, and his voice was like honey.

But I needed help, and I was afraid that if Jin succumbed, if he changed back, I wouldn't get it.

"Yuri!" I screamed.

"No," Logan cried out as the creature Jin was now disappeared from in front of him and reappeared, towering over me. I understood that he had actually just leaped or flown, but it was too fast to track with the naked eye—it seemed like magic.

"Oh dear God," Kabore moaned, and I could tell how truly frightened he was.

The head of the beast moved just like a bird, almost robotic, and when he bumped my chin, I tilted my head back, baring my throat. If he wanted to kill me, I was dead.

"Jesus, Domin," Logan said under his breath, easing closer.

I closed my eyes, trying not to shake as the beak slid slowly up the side of my neck.

"Don't move don't move don't move," Koren chanted at a whisper, his breathing shallow as I felt his hand close around my bicep.

He was trying to offer me his strength, but I was afraid that if he tugged on me, if he jostled or stirred me in any way, Jin would startle and kill me.

"Domin, you stupid fuck," Logan exhaled.

The talons closed on my shoulders, and I felt the ends like nails pressing through my shirt but not breaking skin, closing but not tightening.

"Domin," Logan pleaded. "Please don't send him into that cave after—"

"Yuri," I said, going for broke. I leaning my head forward and slid my palm flat up the curve of the beak. I quivered as he inhaled my scent but also Yuri's, the sweat from his skin, the musk from him marking me, and whatever lingered from us being in bed together. I watched the nekhene and I understood where the term hawk-cat had come from, and maybe even, possibly, stories about Horus.

The eye flicked everywhere but he saw me clearly, and when he tipped his head, like he was listening, I grabbed hold of his shoulder. He reacted and the talons closed instinctively.

Razor sharp claws met through my body, through skin and muscle, and then bone. The cracking made me scream.

"Domin!"

A rush of air and then I was fifty feet off the ground, dangling from what was left of my collarbone and shoulder.

"Jin!" Logan roared below us, and I saw him start to run.

Why doesn't he shift so he can keep up? I wondered vaguely as my head whipped back when we moved from gentle lift to flight.

It was probably what it was like to be carried off by a bird of prey. I couldn't even fathom the speed as we blasted through the dark night toward the rock. At the last second, he dipped, and rock formations, huge stalactites, and vugs were a blur as we passed them. A miscalculation, a wrong turn, and at the speed we were going, we'd be dead. It would be an instant death to be shattered on one of the walls of the enormous cave.

I heard gunfire, but it was ricocheting off rock and not hitting us. They couldn't see us, it was too dark, and we were moving too fast, only the roar of the nekhene cat giving us away.

He released me when he dropped to the floor of the cavern, and the wings did what they had not done to my men—when he whirled around, he beheaded two of the men before the others hurled themselves into the dirt.

"Defend me!" Hanif screamed, and I saw him then—the new semel.

I stumbled forward with my ruined left arm and saw one of the men rise, rifle in hand, and aim for Jin.

Kicking hard, I caught him in the side of the head. He went down fast and I stumbled forward to reach Hanif.

"No!" he screamed, and I saw that it wasn't Jin he was terrified of, but me, bleeding and broken, lurching toward him.

He lifted a pistol.

"Where is my mate?" I yelled.

"I'm going to kill him. You're vile and unclean, and it's a desecration that you are the semel-aten."

I didn't stop moving forward. "I'll trade you your father for my mate," I lied, because Hanif wasn't going to live to see the dawn. "Tell me where he is!"

"Stop walking before I shoot you!"

"Where is my mate?" I thundered as I heard wailing behind us. His men, except for the one I had kicked unconscious, were being eviscerated.

"I'm going—"

"Your father for my—"

"Fool!" Hanif rasped as he fired.

Same shoulder, which was actually kind of lucky.

"Blow it up!" he shrieked into a walkie-talkie I hadn't realized he had.

We were in farther than I thought, so I heard the explosion, but there was no blowback.

I slammed him up against the huge rock he stood in front of and closed my hand around his throat as I felt his gun press against my cheek.

"The priest ordered me to kill your mate, semel-aten, and that I will do."

"Why?" I trembled with pain.

"Only the priest had honor; he was all I could believe in. It was all a nightmare: my father, the things he let his sheseru do to me—all of it. But when I told Asdiel Kovo, he said once I killed your sekhem, once Yuri Kosa was dead, that it would all end… everything would end… all the horror… just end."

"Oh, it's going to end," I promised, and I shifted to my werepanther form, crushing his throat, his windpipe, in my grip.

Everyone always forgot I was a semel. But no matter what they said, no matter how many times they all said kadish, I wasn't. My blood was of the line of Menhit, and I was a werepanther.

Hanif was surprised, and his last expression conveyed that. Asdiel had lied, convinced him I was not a true semel. But I was, and Hanif paid for his mistake with his life. I had a moment of regret that the priest had known about the horrors at Ipis and had done nothing to stop them, but the semel's son had chosen to put his faith in the wrong man.

Releasing his body, I stumbled back and fell down, dropping to my knees in the dirt. Unable to hold on to my half-man/half-panther form, I cried out for Yuri before I stared at the nekhene cat.

"Please," I begged.

Jin shuddered, and I saw that he, too, was losing strength. I had no idea what kind of wounds he'd sustained before Logan's pheromones forced the change, and I was suddenly panicked even as I shivered.

I was getting cold.

"Jin," I said, my voice cracking. "Yuri."

He was gone like he'd never been there. He left no trace of sound, nothing. And it struck me then why Logan hadn't shifted earlier, because if he needed to bring Jin back, he had to be himself to do it. I envied him his reason in the midst of a nightmare.

It was all my fault.

Jin, forced into a new and frightening nekhene form—that was on me. Logan, outside, probably hoarse from yelling, petrified of losing his mate, that too was my fault. No one would be in Ipis if they hadn't followed me. I was to blame for all of it. I had led Rahim and Taj and everyone else to their deaths. I was a horror.

A gust of air, and then the creature was back, coming toward me.

My knees weak, my throat dry, and my chest tight, I felt his eyes fix on me. I wondered if this was how I was going to die.

"Jin."

He inhaled, and suddenly I was seeing a bruised and bloody Jin Church.

"Oh God."

That was worse. If I had to choose, I'd rather die myself than watch him succumb. I was terrified that I wouldn't be able to get him out of the cave. If he was shifted, he could fly out, but reverted now back to just Jin, what was I supposed to do?

He crumpled to the ground, and I was running before I even realized I was moving.

I went to my knees beside him, pulled him into my lap, and curled around him, trying to give him any body warmth I had left.

"Domin." Jin's voice, which I had always teased him about, was now the sweetest sound I had ever heard. "Don't cry."

I couldn't even speak.

"I searched and I saw no trace of Yuri, and I don't sense him in here at all."

I searched his face.

"I swear to you, he's not in here."

There was no way he could know that.

"Please keep your eyes open," he pleaded. "Please, Domin."

But there were spots in front of my eyes.

He twisted around in my lap and put his hands on my face. "You're ice cold."

But he was the one, naked, who was shivering. "You're so strong now. That dragon thing was new."

He shook his head. "It's not, did it once before. Logan hates it."

"I can understand why." I coughed and my whole body hurt. "There's a walkie-talkie back over there by Hanif. If you get it, we can at least see who might answer."

"You should shift to panther, you'll be warmer."

"But I'm not like you," I said softly. "I'm not me when I'm a panther."

He didn't argue, simply rose and shifted, rolling into his panther form in midstride. It was really something to see and never failed to amaze me.

I couldn't keep from sighing. He retrieved the walkie-talkie and dropped it onto my stomach, then nuzzled against my side, head down on my chest.

Pressing a button on the device, I gathered myself and then said, "Is there anyone there? Please. Anyone."

Nothing.

"Yuri." My heart was breaking.

Dead air.

I gazed at Jin. "In case I… just so you know, I killed your father, not Yuri. I mean, I know Crane probably let you know, but he wasn't in there, and he doesn't know what I did and what Yuri did. We never said. I didn't even tell Logan. But for the record, so you know, it was me."

He lifted his head and gazed down at me.

"I wanted to bring him back and kill him again, Jin. I hated him. You deserved so much fuckin' better. I wish it was different, and I wish he had been different, and I wish I could tell you that at the end he recanted it all and realized what he'd done."

He nuzzled under my chin.

"You're a gift, Jin, so please run out of here to Logan."

He just cuddled tighter against me.

"Nobody fuckin' listens to me," I grumbled. "Some akhen-aten I am."

"Domin!"

I was wrong. The voice of my mate was the sweetest sound I'd ever heard.

"Domin Thorne!"

I lifted the walkie-talkie.

"Domin, goddammit! Please!"

Pressing the button, I choked out, "Yuri."

"Oh, thank you, God," he gasped on the other end.

Even over a crackly connection, he sounded so good I was ready to bawl.

"Where are you?" he wanted to know.

"With Jin."

"With Jin? Jin's okay?"

"No, we're not okay. Are you bleeding?"

"No, baby, not my blood. Not Jin's blood. I was the sheseru of my tribe, remember?"

I forgot sometimes. "You're not bleeding?"

"I'll be okay," he comforted me. "Don't you worry."

And everything went dark, my vision going out on me, but it was fine. I didn't need to be able to see to work the buttons. "Hanif's dead. There's only one guy alive in here with us, but he's out cold right now."

"Okay, we're coming in, we just have to get people up here and more men and some bulldozers. It's just a small cave-in, but enough to slow us down. You're all right, though, aren't you? You're not hurt, are you?"

"Come get Jin."

"We're coming for both of you."

"I might not... Jin's cold," I said, and then I heard a low whine from the panther purring on my chest.

There was nothing else.

Chapter Twelve

I HEARD my mate. He sounded hysterical.

"He has to shift."

"If I drag him through it, he could die."

"He'll die if he doesn't!" Logan yelled.

"Yuri." I heard Jin's gentle, patient tone. "What do you want me to do? It's up to you."

"Try," Yuri heaved out the word, and I could hear the tears in his voice.

"Move," Jin ordered, and I heard scrambling. "Domin Thorne, you will shift for me."

But I wouldn't, because Jin had no power over me anymore, and more than that, he wasn't my mate. I'd never had anyone who wanted just *me* before Yuri Kosa. Everyone else let me go. Yuri was holding on.

I felt Jin's power run over me, wash hot and scalding over my skin, and then sink into my bones, chasing away the chill. I took it in, absorbed it, and tried to pull more.

"Oh shit." Jin sounded surprised.

"Love," Logan sounded scared.

"I need—you."

"Here, I'm yours."

I wanted to see the big, strong semel holding his mate, but more than that, I wanted to see Yuri's beautiful blue eyes.

"I can't make him shift anymore—he's like Crane now. My power recognizes him. It runs through my beset, but Domin just absorbs it." His voice sounded shaky. "Oh, Yuri, I'm so sorry, I can't make Domin do anything. He's too strong."

Yuri moaned softly, and his voice was thick with tears when he spoke. "I need him."

Jin was crying, and I wanted to tell him it would be okay, but I was so tired. I'd tell him later.

IT WAS quiet, but there was something tickling my nose. A smell I knew, a smell I liked. The breath on my ear made me shiver, and I felt goose bumps on my skin.

"Domin." My mate's voice was a rumbling purr. "You need to shift so you can heal, because I have things I want to tell you and more you should see."

I felt like I was underwater and needed to swim up to the surface so I could talk to him. And I desperately wanted to talk to him.

"We're back home, and everyone's here."

I was *home*.

"I have to tell you what Logan did," he said, like it was a secret. The conspiratorial tone rolled right through me. "You'll like it."

I burned with curiosity.

"I've brought everyone in here, I even had Koren come to talk to you, and it did nothing," he said, his voice husky and low.

I wanted to touch him so badly.

"And then Jin pointed out that I haven't once been in here all alone," he said, and I felt him slide the palm of his hand over my stomach. "I have to wonder at my own lack of self-confidence. Jin simply knows he's what Logan needs, but it's not just them. Every mated couple, just like regular married couples, assumes that the husband or the wife, or the mate, is the one the other craves. So I thought, what if I am simply missing the obvious?"

He slid his hand up to my chest as he pressed his lips down into my abdomen. It felt so good, and I made a noise in the back of my throat.

"Oh, I like that sound," he growled, and it was low and dark and full of decadent ache.

My cock twitched and my breath caught.

"I had no idea," he said, his voice thick with hunger. "I mean, I knew you enjoyed being in bed with me—you can't fake what we've been doing—but I didn't know that the sex was wrapped up in so much more. Forgive me for doubting. I knew you loved me, knew you almost died getting to me, but I didn't know when you were saying the word 'mate' that it was truly what I was. I'm an idiot, and I can only say in my own defense that you're all I ever wanted, so it's been Christmas for me for the past six months already. I keep thinkin' I'm gonna wake up."

The hot hand closing around my cock made me gasp.

"Doc says that your brain isn't making a connection to your body, and if it did, you could wake up."

Instinctively, I bucked up into his hand.

"Do you want me?" he whispered, and it was sultry and hot and he stroked me until I was throbbing and hard. "Do you love me?"

I wanted to answer.

"I'm leaving if you don't open your eyes and tell me."

It was like rising through layers of thick, heavy fog.

"Okay," he said, and his hand was gone. "I'll be back."

"No." My voice was raspy and full of gravel, and when my eyes fluttered open, I closed them again quickly because it was so bright.

"Oh baby." His hands were back, on my face, and he kissed everywhere he could reach, small, light, soft kisses that felt warm on my cold skin.

I smiled because I could feel it in his clutching hands, taste it on his lips when they grazed mine, and hear it in his halting breath: he loved me.

"Domin?"

"I'm not leaving you."

"Promise," he insisted.

"I swear," I said, opening my eyes again, and I saw how pleased he was, and how tired.

"Why are you scowling at me?" he asked as tears ran down his cheeks.

"Because you look like hell."

He framed my face with his hands.

"I woke up to get laid," I quipped, even though just that much talking was exhausting.

He leaned over and kissed me again, laughing into my mouth, so happy, even as I parted my lips under his, his tongue sliding over mine as he tasted me, savored and ravished me.

"You missed me," I said as he kissed my eyelids and my nose, my cheeks, my forehead, my chin, and then fused his lips to mine once more.

"Sleep," he commanded. "You'll shift when you wake up."

"Stay with me," I ordered. "Right here. I want to smell you when I wake up."

"Yes, my semel."

"And I expect some action then too."

I was kissed again and it was good.

I WOKE up ravenous.

"Shift," Yuri said the second I opened my eyes.

It hurt, my muscles were sore, but I did it and lost time as I always did when I was in panther form. I was starving and there was meat and water, so much food, and I ate and drank my fill. When I was sated, I found my mate outside in the sun, lying down, and I crept over and joined him on a blanket in the grass. It smelled good, there was shade, and I could hear a fountain. I fell asleep curled into his side.

The next time I opened my eyes, I was in bed. I had been bathed; I knew because I no longer smelled like blood and dirt and sweat. I had felt gritty before, but now, smelling good, clean, lying on my back under freshly laundered sheets, I felt better. The best part of all was that when I rolled my head to the left, I found Yuri sleeping beside me on top of the sheets, barefoot, in jeans and a threadbare old T-shirt. The man was gorgeous all rumpled, and I would have reached for him, woken him up to hold me, but the sound of a throat clearing drew my attention. I found myself caught in the gaze of Dr. Pakhom.

"Oh," I said, yawning. "Hi."

She sucked in a breath.

"What?"

Quickly, she shook her head.

"Good Lord, woman, get a hold of yourself," I grumbled.

"You scared me to death," she said, then pursed her lips together in a tight line. "But I guess you're going to be doing that a lot."

"I hope not."

She reached down to take my hand without permission.

"This is a slippery slope," I said with a grunt.

"I want to hold your hand," she confessed.

I shook my head.

"Are you really planning to visit every tribe in the world?"

"Yes."

"And are you planning to take me and my team with you?"

"Yes, if you're up for an adventure."

"I am."

"Then, yes, you're invited along."

Her tears were instant.

"Oh come on," I complained.

"No, you come on!" she ground out. "Scaring me to death, how dare you! Broken clavicle, deep puncture wounds, a bullet, for heaven's sake—and still not fully recovered from an assassination attempt! Who *are* you?"

I let out a huff of air to let her know I was annoyed too. "And? Did you save Taj? Rahim?"

"Of course I saved Taj and Rahim!"

"Where are they?"

"That is for your steward to tell you," she huffed, and I saw her begin to fidget.

"Do you need to hug me so you know I'm well?" I asked bluntly.

"Yes. Do you mind?" She sounded just as practical.

"No."

And with that she bent and wrapped her arms around me for a long moment. When she straightened, I gave her a compliment, telling her that she was very beautiful for a doctor.

"Well, I've seen a hundred more handsome semels."

I chuckled, and she said to get ready for visitors.

"Not in my room," I groused irritably.

"No. Use your eyes, what do you see?"

And she was right; I wasn't in my own room. "Why did we move?"

"It's only while you recuperate. Your sekhem didn't want everyone traipsing through the private quarters he shared with you, but once you're all healed, you can go back up there. It's quite the walk to get up there. Have you ever noticed that?"

"I haven't." I sighed, pleased that he wanted our room to stay just ours. I would have done exactly the same.

"So this is just temporary? Until when?"

"Until you can make the climb without being winded."

"I can do it now."

She studied me. "Let's wait a few more days, all right? Humor your doctor."

I scowled at her.

"The semel-netjer would like a word. I'm going to get him."

"Thank you."

She breezed out, and I turned to Yuri. Cupping his cheek, I noticed the bruise there, the dark circles under his eyes, and the new scar over his right eyebrow. There was a line through it now, the brow almost cut in half. I wanted to know what had happened.

As I opened my mouth to wake him, Logan walked into my bedroom, followed by Jin carrying his son.

"Let me see your child," I ordered.

Jin smiled wide and bent over. I took in the carbon copy of him, except that he had Logan's angular jaw and sharp Roman nose. The rest—the eyebrows that quirked, the long lashes, full lips, and black hair—was all Jin.

"Wake him up so I can see his eyes."

"No," Logan and Jin said at the same time.

"Problem?" I teased.

"Your steward is throwing us out," Jin said playfully. "We are not to come back until *he*, meaning Ilia, has learned to control his power."

"What'd he do?"

"Apparently before I got back a week ago, when Ilia was here with Yusuke and Crane, a lot of your staff were dragged through their shifts on a regular basis."

"Oh, lovely," I said sarcastically. "And Kabore wants you gone? I can't imagine why."

Jin passed Ilia to Logan before he sat and hugged me. "Thank you, Domin."

"For what? You saved me, not the other way around."

"No," he said, holding me tight. "Crane reminds me who I am. You sort of ram the truth down my throat and shove me toward the right path."

I eased him back so I could look into his face. "There's only one place on the planet you belong."

"I know. It's just that you, much like Logan, don't let me get away with anything. I appreciate you helping me through my crisis."

"Thank you for saving my life."

"You saved mine too," he assured me. "Ask Logan."

"Get up," the semel-netjer grumbled at his mate.

Jin rose and Logan moved by, passing Ilia over to him. The second his hands were free, Logan ran a hand through Jin's long glossy black hair, as he always did. Logan could not keep his hands off his mate.

"So what did you do?"

"I didn't kill you for taking Jin into the catacombs and again when we got inside and found my naked mate wrapped around you."

"Thank you. I should be dead."

"Yes, you should," he said, putting a hand on my cheek. "But I have grown fond of your face after these many years."

"And?"

"And it would upset my mate if I eviscerated you, and I never upset my mate."

"It's good to know."

He patted my cheek and then got up. "Crane named Kabore the new maahes of the tribe. That's what you wanted, right?"

"Yes."

"Crane's coming home with us, but you knew that."

"Yes, I did."

He cleared his throat. "I'm also taking Koren."

"Oh, that's a tragedy," I deadpanned.

He grunted. "You did good by him, too, both you and Yuri."

"We try." I grinned up at him, throwing the covers off and then moving to stand up.

"What're you doing?"

"I'm gonna hug you good-bye."

"Okay." He seemed pleased. "Let's see if you can get up. You've been lying around for two weeks, did you know that?"

"You're such an ass!" I scolded the semel-netjer.

Logan made a noise and pointed at Yuri. "Don't wake him up, please don't wake him up. The man has been running around—"

"He's been making everything perfect for when you woke up after he knew that you actually would," Jin soothed. "And I remembered when I saw him discipline your khatyu and your sheseru that—"

"What were Yuri and Taj fighting about?"

"They disagreed about how many of your khatyu should be garrisoned in Ipis."

"You lost me." I was still a little muddled. My brain felt like it was stuffed with feathers.

"Just don't worry about it," Logan chimed in. "Yuri won, and I agreed with the number. Until the two djehus get that tribe in order, they need backup."

"The djehus?" I was confused.

He nodded, helped me sit up, which was harder than I thought it would be.

"Be careful with him," Jin cautioned.

Logan arched an eyebrow.

"Don't say something horrible."

"Fine," Logan rumbled out the word. "Assume I'm going to be gentle, then."

"The djehus?" I inquired, curling my leg under me and straightening up, taking a breath as Logan sat down beside me.

"I put them in charge of Ipis," he explained. "The house of Feran is done; the line is ended."

"Did you kill Hakkan there?"

"No. Crane named Kabore as your new maahes, and for his first act, he read the charges and then had Taj execute him in the pit."

"So Kabore was able with that one act to show everyone that he is not a maahes to be questioned."

"Yes, as well as one who follows you and the law."

"He'll be good, don't you think?"

"Oh yes, I'm impressed. He's very capable, loyal, and no one is going to trip him up on protocol or custom or language. Excellent choice."

"Thank you."

"And by bringing Crane to Sobek in the first place, you built him up, proved to him that he's capable, and let it be his choice to go home or not. He knows that being beset of his reah is of vital importance, and it's a huge deal to others since Jin's a nekhene cat."

"Good."

"He wants to see you. Can you walk out into the main hall and say good-bye to everyone?"

"I think so," I said, reaching for my oldest friend.

Logan slid an arm around my waist, and with him lifting and me using him for leverage, I got up.

"I could carry you."

"In some alternate universe, I'm sure I might let you."

A gentle sound rumbled out of his chest as he helped me out of the room. By the time we reached the hall, I was walking by myself and liking the feel of the marble floor under my bare feet.

I saw Mikhail and Samani, Koren and Danny, and Kabore, Taj, Rahim, Ebere, and Jamal. It was nice that they all clapped as I came shuffling toward them between Logan and Jin.

"Knock it off," I demanded.

Ebere moved quickly to reach me, and I put an arm around her, leaning her gently into my side.

"You gave me quite a scare."

"It will probably continue to happen."

"Please, no." She sounded tired. "You took years off my life."

"Forgive me."

"Perhaps," she agreed. "But there's so much to tell you."

"Let me say good-bye to these nice people first," I said, lifting my arm for Koren.

He moved forward and wrapped his arms around my neck gently.

"You take care," I said, turning my head to kiss his cheek. "And take care of your sweet little mate too."

"I will," he rumbled. "And you do the same."

We parted, and it was good to see him so content.

Danny stepped forward and offered me his hand. He could not control the trembling. "All the blessings on your house, akhen-aten," he said, his voice cracking just a little.

"Thank you." I smiled, covering our clasped hands with my other for a moment.

He stepped back and Koren took his hand in his, lifted it to his lips, and kissed his knuckles. It was very sweet and nothing I had ever seen him do before. The adoration and devotion on Koren's face was good to see. I was pleased and really hoped that he wouldn't break the beautiful boy's heart.

Turning, I saw Crane and Yusuke approaching us.

"Oh, maahen, you're gorgeous," I said sincerely.

She flushed deeply, dropping Crane's hand as she moved by the others and walked into my arms.

"Thank you for keeping my love safe, akhen-aten, and for releasing him now so that he may return home with me and be mated."

I squeezed her tight. "Congratulations. Send me an invitation, all right?"

She nodded into my shoulder.

Leaning back, I offered my hand to Crane.

He took it, holding it tight in his as he stared into my eyes. "I said good-bye to Yuri last night. And you'll come to my mating ceremony, yeah?"

"I will."

"Bring him and the rest of your house, my semel."

I sighed, releasing his hand. "Take care of your reah."

"Always."

"Go." I tipped my head.

He took Yusuke's hand in his, and said his good-byes to the others as Jin stepped in front of me.

"Thank you again."

"I take, I give back," I said playfully, leaning over and kissing his forehead. "Now get out of my villa."

His smile was gorgeous, and when he moved, Logan filled my vision.

"You'll come for the mating ceremony." It was a statement; I wasn't getting out of it even if I wanted to.

"I will."

"And when you do the traipsing around the world you're planning, call me from places where you'll be and I'll meet you."

"Really?"

"Yeah, I'd love to."

"There's going to be more... I sort of signed you up for the deep end with me. I don't know if when I was out you talked to Kabore at all, but—"

"I did, we did," he assured me, taking his son from Jin and then passing Ilia to me. "So I'll be with you when you start your newest adventure. Thank you for wanting me along."

"Wouldn't be real if you weren't with me," I sighed, staring down at Ilia, noticing again how beautiful he was before I looked back up at Logan. "Why am I holding this kid again?"

"You need to kiss him good-bye."

"You know you're not supposed to demand that people give your child attention."

"No?"

Ilia was so small and soft, and his little hand closed on my finger the same instant it felt as though a tuning fork had been struck inside my chest.

"What was that?" I was startled.

"Oh, did you feel it?" Logan asked, his eyes warm as he held my gaze. "That's what he does. It's like he checks the strength of whoever's got him. There's a ping, almost, that he sends out, and it resonates back. If it doesn't come back, he'll cry. But with you, he got pinged back and so... he's good."

Ilia yawned big, there was a quick back-and-forth twist, and then sleep.

"He likes you."

I scowled at him. "Stop. He's a baby."

"Still." Logan was very pleased with me—I could tell. "He's good with you, that's why."

"That's why what?"

"You know."

I was afraid to ask. "Logan?"

He inhaled deeply. "Who else would you have raise the son of the semel-netjer and the nekhene cat? Who else could even attempt it?"

I was completely floored. "You're not serious."

"I am deadly serious. When have you known me to joke?"

He didn't. In fact, Logan was not much for jokes of any kind. He laughed, not often, but he did. I had seen him do more of it since he found Jin than at any other time in his life. But still, words like reserved, serious, and intense described him best. So I knew he was not pulling my leg. If he and Jin died, Ilia would come to live with me.

"Is it wise to make me his guardian?" I swallowed hard. "I mean—what will your parents say and Koren and—"

"I decided," Logan said as his mate moved to my other side and put his hand on my arm. "And Jin agreed. I have faith in you, and so does he. And then, there's Yuri to consider as well. I trust Yuri with my life and Jin's. Of course I would put my child in his care."

My vision blurred, and for a moment I couldn't speak.

"Aww." Jin nuzzled his face against me shoulder. "You have such a soft heart, Domin."

I ignored him, tried to chicken wing him off me.

"You do," Jin said softly, still fawning all over me, not intimidated in the least. "I know you and Yuri are the ones to watch over Ilia."

I cleared my throat. "I'm absolutely certain that Yuri would make a wonderful father."

"So would you Domin," Logan assured me.

My eyes dropped to Ilia, asleep in my arms. "Did Yuri see him? Hold him?"

"Of course," Logan said softly as I passed Ilia back.

"And you all said good-bye to him?"

"Yes," Jin assured me. "I love that you wanted to make certain."

I scowled again.

"Oh, Domin—" Jin's voice broke, and he tried again. "You really love him."

"Could you just go now?" I snapped.

Logan was laughing as he kissed my cheek and then wrapped a tight arm around my neck. "I'll always be right beside you."

It was a greater comfort than he could imagine.

I put my hands on his sides and breathed in his earthy scent a second before pushing him away. He grabbed Jin's hand and headed down the stairs without another word.

Koren and Crane were still standing there with their intended mates, staring at me.

"Better catch him," I suggested.

"Yes," Koren agreed before he, too, turned away.

"Domin," Crane began. "I—"

"I know," I soothed. "Hurry up! You know Logan hates to wait."

He hurried then and led Yusuke down the marble stairs from the second floor to the first.

After several minutes deep in my own thoughts, I became aware of people staring up at me from the main floor, where the others had just walked through. There was the typical number of people milling around the many bookshelves, sitting at tables, and walking in and out from the gardens. It brought to mind a quad at a college. When hands were lifted and people waved, I waved back.

"Stop making a spectacle of yourself." Kabore was irritated. He gestured for me to come away from the open area where everyone could see me and instead into a large alcove.

"You look good," I said before I glanced around at all of them—Ebere, Jamal, Taj, and Rahim.

"You do too," Mikhail chimed in as he joined us.

"Where's Samani?"

"She's enrolling in school. She's taking online courses to finish her master's."

"That's a nice compromise."

"She came up with it after I broke down and gave her the truth."

"And what's that?"

"That I really do want to marry her and have kids."

"Was she happy?"

"Yes," he said irritably. "Why, I have no idea."

It was endearing, his blindness to his many gifts. "Did Logan perform the handfasting?"

"Yes, he did." Mikhail was startled. "How did you know?"

"Makes sense. You would have wanted Jin and Crane to witness it. Did Yuri stand up as your second?"

"He did."

"And were there many people who congratulated you?"

"Yes." He sounded bewildered.

But I understood. People in the tribe respected Samani Baro. She was known to be smart and honorable, and now Mikhail was her mate. It was a good move for the sylvan to take such a good mate, and marrying into the tribe would also serve him well.

"Good." I patted his shoulder before my eyes were back on Kabore. "Logan said he talked to you."

"He did, yes."

"I'm glad."

"As I predicted," Kabore said, leaning close to me, whispering, "Mr. Morris and Mr. Yadin of the Iusaaset will be here next week." He eased back, no longer speaking under his breath. "I let them know that you were well enough to meet with them."

"I'm excited to meet them."

"As, I was informed, are they to meet you."

I gazed into his dark brown eyes. "I'm sorry that I left the execution of Hakkan Tarek to you."

"No." He shook his head. "That was *maat*."

"Yes," I agreed and reached out for Ebere's hand. "Tell me where you're all going. You seem ready to go somewhere."

"I'm on my way to Ipis," Ebere reported, squeezing my hand. "The phocal of the Shu and I are traveling there to check on the two djehus."

"Excellent," I said, reaching out for Rahim, who moved closer so my hand could close over his shoulder. "And are you enjoying being phocal?"

"I suspect I am as you are, my lord—finding my way."

"I'm so glad you're okay."

"I feel the same about you, my lord."

I gave him a pat, leaned in and kissed Ebere's cheek, and then wished them both a safe journey. Once they were out of earshot, I rounded on Taj and Jamal.

"What about the yareah and her daughter?"

"They were relocated here to Sobek, my lord. Masika is being tested and will then be enrolled in school. Alana was the one who begged to be moved. She wants her daughter to have every opportunity. She is entirely focused on giving her the best life."

"Good."

"I am on my way back to Satis," Jamal related. "There is a lot to be supervised there."

"And how many Shu do you have there with you?"

He said that he had twenty-five men with him, and that things were going well. Shahid Alon had returned from delivering Elham El Masry and Rahab Bahur to Mongolia, and when he got back, his mate and twin girls were there waiting for him.

"Twins?" I clarified with Jamal.

"Yes."

"Huh. Okay, and how's Shahid doing?"

"From what Rahim tells me, he's doing well. Your phocal is even thinking of making Shahid his second, which I think is a good choice. Shahid always was level-headed, and it would be hard for Rahim not to consider him for the position. I mean, really, along with his even temperament, there's no panther alive faster except for Jin."

"I think Shahid's to be trusted," I said, yawning.

"We are all in agreement," Jamal assured me.

"You are just newly risen," Kabore said softly. "Hopefully Taj and Mikhail and I might share a meal with you and your sekhem this evening, if you are able."

"I'd like that," I said before I focused my attention on Mikhail. "Bring Samani, okay?"

"I will. Thank you, Domin."

I had no idea why he was thanking me for something that was a given.

"It just means a great deal that you would accept her."

"Of course."

"But most semel-atens would not. You understand that, right? You think of us as family, and not just as sylvan or sheseru or maahes, but more. And I know that's how Logan modeled his tribe for you, but for a semel-aten to run his home the same way is simply extraordinary."

"Agreed," Taj added. "You run your household like a family, and we are all honored to be part of yours."

"I couldn't imagine it being any other way. I trust you all with my life."

"And we are all proud that you do so." Taj blew out a breath, then smiled at me. "Being your sheseru has been a gift."

"Yeah, getting shot, that was fantastic."

"I was in your service. I hope to always be."

"You will be," I said and then glanced over at Mikhail. "Neither one of you is going anywhere. I have to trust my inner circle implicitly."

"You have that," Mikhail affirmed, "and now that Kabore stepped up because Taj and I are both cowards—"

"Coward is an ugly word," Taj said, cutting him off.

"But appropriate."

"I didn't hear you doing it."

"What are we talking about?" I needed to get them back on track.

Kabore crossed his arms. "I'm sorry, my lord, it had to be done. I know the semel-netjer and his reah are like your family, but really, between the baby and the volume of their fights and their—" He cleared his throat. "—other activities, they disrupted everyone here quite effectively. Your entire household needed them out."

I was trying not to laugh. "Everybody wanted them gone, huh?"

"My lord, I can speak for the entirety of the villa when I tell you the consensus is we were all very pleased it was you who won the sepat."

Taj grinned, Mikhail was coughing, and Kabore restated for emphasis, "*Very* pleased, my lord."

It was nice to be appreciated.

WHEN I reached my quarters, I found Yuri still sleeping and noticed that, in my absence, a large fruit platter and a pitcher of ice water had been delivered. I locked the outer door before climbing back onto the bed.

He seemed exhausted, and I wanted him to rest, but when his eyes fluttered open and I was looking into his clear blue eyes, I was too happy to tell him to close them again.

"You're awake," he said, obviously pleased, the gravel in his voice very sexy.

"I am," I said, reaching over to touch his cheek, then run my fingers along his jaw line. "Tell me about the scar on your brow."

"Oh. The night Hanif tried to kill me, one of his panthers caught me across the face with a claw. I was more worried about the eye than the brow."

"I didn't notice before."

He grinned lazily and my heart clenched. "You were so out of it. I'm surprised you knew you were talking to me half the time."

"Why are you so tired?" I questioned, putting a hand on his hip and then easing him closer, until our legs entwined.

"I just wanted everything to be in order when you woke up, that's all. Plus, I've been making some changes to the villa, like making the entrances wheelchair accessible, as well as the stacks. Samani and I are also going to build a shelter to house runaways, battered women, just anyone who needs protection. I think sometimes we assume that because we're panthers that there is always the semel to count on, or the tribe. But if you think about it, even someone as remarkable as Jin was thrown out of his original one. The home of the semel-aten must always be a place that everyone can come to and find safety."

"Yes, but kids from, say, Omaha, Nebraska, aren't coming all the way to Sobek for a place to eat and sleep if they're thrown out of their homes."

"No, but there should be a sanctuary like the one we're building here in every city," he murmured as he slid a hand under my T-shirt, feeling for bare skin, before moving to the small of my back. "It's a change for you to implement."

"I—what?" His warm palm pressing me forward against him broke my train of thought.

"Every city you visit, you'll give the semel money to build a shelter. We'll call them Menhit House, after your tribe."

It was a sweet thought, but Menhit represented everything I used to be, not who I was now or ever wanted to be again. "No, we'll call them Sekhem Shelter, because like you are my arm, there will be arms to protect and embrace all who need it."

His eyes filled.

"Come here."

"I don't—you're still fragile and—"

"I'm okay," I said, opening my arms for him.

He rolled over on top of me and wrapped his arms under and around me, and then he shoved one hand down the back of my pants.

"I know tears of joy when I see them," I said, trying to be sensitive even as I bucked off the bed, grinding my groin into his. "But it's not like you to go all maudlin on me."

"I'm just tired," he rumbled, hand on my thigh lifting my leg over his hip. "And you're saying good stuff like you love me and—"

"Oh, baby, I love you." I laughed softly, playfully, squirming under him, pushing him off me just enough so I could get to the snap of my jeans and my zipper. "I love you so much."

He scowled and I lost it, laughter rolling up and out of me, full of relief and happiness. Amazing that being in bed with this man changed everything in so many ways. I owed him, and I was happy to repay him for the rest of my life.

"You don't love me." He huffed indignantly, shucked my jeans and underwear and then tossed both away as I yanked my T-shirt over my head. "You just wanna get laid."

"I do love you," I said honestly, twisting under him, reaching for the nightstand as I heard the jingle of his belt buckle.

"The lube is under your pillow."

I met his hot gaze. "Is it?"

"What? Why am I being teased now?"

"Because I can't believe you! You're giving me grief for not being romantic when you stashed lube under the pillow!"

"I—what?" He was laughing as he stood up on the bed to get his jeans off faster.

I grabbed the lube and tossed it to him as he stepped down off the bed to the floor.

"Me? Are you sure?"

"Oh yes," I whispered, and I saw the effect my words had on him. All his playfulness was instantly replaced with raw, primal hunger. "Oh please."

He slicked his cock, fast. I was never that rough with his flesh, more careful because he was mine. I understood the haste, though, and his absolute need.

"Come here." His voice bottomed out with the command, and I scrambled over to him and lifted my legs in invitation.

He dropped the lube, gripped my thighs, and jerked me toward him. He then spread me wide as he positioned himself between my legs.

"I'm okay," I assured him. "You don't have to be careful with me."

"Yes, I do."

"No, don't you dare be gentle."

He draped my knees over his forearms as he nudged against my entrance. "You're not in charge here, my semel." His voice hitched as he began pressing forward. "Never here."

I arched off the bed, head back, mouth open, panting as he slid inside me.

"You belong to me, Domin Thorne," he growled as a surge of heat tore through me. "And only me."

"Yes," I gasped as he pushed deep and my body opened and welcomed him home. "I've only ever been yours."

"This is your vow to me," he said as he lifted me higher and curled his arms around my thighs. "Your promise."

"Oh yes," I breathed, raising my arms, reaching, wanting, aching to touch him. "Give yourself to me."

And his smile—the blinding, heart-stopping joy I saw on his face—let me know that whatever sliver of doubt had remained in the man was gone. When he bent to let me wrap him in my arms and seal his lips to mine, I knew he was finally, and undeniably, my mate.

"You're mine," he whispered.

There was never any doubt.

Check out
this excerpt of

Forging the Future

By Mary Calmes

A Change of Heart Novel

Jin Church is back where he started, alone, wandering, and uncertain of his path. It's not by choice but by circumstance, as he remembers he's a werepanther… but not much else. He knows one thing for sure—he needs to find the beautiful blond man who haunts his dreams.

Logan Church is trapped in a living hell. His mate is missing, his tribe is falling apart, and he's estranged from the son he loves with all his heart. His world is unraveling without his mate by his side, and he has no one to blame but himself.

If Jin can regain his memory and Logan can overcome the threats to his leadership, then perhaps they can resume their lives. The question is: Is that what they want? Back to the same house, the same tribe, the same troubles? They can choose from various roads leading to their future… or they can forge their own path.

Available at
http://www.dreamspinnerpress.com

Chapter One

"SMITH?"

I lifted my head because my manager called everyone by their last names—easier to keep track—and since I didn't know my real one and had adopted the generic, "Smith" was me until I got my memory back.

I said *until* all the time. The other word I used was *when*. It was beyond imagining that I would spend the rest of my life not knowing who I really was, so to remain positive, *if* had been stricken from my vocabulary. There had to be an end. But I couldn't stop the questioning and the worrying.

"Where's Keith?" Eliza Abernathy asked as she stepped around in front of me.

I gave her a huge grin, way over the top, but said nothing. She smiled back, couldn't help it, and we'd figured out why weeks ago. She really liked me. I was a stray she'd taken in off the street, and seeing me get my footing, my confidence, pleased her. So as she stood there and I acted like a dork, Manager Eliza melted away, and there was only the warm, maternal woman left. And then, of course, she realized that I'd gotten her to switch gears, and after a moment of us standing there like idiots, she turned a glare on me.

"What's with the face?"

"Really?" she prodded me.

"Pardon?" I asked innocently.

"This makes nine days straight."

I cleared my throat, hitting her with another smile. "Do you want the long version or the short one?"

"Oh God, please, short. I can't deal with long at this point."

"Okay, so he's stuck in Vegas, but he says for sure he'll be here tomorrow."

Her sigh was long and exasperated. "You know I'm about done with everyone taking advantage of me."

"Oh, no, I would nev—"

"Not you," she corrected, reaching out and taking hold of my bicep.

I ignored the pain. I'd found that anyone touching me at all, gentle bumps, a hand squeeze, a hug, or a pat on the back, all shot excruciating bolts of pain to my nervous system. If I was hit with a tray or a door, that was normal—or what I perceived as so—and caused only a moment of surprise. But hands on me, anyone at all doing that, forced me to steel myself against the wall of hurt I slammed into. But I allowed normal interactions like Eliza hugging me because I truly liked her, and the momentary discomfort was worth it to strengthen our bond.

She had continued talking. "I appreciate you working all the doubles and the extra days, and you must believe me when I tell you that it's been no hardship for me having you here."

I knew that, logically, but she'd taken a huge chance on a drifter she didn't know from anywhere, and I wanted her to understand how much it meant to me. I lived with the constant fear that something was going to change and she'd throw me out on my ass with nothing. It woke me up in a cold sweat some nights.

"You're the best bartender I have," she said. "You're charming and funny, the customers love you, the staff adores you, and you're the only one Hector doesn't want to skin."

The head chef and I had a mutual appreciation. He liked that I remembered all the specials the first time, listened when he explained how they were prepared, and never, ever, asked any questions. He'd been pleasantly surprised by the number of people eating at the bar because I talked up his cuisine. I liked his food and told him often, and now he never sent me home at night without dinner. Without fail, the last thing he made was a meal for me to take home. It had started when I had nothing, but even now, when I had a little, he still thoughtfully cooked so I didn't go hungry. He was a blessing, as was his boss, our boss, Eliza.

"Jim."

Back from my wandering thoughts, I met her gaze.

"And I'm sorry I made you cut your hair, but there was no way around it with the new investors I was forced to take on."

She still felt bad about me going from having hair that fell long and wavy almost to my ass to a style short in the back and on the sides, and longer on top. I was clean-cut, without the beard and mustache I'd been sporting when I arrived, and I looked a lot younger than I had when I'd walked in, hoping to wash dishes or bus tables. Of course I had no idea how old I was, but late twenties seemed a pretty safe bet. "You know I don't give a crap about my hair."

"It was so pretty, but just not our aesthetic here."

I shrugged. "I'd rather be part of your family than have a ponytail."

That made her sigh. "You know I'd make you an assistant manager, but you make more with tips behind the bar."

I was overwhelmed, as I was on a daily basis. She had so much faith in me after only three months, and though I didn't understand why she did, I was touched.

"I know you don't have your memory back, but honey, you took to this job like a duck to water. I'll bet you you've done this kind of work before."

Perhaps.

"But seriously, I need you to start taking your days off so you don't get burned out. Do you understand?"

"Yes, ma'am," I agreed, patting her hand still on my upper arm. "So what do we think? Can I get some drinks made for my customers, or should we bond more?"

She chuckled before tugging me close and holding me tight.

I hugged her back, even though it hurt, and then when we parted, she was smiling for a moment before she suddenly jolted.

"Eliza?" I asked, concerned.

"Oh dear Lord," she said quickly, "I almost forgot why I came back here in the first place. Our semel, Alaine Boucher, is having dinner with his mate and his entourage, and he said he'd love to finally meet you. I already explained to him that you're under my protection, and I vouched for you, so it's really just a formality. But you know how much semels like their posturing and tradition."

But I didn't.

"They love to bore everyone to tears."

I nodded, nervous, felt my hands shaking as my stomach twisted into a knot.

"You don't have to worry. I explained that your memory has been affected by whatever you've been through and that you can't speak your lineage to him."

"And he accepted that?"

"Of course, why wouldn't he?"

"That seems awfully trusting."

"Sweetie, a semel has to trust his people."

"Okay."

"You have no idea what I'm talking about, do you?"

I shook my head.

"A good semel knows the names of every member of his tribe. He cares about them all and takes on the role of father and brother, leader and protector, confidant and counselor."

"It sounds like a big job."

"It is, and that's why only a select few who are born to lead actually do so."

"Sure."

"But semels get their strength from their tribes, and what makes up the tribe is individuals. So when I tell you my semel values me, he does."

"I believe you."

"Good," she said, putting a hand gently on my cheek. "I told my semel you were to be trusted, and he took me at my word. You'll be fine."

I took a breath. "Thank you."

Her smile was meant to be encouraging. "So just go on back there to the private room when you get a minute, and—what? Why are you making that face?"

"The back room?"

She rolled her eyes. "Oh, for heaven's sake, Rosario and Val don't have you believing that crap about those rooms being haunted, do they?"

I grimaced.

"I've had it checked out, for goodness sakes—just go!"

Moving quickly, I walked down the hallway leading to the dining room floor while I heard her yell for Suri to take my place.

I crossed the dining room and walked down a short stained glass–lined hallway—it felt like moving through a miniature cathedral—to the private area in the back. Once there, I slipped under the archway and bowed, waiting for someone to spot me. As loud as the conversation was, it would probably take a few minutes to capture anyone's attention. Not that I cared, they could ignore me all night if they wanted. I was terrified of speaking to anyone, especially the semel. It wasn't that I doubted Eliza—I didn't—but she was the known and I was a stranger. She honestly had no way of knowing what her leader's reaction to me would be.

There were twelve people in the room, nine men and three women, and everyone was dressed well: suits for the gentlemen, elegant dresses for the ladies. It didn't help me feel any less intimidated by the gathering, with them all decked out and me in my uniform.

I thought I might need to leave and come back, but suddenly a man's voice cut through the din.

"My semel, we have a visitor."

The room fell silent.

"You may approach."

Straightening, having spied the man who spoke, I moved quickly to the head of the second table, stopping in front of him and dropping down to one knee.

"You're Jim Smith?"

"Yes, my semel," I replied, adding the honorific "my" as I'd been told custom dictated.

Alaine Boucher nodded. "Eliza tells me that you've had a memory lapse and are unsure of your tribe or of your standing therein."

"That's correct," I replied to the handsome man regarding me. He was, I guessed, in his late forties, striking, with gray hair and piercing cobalt blue eyes.

"And is Jim your given name?"

I wasn't sure, but it felt *almost* right. If it wasn't Jim, it was something very close. "I believe so, my semel."

"Well, I've sent an e-mail off to the office of the akhen-aten, and since it's not like it was before he took over, since everything is centralized now and he acts on information right away, I might actually get an answer about where you belong."

"Yes, my semel."

"I'm a great admirer of Domin Thorne. I met him when he came on his tour of the US a year ago."

I remained quiet, listening.

"You know he traveled the world for five years total. The US was the last leg of it."

"Oh."

"Did you know that?"

"No, my semel."

"Do you recall seeing him?"

"No, my semel."

"Rise."

I stood, and he and everyone else in the room did as well. The women all rose seamlessly with the grace panthers had, and the men were menacing, probably not on purpose, but I could have been wrong. I had a hard time reading people.

"Let me present to you my yareah, Catherine."

Quickly I bowed, and his mate reached out and touched my shoulder. I lifted my head so I could see her face and found her smiling, which was nice.

"It's a pleasure, Jim."

"I assure you, my yareah, the pleasure is all mine."

"Oh, such lovely manners," she sighed, beaming. "You know, it's odd, there's no scent coming off you. I don't sense that you're a panther at all."

"Others have also remarked on that fact, my yareah."

"You're certain you're not human?"

"I have shifted since my memory was lost," I told her.

"Have you shifted since you've been here?" Alaine asked, testing me, I was certain. Eliza had warned me that he would try to find out if I'd broken protocol.

"No, my semel, I would not think of it without your permission."

"You know your law well," another man said.

I turned to him. "It seems to be the only part of my memory that remains intact," I lied.

It was *all* gone. All my memories, and even the smallest questions, like did I like vanilla ice cream, had answers I could not provide. Every day I found something terrifying to ponder, sometimes stupid things like did I have a favorite season, and at other times, were my parents still alive? I spent hours sitting in my apartment, on the window seat looking out across the French Quarter, and wondered if I'd ever have a real home. It was too easy to get lost in the self-pity, so I worked hard to not succumb. But sometimes, especially late at night when I couldn't sleep... it was overwhelming. At those times I took stock of the small number of things I did know. For instance, I knew I was a panther, but that was no different than other people knowing they were human. But the laws themselves, the protocol—Eliza had given me a quick lesson, the dos and don'ts, so I wouldn't screw up when I met the semel. One of the big don'ts, it turned out, was to shift in a territory without first being recognized as part of the tribe inhabiting said area. That was taboo.

"It's a good beginning," he said, smiling at me. "And you couldn't have picked a better shield than Eliza Abernathy."

A shield, I had come to understand, was a person who was basically your guardian. You could speak their name to others, and they were responsible for what you did while you were visiting. Their name carried weight and protection.

"She's been very kind to me," I replied.

The man who had spoken came around his semel and held out his hand. "I'm Luther Hockney, sylvan of the tribe of Kynum."

I reached out, but our hands never met.

"Wait," the man on the other side of the semel cautioned sharply before he stepped around the sylvan to face me.

"Nazar?" Alaine asked, concern in his voice.

"I—" The man in question began before suddenly grabbing my bicep, spinning me around, and shoving me over the end of the table to hold me down.

"Please don't hurt me," I pleaded, struggling to get free, poised to run at any opportunity even as my stomach roiled from the instant pain and threatened to empty.

How the story started

Change of Heart

By Mary Calmes

CHANGE *of* HEART
Mary Calmes

As a young gay man—and a werepanther—all Jin Rayne yearns for is a normal life. Having fled his past, he wants nothing more than to start over, but Jin's old life doesn't want to let him go. When his travels bring him to a new city, he crosses paths with the leader of the local were-tribe. Logan Church is a shock and an enigma, and Jin fears that Logan is both the mate he fears and the love of his life. Jin doesn't want to go back to the old ways, and mating would irrevocably tie him to them.

But Jin is the mate Logan needs at his side to help him lead his tribe, and he won't give Jin up so easily. It will take time and trust for Jin to discover the joy in belonging to Logan and how to love without restraint.

Trusted Bond

By Mary Calmes

Sequel to *Change of Heart*
Change of Heart: Book Two

Jin Rayne is having trouble adjusting to the new life he's supposed to love. Instead of adapting to being the mate of tribe leader Logan Church, Jin can't get past the fact that his lover was straight before they met. He's discovered the joy in belonging to Logan but fears his new life could disappear at a moment's notice, despite Logan's insistence that they are forever, end of story.

Jin wants to trust Logan, but that desire will be put to the test both by a rival tribe leader and by a startling revelation about Jin's existence. At stake is Jin's life and his place in the tribe. If he's going to survive to see Logan again, he'll have to release his fear and freely accept the bond, for only then can he truly trust.

Available at
http://www.dreamspinnerpress.com

Honored Vow

By Mary Calmes

Sequel to *Trusted Bond*
Change of Heart: Book Three

Jin Rayne is still growing into his frightening new powers as a nekhene cat and his place as reah of Logan Church's tribe when he learns that a sepat, an honor challenge, has been called. Logan, who has never wanted to do anything but lead his small-town tribe, must travel around the world to Mongolia and fight to become the most powerful leader in the werepanther world.

Logan won't be the only one making the journey. As his mate, Jin must fight with him to honor his commitment to Logan, his culture, and his tribe. But the trial is long, involving a prolonged separation between the two men, and Logan's humanity is at stake. In order to make it through the nightmarish sepat, Jin and Logan must accept their fates, trust each other, and honor the vows between them no matter the cost.

Available at
http://www.dreamspinnerpress.com

MARY CALMES lives in Lexington, Kentucky, with her husband and two children and loves all the seasons except summer. She graduated from the University of the Pacific in Stockton, California, with a bachelor's degree in English literature. Due to the fact that it is English lit and not English grammar, do not ask her to point out a clause for you, as it will *so* not happen. She loves writing, becoming immersed in the process, and falling into the work. She can even tell you what her characters smell like. She loves buying books and going to conventions to meet her fans.

http://www.dreamspinnerpress.com

A Matter of Time Series from MARY CALMES

http://www.dreamspinnerpress.com

Mangrove Nights from MARY CALMES

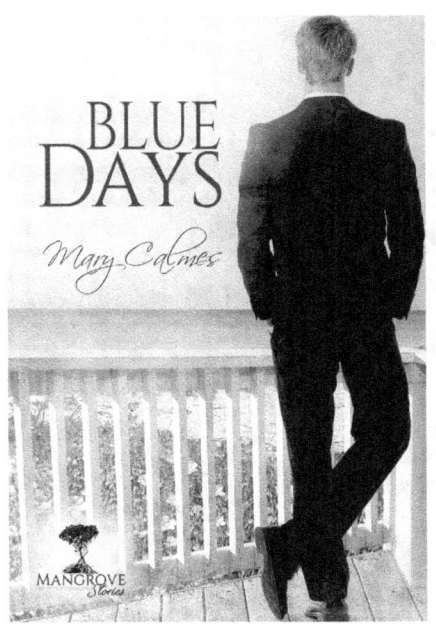

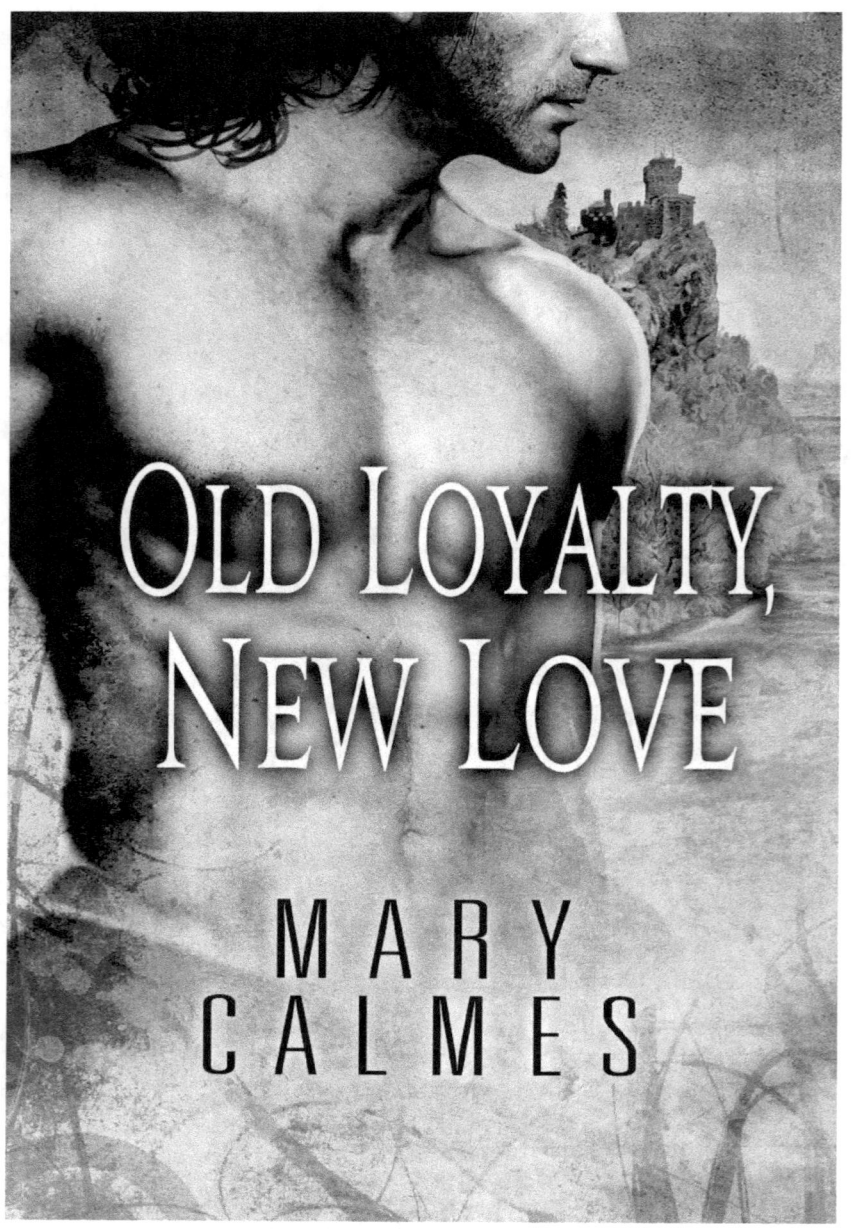

OLD LOYALTY, NEW LOVE

MARY CALMES

http://www.dreamspinnerpress.com

FIGHTING INSTINCT

MARY CALMES

http://www.dreamspinnerpress.com

Acrobat

MARY CALMES

http://www.dreamspinnerpress.com

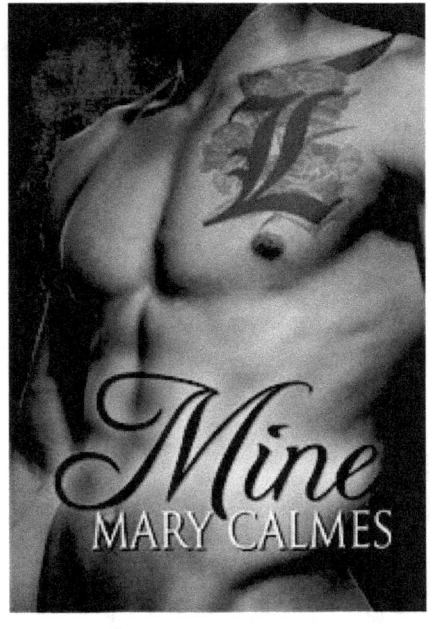

http://www.dreamspinnerpress.com

The Warder Series by MARY CALMES

The Warder Series by MARY CALMES

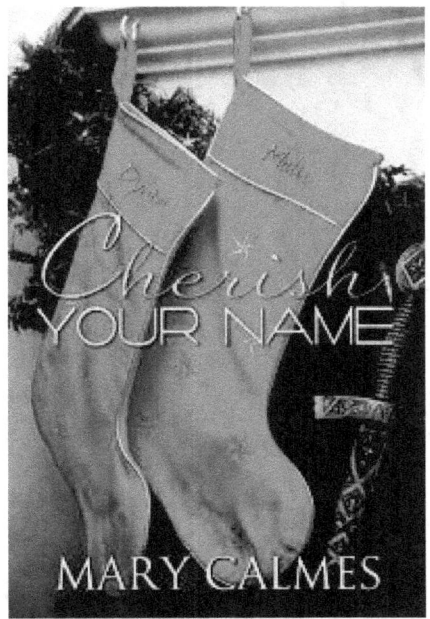